MAKE IT STOP

MAKE IT STOP

a novel by

JIM RULAND

RARE BIRD
LOS ANGELES, CALIF.

RARE BIRD

THIS IS A GENUINE RARE BIRD BOOK

Rare Bird Books
6044 North Figueroa Street
Los Angeles, CA 90042
rarebirdbooks.com

For more information, address:
Rare Bird Books Subsidiary Rights Department
6044 North Figueroa Street
Los Angeles, CA 90042

Set in Dante
Printed in the United States

10 9 8 7 6 5 4 3 2 1

Library of Congress Cataloging-in-Publication Data

Names: Ruland, Jim, author.
Title: Make it stop : a novel / by Jim Ruland.
Description: First Original Edition. | Los Angeles, Calif. : Rare Bird, 2023.
Identifiers: LCCN 2022048819 | ISBN 9781644283035 (trade paperback original)
Classification: LCC PS3618.U563 M35 2023 | DDC 813/.6—dc23

LC record available at https://lccn.loc.gov/2022048819

In memory of
Jeremy Richman
and Shanna Mahin

PART I
WESTERN PSYCH

LOS ANGELES

1

FIERY CAT

MELANIE WONDERS HOW MANY OF the vehicles clogging Wilshire Boulevard contain operatives for an underground vigilante organization. This one has three. Vinnie drives and Melanie rides shotgun. Trevor, her case manager and Make It Stop's tech expert, sits mashed in the middle seat of the nondescript box truck. They're going on a mission to Western Psychiatric. Scratch that. *She's* going on a mission. These puds are staying in the truck. And now Trevor's badgering her about her cover story.

"Seriously?" Melanie asks.

"One more time," Trevor insists. "Who are you?"

Melanie hesitates, and that means trouble. In her line of work, thinking on the job can be dangerous—even deadly.

Here's to thinking. Melanie pulls a pint of Fiery Cat from her leather jacket and takes a swig. Terrible stuff, like drinking the dregs of a salsa jar. The truck hits a pothole and jalapeño-flavored vodka spills down her neck, soaking her tank top. Even her bra is soggy. She's a walking body shot.

"Shit."

"You're drinking?" Trevor asks. He can barely keep the aggravation out of his voice.

"Trying to." Melanie wipes her mouth with a studded sleeve, which isn't a hot idea.

"I told you she was trouble," Vinnie says.

"Suck my dick, Vinnie," Melanie says.

Trevor sighs. He's nervous, and nerves are contagious before a mission. He hates it when she drinks, but no drunk shows up to a detox facility sober. Melanie ought to know. She's been in and out of them her whole life.

"Melanie…"

"Melanie's not here," she says, finally getting into character. "This is Rachel, and Rachel likes to party!" Her hair feels heavy on her head. This morning she'd shaped it into a shiny pink mohawk, something she hasn't done since she was a teenager. It's already starting to wilt in the truck's rearview mirror.

"Rachel who?" Trevor asks.

"Rachel Roark," Melanie says. The name still strikes her as absurd, but she's stuck with it for the next few weeks—or however long this operation is supposed to take.

"Again," Trevor says.

"Rrrrrrrrrrrachel Rrrrrrrrrrrrroarrrrrrrrk!" she shouts like an announcer at a boxing match.

"Mel," Trevor pleads, "we don't have much time. Let's go over your cover story again."

Melanie checks the dashtab. ETA: five minutes.

Five minutes to tell Trevor how she *really* feels about him.

"Rachel Roark. Twenty-three-year-old female chameleon. Alkie, addict, self-harmer—"

"Chameleon?" Trevor interrupts.

"What?"

"You said chameleon."

"No, I didn't," Melanie says.

"Yes, you did," Vinnie says without taking his eyes off the road. Drivers aren't supposed to interact with ops before a mission, but Vinnie's an irascible old prick who does what he wants.

"Chameleon. Caucasian. You knew what I meant."

Did she really say chameleon? That's not good. She takes another swig and coughs up fumes. She pounds the door with her fist until the burning subsides. Maybe the Fiery Cat wasn't such a hot idea.

"Are you all right?" Trevor asks.

"Fine," she spits, and sets the bottle on the floor so she won't be tempted to drink any more. Melanie rattles off the details of Rachel's profile, data she's spent the last two weeks memorizing. Rachel Roark is Melanie's cover, a fake person with real issues.

"Two minutes," Vinnie announces even though the dashtab says three.

Now it's two. Shit. She needs air. Melanie rolls down the window.

"Are you ready?" Trevor asks.

"Ready when you are!" Melanie is incapable of saying anything that isn't a total cliché. That's what even a little bit of alcohol does to her. It speeds up her tongue, slows down her brain, messes with her emotions. Feelings get Melanie in trouble every time. *No feelings, only choices* is Melanie's mantra—and that goes double when she's drinking.

"You have your mayday device?" Trevor asks.

Melanie pats the pin affixed to the lapel of her leather jacket. It's a simple GPS that triggers an alarm at HQ. If the mission goes sideways, she can call in the calvary with a click of a button. She's never needed to use it but likes knowing it's there. On her previous mission, it was a brooch in the shape of a pentagram. This time it's a button with the logo for a punk band called Swallows. Great name. Terrible band.

"Good," Trevor continues. "Remember, this is a deep-cover extraction, not a bust-out, so go slow. There's no need to rush this assignment, all right?"

Melanie nods but she's not really paying attention. There's hardly any time left on the clock. She glances out the window. Condos are going up where the Federal Building used to stand before it was blown up by the Subsubhumans, a group from the San Diego-Tijuana-Tecate triangle. Soon the truck will come to a stop in the mini mall parking lot across the street from Western Psychiatric, and she'll be on her way. If there's anything she wants to say to Trevor, now is the time. Operation details. Target info. Feelings of infatuation. How she loves the lock of dark hair that's always falling into his bright blue eyes that seem to take in everything at once. The way he'd looked at her the one and only time they'd kissed...

"Tell me I'm beautiful," she says through a belch that catches her by surprise and leaves the cab smelling like a soup kitchen.

"Mel..." Trevor complains.

"Tell me or I'm aborting the mission!"

Is she really doing this? Screaming at her supervisor in front of Vinnie? She might as well be twelve, her bedspread overflowing with stuffed bunnies and bears. Melanie had used her menagerie as a receptacle for drugs she sold to her friends at school. (She kept the Adderall in the ape, the skunk got her edibles, and she shoved Oxies up the ass of her favorite bear.) Every few months, she'd get wasted and forget who was holding what and tear the animals to pieces, which freaked out her foster parents.

Trevor relents. "You, Rachel Roark, are a beauty beyond compare."

"Rachel isn't real."

"She better be."

"We're here," Vinnie says as he turns the truck into the hospital's parking lot. Melanie picks up the pint of Fiery Cat and brings it to her lips, but the bottle is empty. She hurls it out the window. Glass smashes on the pavement.

"I'm not cleaning that up," Vinnie says.

Melanie catches a whiff of exhaust and imagines the truck filling up with fumes. She's already starting to get a headache, which strikes her as unfair. It's time to embrace the assignment.

Get in tune with her inner lush and *become* Rachel, a lost soul searching for...she isn't sure yet. She'll figure out that part later.

Melanie ambushes Trevor with a kiss on the lips but doesn't press her luck. She jumps out of the truck before he can ruin the moment. The ground sends a jolt through her legs. *Steady, girl.* She's ready for whatever the hospital has to throw at her. She's a spark, a match, a goddam flamethrower, and she'll blow this whole shit show sky-high if she has to. She flips Vinnie the bird, pulls her leather jacket tight around her body, and strides toward the entrance to Western Psychiatric like a goddess walking through a dream.

"WHAT DID YOU SAY YOUR name was, sweetie?"

Melanie tries to be patient, but she's just about had it. She's given her name to the middle-aged woman at the hospital's admittance desk three times already.

"Roark. Rachel Roark."

"Roark?" the woman asks, lifting her eyeglasses from the nest of her tremendous bosom as she peers at a computer screen.

"Roark! Last name. R as in Romeo. O as in Oscar. A as in Alpha..."

"That's enough of that." The woman looks up from her screen, clearly annoyed. "You have a seat while I get this sorted."

When you sit, you give people permission to forget about you. It's harder to ignore someone standing over you. "I prefer to stand."

"You do what you gotta do," the woman says.

"Doing it."

The detox ward is housed in an ancient wing of the hospital that's been renovated many times and still looks like a dump. Though the paint is fresh and the floors are clean, the place feels dingy and smells strongly of floor wax. It's got a purgatorial vibe Melanie wants no part of. The sooner she gets this operation underway the better.

"You got insurance?"

"Of course."

"You do know this is a conditional release facility?"

Melanie knows all about Western Psych's patient policies. That's why she's here. Once patients are admitted to Western Psych (and scores of hospitals like it), they aren't released until they meet two conditions: they're medically cleared and financially paid up. In other words, if you can't pay your bills, you don't go home. Patients who can't pay are remanded to the hospital's detention center until their financial obligations are met. Or, if they're lucky, until someone like Melanie comes along and busts them out.

"Stay until you pay," Melanie says. "Got it."

"I don't know about all that..."

"What *do* you know?"

Stalemate.

"Let's see if I can find someone who can help you," the woman says.

"You do that."

The woman rises from her computer, peers at Melanie over the top of her glasses, and shuffles through the door at the back of the office. Melanie counts one, two, three beats before she blows through the double doors to her right and into the hospital proper.

Is this a good idea?

No, definitely not. Trevor told her to take it slow. This is the opposite of that, but it's too late for second-guessing. She's in.

Melanie has the hospital's layout memorized. Inpatient processing is surrounded by back-of-house operations: kitchens, laundry services, maintenance workshops. The first thing she does is lose the leather. She wads up her jacket and stuffs it into a trashcan, then pushes through the doors to the massive laundry room. It's lunch time so there isn't anyone around. She rifles through a bin and finds what she's looking for: a relatively clean set of hospital scrubs and a nurse's bouffant, which she slips over her head, wrecking the Mohawk she'd worked on all morning.

Melanie hurries down the hall and takes the elevator up to the second floor, where the cafeteria is located. It smells like hot milk and boiled meat. Institutional chow. She gets in line, fills six paper cups with black coffee, and wedges them into a cardboard tray.

"You want cream and sugar?" the cashier asks with a weary look.

Melanie nods, clocks his nametag: JUREYL. He dumps packets of sugar and non-dairy creamer on her tray without bothering to count them out.

"These all for you?" he asks.

"Don't be a bitch, Jureyl," Melanie says with a wink.

Jureyl smiles. "I can't help it."

Back in the elevator, Melanie breathes in the aroma of the coffee, willing the caffeine to light up her brain. Melanie has never blown her cover or botched a bust-out, and she doesn't intend to start now.

The target's name is Michael, but he goes by Mick. Twenty years old. Son of a CEO. Part-time construction worker, full-time fuck-up. Mick likes pills (who doesn't?) and has a girlfriend he may have knocked up. Western Psych cut off his visitation privileges and stashed him in a private room. This wasn't a case of a family who couldn't afford to pay for Mick's care; this was straight up extortion.

Enter: Make It Stop.

There's no elevator access to the detention level on the fifth floor, so she'll head to the sixth and take the stairs down. The hospital's security staff is headquartered on the sixth floor, but she's got a plan for that.

The bell dings and the doors slide open. "Corp" is MIS slang for the corporate cops hospitals employ as private security. There are corps everywhere but Melanie walks right in. She smiles at the men as she passes. Whether it's the aroma of the coffee or the wiggle in her walk, no one gives her any trouble.

"Jureyl sent these up for the boys," she says to no one in particular as she puts the coffees down on the counter.

The men on duty brighten. They are muscular and thick. Crew cuts and hairy knuckles. Most are fatter than regular cops.

"What, no donuts?" one of them jokes, and they all laugh. A jovial bunch of head crackers. A female corp with a confrontational demeanor sticks her head out of an office down the hall.

"Who sent those?" she wants to know.

It's always the women who make trouble for her, trying to prove how hard they are.

"Jureyl," she says with a fake smile. "Down in the cafeteria?"

"Who?" she demands like it's a matter of earth-shattering importance.

Melanie sighs. "J as in Juliet. U as in Uniform. R as in Romeo…" The woman loses interest and returns to her office. A couple of the corps chuckle.

"Bathroom?" Melanie asks.

One of them points the way with a beefy finger. "Across from the locker rooms."

"Thank you," she says, flashing a smile. She pivots and goes down the passageway. The locker rooms are on the left. The all-gender restroom is just past it on the right. An exit sign glows at the end of the hall. That would be the stairwell.

She ducks into the lady's locker room. The air is damp and humid. She can hear two women talking in the shower. One is complaining about something, the other urges her along, their voices echoing off the tiles.

"I told him I was done with his bullshit."

"Yes, you did."

"But he was trying not to hear me."

A sign on the wall reminds patrons the hospital is not responsible for lost or stolen items. The idea of things getting stolen out of a security station locker room strikes Melanie as funny, but she supposes it happens. Crimes of desperation. Crimes of opportunity. And what do we have here… A large gym bag has been left unattended on a bench in front of a bank of lockers. Melanie rifles through the bag and finds all kinds of useful supplies: a key card, pepper spray, a bundle of red plastic zip ties, a short stack of paper masks, a bottle of pills, and a can of pomegranate juice. She cracks open the can and drinks the juice down in one go while reading the prescription bottle.

Hydrocodone.

Hello.

Melanie stashes everything in her pockets just as the showers turn off. Water gurgles down the drain as if into a colossal stomach. The echo of flip-flops slapping the wet tiles tells her it's time to go. She breezes through the door, goes down the hall to the stairwell, and double-times it to the detention level. On the landing, she listens for a sign she's being pursued, hears nothing. She gives herself a few seconds to catch her breath and orient the map in her head before she proceeds.

She opens the door, clutching the pepper spray at her side. She prefers to fight with her hands, but it's foolish not to use all the tools at her disposal. The nurse's station sits in the center of the room with hallways leading left and right. A startled young woman wearing a nurse's uniform and long braids looks up from her computer.

"Can I help you?"

"Emergency!"

"Where's your badge?"

"I have it right here…" Melanie holds up the pepper spray.

"That's—"

"Gonna hurt." Melanie blasts her in the face.

The woman coughs and gags. Blinded, she lashes out at Melanie with her feet.

"Easy now," Melanie says, but this only eggs the woman on. Melanie knocks the nurse to the ground, straddles her, and binds her wrists with the zip ties, which she is delighted to have found a use for so quickly. She stands while the nurse yells and thrashes around on the floor. The nurse's skirt hikes up, revealing baby blue panties decorated with little fluffy clouds. Adorable. The nurse ends Melanie's reverie with a kick to her knee.

"Ow!"

Melanie drags her by her braids into the back office and locks the door. It only takes a few seconds of poking around on the desktab to find what she's looking for: M. MORIARITY, 505.

"Gotcha."

Melanie goes down the corridor to her left and follows it until she reaches room 505. She turns the knob and pushes it open.

Her target, a well-built young man, sits on the bed in his underwear, braiding a rope out of strips of cloth ripped from his bed sheets. Upon closer inspection, Melanie realizes he's making a noose. How creative.

"Okay, Tarzan," she says, stepping into the room, "arts and crafts time is over."

Mick blinks as Melanie takes the crude noose away from him. He's a good-looking kid with strong features and thick, dark hair combed back into an unruly pompadour, but his teeth are like a trailer park after a tornado. He is either heavily medicated or not particularly bright. Either way, he doesn't seem surprised to see her.

"You're one of those Make It Stop vigilantes, aren't you?"

The question catches her off guard. Mick's tone suggests he knows exactly what he's talking about, like he'd just watched a documentary about the suddenly not-so-secret organization.

"We're not vigilantes," Melanie says. "We help people."

"You're, like, famous!"

"On your feet."

"I'm not leaving. There's only one way out for me." Mick nods at the noose.

This has never happened to Melanie before. She's heard other ops talk about it, but this is the first time a detainee has refused to cooperate during a bust-out.

"Look," Melanie says, "that's a real nice hobby you've got there, but we need to get moving."

"You don't understand. I'm checking out on *my* terms."

"I can't let you do that," Melanie says.

"Gimme a reason."

She rattles the bottle of hydrocodone. "I've got about thirty of them."

That gets Mick's attention. "Gimme."

"Whoa, cowboy. We'll talk after we get you out of here."

"Let me see." Mick scrutinizes the label on the bottle with an intensity Melanie finds unnerving. She has no intention of giving Mick any of these pills, but at least he's stopped crying goodbye cruel world.

"Get up," she says.

"There are sensors in the bed. I get up, the alarm goes off."

Melanie thinks this over and whips off her scrubs. The odor of jalapeño-flavored vodka fills the room.

Mick whistles. "I *knew* you liked to party."

"Shut up and put these on," she says, ignoring Mick as she shimmies out of her pants and tosses the scrubs at him.

"Our first date and we're already playing doctor!"

Melanie rattles the bottle again. It's like flipping a switch. Mick's eyes glaze over and he dons the mask without further complaint.

"Good boy." Melanie checks the hallway to make sure the coast is clear. It's eerily quiet. "Let's go."

Mick gets out of bed and, sure enough, she can hear an alarm sound at the nurse's station.

"Give me your hand," she says.

"What for?"

"If the bed is monitored, chances are your ID bracelet is, too."

Mick does as he's told. Melanie rips the bracelet off his wrist, kicks it into the cell, and slams the door shut.

She leads Mick back to the nurse's station and down the stairs. The stairwell is as empty as the hallway. Where is everyone?

They make their way down the stairs to the second floor when she hears a noise. Melanie stops and peers over the railing. Corps crash onto the landing on the level below. Their steel-shod boots clang on the iron stairs and echo up the shaft of the stairwell. She can hear more of them above. She's trapped. It's time to send the mayday signal and call in the troops. She goes to push the pin and realizes it's not there because she left it in the laundry room with her leather jacket.

"Shit!"

"What?" Mick asks.

"This way," Melanie hisses, and pushes Mick through the door and toward the cafeteria. Doctors and nurses go about their business with varying levels of urgency. She lets out a loud moan and doubles over as if in pain. The only one who pays any attention to her is Mick.

"Are you okay?"

"Don't stop," she whispers. "Keep moving."

They shuffle toward the elevators and get on when the doors open. Melanie gasps and groans as the elevator car descends. Mick hovers over her. He's broken a sweat and seems genuinely concerned.

"Follow me," she says when the doors open. They fall in behind a gurney and follow it to the end of the hall. The gurney goes one way and Mick and Melanie go the other. She can see sunlight streaming through the wide glass windows of the hospital's front lobby, but she doesn't let up. She continues to whimper and moan.

"What's the matter?" Mick asks as they pass through the doors.

"Keep going," she says, standing a little taller, walking a little faster.

"Hey," Mick says, jogging to keep up.

They go out the door and into the parking lot. They're going to make it.

"You were faking it!" Mick yells.

"The best way to get ignored in a hospital," Melanie says, "is to be a woman in pain." She yanks open the rear door of an ambulance. "Get in."

"We're stealing an ambulance?"

"Borrowing." Melanie shoves Mick inside and slams the door.

A burly EMT pops out of the driver's seat. "Ma'am, what are you doing?"

Melanie drops him with a kick to the head he never sees coming. "Leaving."

Melanie climbs behind the wheel, turns on the siren, and hauls ass out of the parking lot. She glances in the rear view and sees a cadre of corps storming out of the hospital, but they're too late. The GPS starts squawking at her.

"Where would you like to go today?"

"Fuck off."

"I don't know that location. Where would you like to go today?"

A flashback from her training floats through her consciousness: *A device that can take you somewhere can lead others to you.* She either needs to ditch the van or disable the GPS.

Melanie makes a hard turn and goes barreling into the parking lot at Howdy's Biscuits. She parks the ambulance, taking up three spaces. She hops out and opens the rear door.

"Everything okay back here?"

"Oh, yeah," Mick says, reclining on the gurney.

"Wonderful."

Melanie grabs a bag of tools and slams the door. In the parking lot, a big bearded dude leans out of the window of a white pickup truck.

"Move your vehicle, you stupid cooze!"

Melanie puts on a fake smile. "Sorry! Broke down!"

The driver shakes his head and steers his truck into the lot. Melanie curses under her breath. She doesn't know anything about GPS systems, but she knows how to break things. She climbs into the ambulance and hammers away at the dashtab and then uses the claw end to rip it out.

She strides across the parking lot, finds the white pickup, and tosses the GPS system in the bed with a thud, which somehow activates the computer.

"Where would you like to go today?"

2
SCARY GARY

TREVOR AND VINNIE RIDE THE elevator up to Make It Stop's headquarters on the fourth floor of an office building in the Sherman Oaks Galleria. Sitting at the crossroads of the 101 and 405 freeways in the heart of the San Fernando Valley, the Galleria was once the apogee of eighties mall culture, but those days are long gone. Now the mall is presided over by a monolithic glass-walled skyscraper that is every bit as outdated as the aerosol can of hairspray the building vaguely resembles. MIS has only been at this location for a few months and Property Protectors, the building's management company, believes its fourth-floor tenants operate a high-end meditation center. Sometime next year, Doyle will break the lease and move Make It Stop to another part of the city. All part of the MIS plan to stay mobile and hide in plain sight.

The elevator shudders, causing Trevor to grimace.

"What's the matter?" Vinnie asks.

"I have a bad feeling about this operation," Trevor says.

"No shit," Vinnie says. "Melanie's a train wreck."

"She's a little high maintenance," Trevor clarifies.

"*I'm* high maintenance," Vinnie says. "*She's* a dumpster fire."

Trevor can't argue with that. He'd hoped the bad feeling would dissipate once the operation got underway, but it's only gotten worse. Trevor makes it his business to pay attention to these feelings, but Vinnie is right. High-maintenance doesn't even begin to describe Melanie. He's known for a while that she has feelings for him, and he has only himself to blame.

Shortly after Melanie arrived at Make It Stop, Trevor made a clumsy pass at her. That was almost two years ago, and since then his duties at MIS have expanded. When he became Melanie's case manager, he resolved to be *extra* professional with her. At first, she buried whatever feelings she had for him under layers of sarcasm and humor, but as the months wore on, she became more brazen. MIS isn't big enough to be a bureaucracy, but a group in Florida known as The Everyday Satans was exposed when an op who'd fallen for his section leader snitched to the feds after she started sleeping with another agent. MIS doesn't have a handbook, but its operating procedures are clear: No fraternization between members.

Maybe that's the source of the bad feeling, his growing anxiety about what he's going to do about Melanie now that she's putting her feelings for him out in the open.

The elevator stops and the doors open onto an expansive lobby painted in earth tones. Watery light shines down on the reception area's high-traffic carpet with a gingko leaf pattern. A woman Trevor has never seen before sits behind the reception desk wearing a headset.

"Doyle wants to see you," she says.

"Both of us?" Vinnie asks.

"Just Trevor."

Vinnie scowls.

"Where is he?" Trevor asks.

"In the dojo."

Trevor nods and heads down the hall. In a former life, the dojo was a yoga studio and still resembles one, but now on the far wall swords and staffs hang on a rack. Trevor finds Doyle doing tai chi, which always embarrasses him to watch. Doyle is an ex-Marine whose buzz cut and linebacker physique ensure he will always look the part. While some people look like trouble, Doyle's vibe screams authority. Trevor has seen gangbangers cross the street to get out of his way. Even cops mistake him for one of their own.

"We lost an op today," Doyle says as he continues his routine.

Whatever Trevor was expecting, it wasn't this. "Who?"

"Gary Gray."

"Scary Gary?"

"Lancaster assignment," Doyle says by way of an answer. "Mojave Critical Care."

"How?" Trevor asks, feeling suddenly lightheaded.

"I don't know. He must have blown his cover." Doyle stops his routine and picks up a towel to wipe his face. "They killed him, Trevor."

Scary Gary was a reformed junkie. A seemingly indestructible cockroach of a man who'd overdosed countless times and flatlined twice before MIS recruited him. Scary Gary was in his late thirties and still looked like his high school yearbook photo, which he loved showing to new recruits. It was true, he did resemble the photo, but by eighteen he was already a hardcore addict. Over the years, he added scars and tattoos and never stopped looking like a terrifically sketchy dude. Hence the nickname. Scary Gary was an outstanding undercover operative, one of the best in the organization. He was smart, loyal, funny, and great with the younger ops. A tremendous asset to MIS. He was also really tight with Melanie, who would take the news hard. It was never easy when they lost an op, and if Scary Gary could get taken out, anyone could.

"Was Melanie drinking when you dropped her off?" Doyle asks.

Trevor snaps out of his reverie. "Yes, but—"

"We can't have our operatives," Doyle interrupts, "compromising the integrity of an assignment by getting impaired."

"She wasn't impaired."

The door opens and Vinnie sticks his head in the dojo. "Uh, excuse me…"

"What is it, Vinnie?" Doyle snaps.

"It's Melanie."

"Is she all right?" Trevor asks, suddenly worried.

"She's here," Vinnie says.

That makes no sense. The extraction was supposed to take weeks.

"And the target?" Doyle asks.

Vinnie shrugs. "She says she needs assistance in the garage."

Doyle glares at Trevor. "Take care of this. And then send her to my office." Doyle throws his towel on the floor and leaves.

Trevor curses himself for not acting on the bad feeling sooner. He'd been right all along, and when it comes to Melanie, it's always better to be wrong than right.

Bubba McArdle pilots his pickup truck down the boulevard with one hand, while holding a fried chicken biscuit in the other. Life, in his opinion, is short, brutal, and mean. While the pleasures of existence are few and far between, one of its most reliable is a chicken biscuit from Howdy's.

"You're never lonely," he sings along to music only he can hear, "with a biscuit in your hand…"

No one has ever told Bubba he has a decent voice, but he harbors elaborate fantasies of rising to the top of the charts as an outlaw country singer. He is in the middle of such a daydream, performing as a spokesman for Howdy's Biscuits, when a black SUV swerves into his lane, cutting him off.

"What in the heck," Bubba says as he jerks the wheel and slams on his brakes, holding his biscuit aloft like the statue of liberty clutches the torch of freedom.

Two more SUVs close in from behind, boxing him in. Armed men pour out of the vehicles. Bubba steps out of the truck, arms in the air, still holding the biscuit.

"Don't shoot!"

A man in a dark suit slips out of one of the SUVs. He calmly approaches Bubba, sizing him up.

"And who might you be?" he asks in an English accent. Bubba swears he's seen him somewhere before. Something about the teeth, which are whiter and brighter than God ever intended.

The armed men begin to search Bubba's vehicle, which he doesn't care for one bit. "Listen here," he says, "I'm a taxpayer and—"

The man in the suit explodes. "Who! The fuck! Are you?"

"Boss?"

Both Bubba and the man in the suit turn toward his pickup truck, where another man is standing in the bed holding up what looks like a mangled GPS system.

"Where would you like to go today?" the GPS inquires.

The man in the suit shakes his head in disgust. "Let's go," he says and slaps the biscuit out of Bubba's hand.

"My biscuit!" Bubba blurts.

DEREK HANSEN NEEDS TO CALM down.

Usually, the founder and CEO of Health Net Secure feels a sense of tranquility after eliminating an infiltrator, like he did this morning at Mojave Critical Care, but the fiasco at Western Psychiatric has him seething. Seated in the back of a black SUV, he holsters his weapon and closes his eyes, taking solace in the memory of how it went down this morning.

An hour before dawn, an elite squad of his security staff dragged the vermin out of his cell and into a fenced-in yard lit up as bright as day. They tossed the man to the ground and formed a semicircle around him. Then it was Hansen's show.

"Listen here, my little vigilante friend," he said, "you've got one option." Hansen pointed at a gate in the security fence as two of his men pushed it open. "If you make it past the gate, you're home free. If not, well, you've had a good run, haven't you?"

The prisoner sensed it was a set up. "Fuck you," he spat. "I don't run."

"A noble junkie," Hansen said. He had to give the man credit. He didn't seem scared. Nor did the semiautomatic Hansen pointed at his head seem to have any effect on him. The fucker didn't even flinch. Hansen pulled the gun back and considered his options.

"You want a second chance? It's what all you junkies want, isn't it?" Hansen tossed the weapon in the dirt in front of the man.

"Take your shot."

The scum lunged for the gun and his men lit him up with their assault rifles, turning the scene into a bloodbath. A happy memory ruined by the debacle at Western Psych.

Hansen's tab lights up with a message from Bethany Webster, his crack director of public relations and a so-so piece of ass. *TV crews setting up. Coming?*

Be right there, he types.

"Driver," he says, raising his voice to ensure he will be heard. "Take me back to the hospital."

MELANIE IS LEANING AGAINST THE rear doors of the ambulance when Trevor and Vinnie emerge from the elevator. She takes a deep breath. No feelings, only choices.

"Miss me?" she asks.

She can tell Trevor wants to be mad at her, but he isn't, which is weird. "You want to tell me why you're here?" he asks.

"I saw an opportunity and I took it," Melanie says, but she isn't fooling anyone, especially not Trevor. She knows she fucked up and is overcompensating with a show of bravado she isn't really feeling.

"And the target?" Trevor asks.

"Yeah, about that." Melanie opens the ambulance door and steps to the side. "We had a mishap."

A gruesome stench wafts out of the ambulance. Vinnie pulls the collar of his shirt up over his mouth. "What is that?"

"The target," Melanie says.

"Already?" Trevor asks.

Melanie doesn't have an answer for that. The last time she spoke to Mick was at Howdy's, but when they pulled into MIS HQ, he was stiff and blue and, by the smell of things, in an advanced state of decomposition, which makes no sense.

Trevor and Vinnie cautiously approach for a closer look. Although a sheet covers Mick's body, it doesn't conceal the fact that he's sporting an enormous erection.

"That's something you don't see every day," Trevor says.

"Maybe *you* don't," Vinnie says with a smirk.

"What happened?" Trevor asks Melanie.

"He was fine when we left the hospital," Melanie shrugs, feigning indifference, "but I found this on him."

Melanie hands Trevor a bottle of pills. He scans the label. "This isn't a hydrocodone overdose," he says.

"What is it then?" Melanie asks.

"I don't know," Trevor admits.

Melanie softens. "I thought you'd be mad at me."

"I'm just glad you're safe."

"You sound like you mean it."

"I do."

Normally, Trevor would be furious at her for botching the op, but he's curiously calm.

"Is everything all right?" Melanie asks.

"We lost an op today."

Oh, shit. Here it is. "Who?" she demands.

"Scary Gary."

Horror and disbelief surge through her and she pukes on the parking garage floor. "Not Gary," she says when she's done.

Trevor puts an arm around her but addresses Vinnie. "Put the target in the truck and get rid of the ambulance."

"Roger that." Vinnie snaps on a pair of black latex gloves and slides a paper mask onto his face.

Melanie regains what's left of her composure. "I want to talk to Doyle," she says.

"Good," Trevor says. "Because he wants to talk to you." He leads Melanie to the private elevator for MIS.

"You're not coming with me?" Melanie asks.

"I gotta clean up your mess."

The doors open and Viviana Sanchez steps out of the elevator dressed in skintight workout clothes. She looks like she's just left the set of a photo shoot for a line of high-end yoga gear. She's tall, fit, and incredibly attractive, but that's not the problem. Melanie despises Viviana because she's taken her spot as the top op at MIS.

"Thank goodness you're alive!" Viviana exclaims.

"Bite me."

"Easy," Trevor chastises.

"It's okay," Viviana says. "She's had a rough day." Viviana does an extravagant hair flip as she walks past them. "Going for a run, Trev."

"Going for a run, Trev," Melanie mimics.

"Mel..."

Melanie ignores him and storms into the elevator. She turns and crosses her arms as the doors close. When they open again, a half-dozen staffers and data analysts mill about Make It Stop's lobby. Vernon and Max, two of the newer ops who follow Viviana around like puppies, turn their heads when Melanie enters and then quickly look away.

So, it's gonna be like that...

Melanie cruises through the lobby. When she reaches the end of the long hallway, she knocks on the door to Doyle's office and barges in, but no one's there. She considers going to look for him but decides to wait. She plops down in a chair across from Doyle's desk and stares out the window that faces the Hollywood Hills, watching clouds sail by and palm trees sway in the breeze. Usually, the slivers of light sliding up and down the rustling fronds would have a calming effect, but her mind is a mess. She blew the assignment. Mick must have gotten a hold of the pills she'd copped in the locker room when they were leaving Western Psych, and now he's dead. She has no idea how, but this is bad. Very, very bad. Not as bad as Gary dying, but she didn't have anything to do with that. This is all on her. On any other day she'd be devastated, but this is not any other day.

She knew Gary had gone on a long-term assignment in the desert, an infiltration job that was expected to take weeks—just like hers. He'd left the day before yesterday. How did they sniff him out so quickly? Did he screw up? Or did someone know he was coming?

Trevor should be here. He's her case manager. This is his job. She never meets with Doyle one-on-one.

Doyle steps into the office with a grim expression on his face and closes the door behind him. He's wearing an old school sweatshirt and sweatpants that are two different shades of gray. It *kills* Melanie they don't match. Who does that?

Melanie decides a proactive approach is in order. "What the hell is going on?"

"That's what I should be asking you," Doyle says as he settles into the chair behind his desk.

"Where's Gary?" she asks.

"At the morgue."

Melanie sits up. "What are we waiting for? We have to go get him!"

"You know we can't do that."

"What are you talking about? We're his family!"

"Of course we are, but if we go down there…"

"I'll go." Melanie gets up from her chair so quickly she has to hold on to one of the armrests to maintain her balance.

"Sit. Down."

Melanie snorts and throws herself into the chair.

"We're gathering intel on his family," Doyle continues. "He has an older brother. Did Gary ever talk about him?"

"Yeah," Melanie replies. "He said he was a homeless junkie shitbag."

"We're doing everything we can. Steps—"

"Are being taken," Melanie says, anticipating Doyle's half-assed explanation. She didn't come here to listen to bureaucratic doublespeak.

Doyle isn't amused.

"Let's turn our attention to your disaster of an operation." Doyle sets the bottle of pills on his desk. "Where did these come from?"

"Trevor gave them to you?"

"Really, Melanie? That's how you want to do this?"

Melanie sighs. She can handle Doyle when he's angry but not when he's disappointed. "I acquired them during my mission."

"The target didn't have them in his possession when you found him?"

Melanie shakes her head. "He must have taken them from me somehow. He—"

Doyle holds up his hand. "He got them from you?"

Her head feels like a kettle getting ready to blow. She decides to change tactics. "Yes, but the target was getting ready to kill himself when I came along. I basically saved him."

"Before you killed him."

"That's not fair."

"Fair? A young man is dead."

Melanie doesn't know why she's arguing with Doyle. She screwed up and they both know it.

"Your mission was to infiltrate," Doyle continues. "What you did was nothing short of a raid."

Melanie tries counting to ten. She looks at the clouds, then the palm trees. She makes it to three before blurting, "I did what I had to do."

"Is that what you call ignoring operation protocol?"

"You can call it whatever you want."

"How about reckless, irresponsible, and detrimental to the perpetuity of the organization?"

"How about the perpetuity of *me*?" Melanie practically shouts. "If I'd followed your precious protocols, I'd probably be dead like Gary!"

Doyle studies Melanie with his intense blue eyes. "I'm taking you off the operations team until further notice."

Melanie can't believe what she's hearing. "You can't do that!"

"Let's review," Doyle says. "To establish your cover, you relapsed to present yourself as a more convincing candidate."

"I always do that!"

"Right, but when you turned the infiltration into an extraction, your impaired judgment became a liability."

"You don't know what it's like in there!"

Doyle gives her a look. He knows better than anyone what it's like to work undercover. When Doyle started Make It Stop, he was a one-man wrecking crew, busting out patients on his own with no one looking out for him on the outside.

"Okay, maybe you do," she admits.

"If we can't do what we do with discretion," Doyle says, "we might as well not do it at all. Your poor judgment led to a young man's death."

"Gary was murdered. Mick *wanted* to die."

"Some of us feel you've become too aggressive."

"You mean Trevor," Melanie says. "Is that why he isn't here?"

"I asked him not to come. Are you two sleeping together?"

Melanie is so surprised she isn't sure she's hearing him correctly. "What kind of question is that?"

"The kind that requires a yes or no answer."

"No," it pains Melanie to admit.

"Then stop acting like it. You know the policy here. I don't want to have this conversation again. Are we clear?"

Melanie nods.

"Your social skills need work. I want you to learn how to connect with people again. Ops must stay balanced, both physically and mentally."

"Here we go with the Yoda shit." The headache Melanie has been fighting has finally arrived. The sunlight stabs her eyes. She wishes she could close the blinds, curl up on the floor, pretend like none of this is happening.

"I want you to stay away from the facility for a while."

Melanie sits up in her chair. "Are you kidding me?" Doyle doesn't answer because Doyle doesn't kid. "I'm suspended?"

"Lay low. Get some rest. Your case manager will be in touch."

"I thought we were a family!"

"Make It Stop is your family," Doyle says, "but it shouldn't be your world."

Melanie feels like she might lose it, a fit so ferocious she won't be able to control herself. She yanks open the door and storms out of Doyle's office. Melanie is halfway down the hall when she hears him call her name. She does an about-face and marches back.

"What?"

"No more drinking," Doyle says. "Relapse again and your suspension becomes permanent."

That does it. Doyle's final directive flips the switch on Melanie's restraint. She exits the office and slams the door behind her. An op named Natalie approaches from the other end of the hall.

"I just heard about Gary. I'm so—"

"Save it." Melanie pushes through the door to the locker room. She opens her locker and starts stuffing her gear into a duffel bag. She's nearly done when she finds a photo of Scary Gary, sitting on the hood of a car in a parking lot, enjoying a private joke.

Oh, Gary.

He was more than a friend and a mentor; he was the best sparring partner she ever had. He could take punishment as well as he could dish it out, which is rare. One time they were sparring with staffs. Gary was the stronger combatant and better with weapons, but Melanie was determined to beat him. She came in for a headshot, but Gary anticipated the move. He ducked out of the way and clipped her in the knee. Not enough to hurt her but it sent her sprawling to the mat.

"You mad?" Gary teased.

Melanie gritted her teeth and launched a furious assault that backed him into a corner. She planted her staff on the mat and vaulted into the air with a flying kick to his face that knocked him flat on his back. When he lifted his head off the mat, he was missing a tooth and blood gushed from his mouth.

"Holy shit that was awesome!" he said.

"Uh, your tooth…"

"Didn't need it anyway."

Melanie stuffs the photo into her bag and exits through the door that leads directly into the dojo. She scans the room for Trevor and spots him in the corner by the racks of free weights, locked in an embrace with Viviana-fucking-Sanchez.

Melanie's brain momentarily freezes before feelings of sadness, shame, and rage flash through her all at once. She storms out of the dojo, puts both hands on the door, and slams it with all her might. She slams it with such force it pops open, so Melanie slams it again and again and again until not only Trevor and Viviana, but everyone at Make It Stop knows she has completely lost her shit.

TREVOR AND DOYLE WALK ALONG the main promenade of what's left of the Sherman Oaks Galleria. In the nineties, a major renovation inadvertently turned the walkway that runs through the center of the mall into a wind tunnel. Walking from one end of the Galleria to the other feels like traversing a blustery desert canyon.

"Well?" Doyle asks with an intensity that makes Trevor squirm.

"I think she's experiencing mission fatigue," Trevor says.

"You mean she's burning out."

Trevor chooses his words carefully. "I don't think she's there yet, but she could be headed in that direction."

"I want to show you something." Doyle takes out his tab and plays footage from a news broadcast. The screen shows a familiar scene: the entrance to Western Psychiatric.

"Is that…?"

"Melanie's mess," Doyle answers.

A reporter stands in front of the hospital. LAPD, corps, and men in suits cluster around the entrance. The screen splits to reveal another crime scene. A team from the coroner's office loads a shrouded body into the back of an ambulance.

"That's Gary?" Trevor asks.

Doyle nods. "And that's bad news. If the media is connecting the two incidents, that means someone's feeding them information about us."

"That is bad," Trevor says.

"Real bad."

The screen reverts to Western Psychiatric, where a press conference resumes. Derek Hansen, CEO of Health Net Secure, addresses the small crowd. Doyle turns up the volume and the two men stop in front of an empty hologram repair store to listen to his spiel.

"I speak for the administration of this hospital," Hansen begins, "and every hospital in the Health Net Secure network, when I say we will not be cowed by vigilantes who take the law into their own hands and put our employees and patients at risk."

"Bastard," Doyle says.

"Today," Hansen continues, "I'm pleased to announce the addition of a dozen more hospitals to our network in Southern California, news that should give those who operate outside of the law pause. You mess with one of us, you mess with all of us."

A reporter shouts a question at Hansen. "What do you have to say to the accusation that conditional release is turning Health Net Secure facilities into militarized debtors' prisons?"

"Thank you for your question! That's all the time we have today."

Polite applause from the small crowd dissipates as corps move in. Doyle shuts off the tab and puts it away.

"Can you guess what all of these new HNS hospitals have in common?" he asks as they resume walking.

"Conditional release?"

Doyle nods. "By the end of the year, the majority of rehab and detox facilities in LA will be holding its patients hostage until they can pay their bills."

Trevor collects himself. "What does this have to do with Melanie?"

"This is bigger than Melanie. This affects all of us. If conditional release facilities are sharing information with each other, we're in for a tough, tough fight."

"We've lost ops before..."

"Not like this."

"Gary knew the risks."

"Did he?" Doyle asks. "Gary's mission was almost identical to Melanie's, a long-term extraction. He lasted less than forty-eight hours."

"Are you saying we have a rat?" Trevor asks.

"I'm saying we can't have ops with mission fatigue."

"But if Melanie had followed the mission the way it was designed..."

"She'd be dead," Doyle says.

"It hardly seems fair to suspend her."

"I'm not just suspending Melanie," Doyle says. "I'm suspending *all* operations until we figure out what we're up against."

They reach the end of the promenade. Doyle stops and shakes his head. Trevor has never seen him look and sound so defeated.

"What does that mean exactly?" Trevor asks.

"It's time to clean house, Trevor."

"We're just going to cut loose one of our best operatives?"

"No," Doyle says. "I've got a plan for Melanie."

Trevor doesn't like the sound of that, but he's glad Doyle isn't kicking her out of MIS.

"And the target?"

"I'll take care of it," Doyle says as he turns and heads back to headquarters.

Trevor's tab buzzes. He imagines its Melanie, ready to give him an earful, but the name on the screen reads Viviana Sanchez.

WHILE THE CAMERA CREWS BREAK down their equipment in front of Western Psychiatric, Hansen glad-hands a brace of hospital administrators and local politicians who have shown up to get their faces on television.

"You're all doing a wonderful job," Hansen says. "Keep up the good work." What he'd really like to do is pistol-whip every last one of their faces into mincemeat.

"Mr. Hansen?" Bethany steps out of the crowd.

"What is it?" On most days he likes Bethany. He finds her infinitely more companionable than his last few assistants. But today is not most days.

"We have video of what looks to be—"

Hansen rips the tab from her hands and watches a short video captured from security footage of a young woman with a pink Mohawk wearing a leather jacket.

"What am I looking at?" Hansen asks.

Bethany pushes a strand of hair behind her ear. "We believe that's the operative who kidnapped Mr. Moriarity this afternoon."

"Who is she?" Hansen barks. "What do we have on her?"

"Not much, but we did find this." Bethany holds out a pin with an illustration of a swallow with its eyes crossed out.

Hansen gives Bethany the tab and takes the pin from her. "What is it? And if you tell me you don't know, I'll put you over my knee." Hansen stares Bethany down in case she gets the notion he's testing her. His last assistant got it into her head he wanted her to stand up for herself, a mistake that cost her dearly.

Bethany doesn't bat an eye. "We're working on that."

Hansen smiles as he returns the pin to Bethany.

"Then get to it."

3

THE COLONY

MELANIE SITS IN HER CAR in the parking lot outside of Buddy Liquor, wondering if she should destroy her life. She's been here hundreds of times, as recently as this morning when she'd picked up a bottle of Fiery Cat for her mission. Now she's back to finish what she started.

Buddy Liquor is a short stroll from her East Hollywood bungalow. When she first moved into the neighborhood, she was obsessed with the store's name: Was there an actual person named Buddy? Did "buddy" signify "friend"? Or was the name some terrible joke?

The front windows are filled with signs with cheesy slogans: EVERYBUDDY NEEDS SOMEBUDDY and WE'RE ALWAYS OPEN (EXCEPT WHEN WE'RE CLOSED). The store carries all the things a single woman who doesn't have her shit together might need. She can find anything from spaghetti sauce to contraceptive sponges on its disorganized shelves, but that's not why she's here.

It's late evening, and men and women who look like they just got off work are stopping by to pick up something to take the edge off the day, make the ride home a little smoother, ease the transition into a domestic wavelength she has zero interest in tuning into. Her car faces the front of the store, and she watches as people exit with their evening fix: construction workers clutching tall boys in paper bags, office drones carrying six-packs, soccer moms stuffing Chardonnay into oversized totes, and executive types slipping tiny bottles of vodka into suit pockets. The more one had to lose, the greater the denial.

A junkie, limping badly and clutching his right arm with his left, shuffles inside the store and is immediately chased out. The man's face is gray and his arm is puckered with yellow sores. He and Melanie lock eyes as he limps past her car, leaving a foul odor in his wake that is nauseating in its sweetness, like sulfur and jizz mixed together. She can't roll up the window fast enough.

It's all getting to be too much. First Gary, then the drama with Doyle, and finally Trevor's betrayal. What a fool she's been. She knows she needs to give the pity party a rest, but Viviana? Really? Of all the people in the world, he has to fall for that fake-ass skank?

She considers Doyle's warning and wonders what her life would be like without MIS. She loves being on the operations team, but the rest of it is starting to wear thin. The inflexible discipline. The insufferable routine. Maybe it's time she moved on to another organization, one that isn't so incestuous. She's heard that groups like Vigilant California were even offering signing bonuses for experienced ops.

Her thoughts keep returning to Scary Gary. She can't believe she's never going to be on the receiving end of one of his rib-crushing hugs again. It's hard to accept he's really gone. That's the problem with MIS. Everything is so secretive. Anything can happen on a mission. Everyone understands that. It comes with the territory. But when things go south—like the time Natalie blew her cover and MIS had to go dark while it established a new headquarters—a black shroud of secrecy falls over the organization and she's never sure what to believe. She knows Doyle keeps things from her. Of course he does. That's what underground organizations do. But does he know about Trevor and Viviana?

Trevor is Melanie's case manager, not Viviana's, but the same edict against fraternization applies to everyone. The hypocrisy of it all infuriates her, but it doesn't matter. When she thinks of her friend stuffed in a drawer in the morgue, or Mick in the back of the MIS truck, the waterworks start up again. She's already gone through all of her tissues and the three Pepsi Starbucks napkins she'd found in the glove box.

She has no idea what she's going to do with herself. Sleep? Work out? Get drunk on Fiery Cat and try to burn the pain away?

Even though Doyle has made it clear he will kick her out if she relapses, technically speaking she's still under the influence from this morning's escapades. If she buys a bottle *right now* it won't be a relapse but a continuation.

Doyle wouldn't see it that way.

She checks her reflection in the rearview and is surprised to see Rachel Roark staring back. Girls like Rachel don't cry in liquor store parking lots. What would Rachel do in this situation?

She wouldn't have anything to do with an organization that tells her what she can and cannot do, that's for sure. And she wouldn't pine after a guy who has his sights set on someone else.

Melanie can see the booze stacked on shelves behind the counter, so she knows they have plenty of Fiery Cat in stock. It's truly terrible. The vodka of choice for teenagers and unsheltered people. You don't *drink* Fiery Cat, you *use* it. It would be so easy to go inside, get another bottle, and finish the job she'd started this morning. Then, when she's good and toasted, she'll decide if she's done with Make It Stop.

She opens the door and puts a foot down on the asphalt when a man carrying a large black and white cat stops in front of her car. The man's name is Lou Johnson; the cat's is Abigail. She knows this because Lou is her next-door neighbor and Abigail is her cat.

"What are you doing here?" Lou asks, peering into her car.

"I, uh…"

Melanie can feel her face flush with embarrassment. Lou takes care of Abigail when she's away on missions. It's an informal arrangement, but he's so reliable that Lou has a key to her place. Abigail is indifferent to most people, but she *loves* Lou. When she gets hungry, she goes through the cat door and waits on Lou's porch until he lets her in. Sometimes she does this when Melanie is home. Though she's offered to pay Lou for his trouble, he always refuses. She leaves money for him in an envelope alongside the cans of cat food Abigail favors, but he never takes it.

"Aren't you supposed to be out of town?" Lou asks.

"Oh, that," Melanie says. "Change of plans. Looks like I'll be sticking around for a while."

"So, you won't be needing me to look after this girl?"

Abigail purrs as Lou strokes her head.

"No," Melanie says, "I'm afraid not."

"Abigail and I had big plans for the evening," Lou drawls, "but we'll just have to make it some other time." Abigail purrs contentedly as Lou strokes her trim little head.

It takes Melanie way too long to realize Lou is joking. "Ha-ha! You're a huge help, Lou. I don't know what I'd do without you."

Lou's smile brightens. He's a big, slab-shouldered dude from West Virginia who came to LA to write screenplays. He knows a lot about banjos and has a thick, nasty-looking scar on his neck. When Melanie asked him about it, he told her he got it in Boone County, but there was something in his tone that suggested if she didn't know what that meant, he didn't have anything more to say on the subject.

"Would you like to come over for some tea?" Lou carries Abigail in the crook of his massive arm like a musical instrument. She looks very content there, which annoys Melanie. Has her cat turned on her, too?

"Maybe later," Melanie says, meaning definitely not.

"Okay, then."

"Some other time." She hates small talk and is absolutely terrible at it. She feels obligated to engage Lou in some meaningful way but doesn't know how. It seems to be the kind of thing a normal person could do with ease. It occurs to her this is exactly what Doyle was talking about: she's lost the ability to connect with people on a one-to-one basis. Well, she has a news flash for Doyle: you can't lose what you never had. And how exactly is a member of a super-secret underground resistance movement supposed to make new friends? It's not like she can bullshit about what she does for work, where she goes, how she spends her time. What else is there to talk about? The fucking weather?

All she wants to do is take a shower and sleep through the weekend, but Lou seems nervous, like there's something else on his mind.

"I'm gonna go inside," he says. "Need anything?"

Melanie shakes her head, but then she changes her mind. "Well, yes, actually, there is something you can do for me."

"What's that?" Lou asks, his smile reappearing. Lou is an easy smiler, which makes disappointing him that much harder.

"Can I have my cat back?"

"You mean right now?" Lou asks.

Abigail hasn't so much as twitched her tail, is fine right where she is.

"If you don't mind."

"No, not at all," Lou says. He edges closer to the car and ducks so Abigail can climb through the window, but Abigail is having none of it. Lou keeps pushing her closer and closer until the cat spills into the car and onto Melanie's lap.

"Sorry," Lou says.

"You have nothing to apologize for."

Melanie cranks the engine, jerks the car into reverse, and guns the gas, leaving Lou standing there with a puzzled look on his face. Abigail peers out the window so she can watch Lou as the car slides out of the parking lot.

"Maybe you'd like to stay with him," Melanie says.

Abigail looks up at her, searchingly it seems, and for a moment Melanie expects her to reply.

MELANIE LIES IN BED, STROKING her cat and bubbling through photos of Scary Gary on her tab. The bed is her favorite thing about the tiny bungalow she calls home. It's a big, sturdy canopy bed with heavy curtains that block out the light. Its poles are elaborately carved and richly stained, and the headboard displays some kind of hunting scene. It belongs in a castle high above Swan Lake, not in some crappy East Hollywood studio apartment. The bed is too big to pass through any of the doors or windows, and she often wonders how it got here. She imagines a homesick Bavarian carpenter assembling the bed in this room, knowing he wouldn't be able to take it with him.

She lingers on a photo of Trevor and switches to a display of her recent calls, all of which are to or from her case manager. She considers calling him but throws the tab across the room in disgust. She pulls Abigail close and cuddles her.

"You love me, don't you, Abby?"

Abigail squirms free and leaps to the floor. Great. Even her own cat is sick of her.

She climbs out of bed and pulls on black Lycra pants and a black long-sleeve shirt that clings to her body. She wraps her hair in a black bandana and zips herself into a tight black jacket. Her shoes and socks are also black. No lights, no reflective gear, not a stitch of color anywhere. She doesn't worry about not being seen. The whole point is to become invisible.

She can feel a monster headache coming on. Melanie opens the medicine cabinet looking for pills she knows she won't find. She drinks a glass of water from a plastic cup she hopes isn't the same one she'd used to empty the toilet when it overflowed last month. She's been drinking from it for weeks and it hasn't killed her yet, so she drinks another, and another after that. In spite of the alcohol she'd put into her system earlier today, she's more wired than tired.

Melanie sets off on a run. The streets are eerily quiet. Not many people around. She sticks to residential neighborhoods and glides through the night unseen. She loves the feeling that comes with running not to get somewhere but to avoid detection, of being invisible. She can run like this for hours. There's only one rule: if someone sees her, she adds another mile to her run. One night she ran so far and for so long that she found herself outside a twenty-four-hour donut shop in a part of the city she didn't recognize. Exhausted and disoriented, she had to call a car to take her home.

Melanie isn't the fastest runner, but she's a quiet one. She regulates her breathing. Fine-tunes it. She doesn't run with headphones on, so she can hear the sounds her feet make on the forest paths, the hillside trails, the asphalt streets. She pushes herself to pick up the pace and reminds herself what running is *for*. Running is medicine for the mind and a crucible for the body, a test of the place where body and spirit come together to determine one's limits. This is the place Melanie is always trying to reach.

A sliver of light knifes through the trees, silvering the limbs as if sheathed in ice. She slips into the shadows and imagines the asphalt is a black river. She reaches out to graze the branches with her fingertips and the leaves feel cold to the touch. Is she even in Los Angeles anymore?

As she gets into the rhythm of her run, images come to her:

The little fluffy clouds on the nurse's ridiculous underwear.

Mick's blue face in the back of the ambulance.

Gary's body-bagged body being carried away.

Goddam it, Gary. You weren't supposed to go out like that.

It was Gary who made her feel like she belonged at MIS, like she mattered. She can see his big toothy smile. His intense stare used to make her wonder if he was on something, a suspicion that persisted for months until she realized that's just how he was. Always upbeat. Always *on*. He had a huge heart that was never closed off to her or to anyone else. A good, good man. And now he's gone.

His loss brings her back to her earliest days with MIS, a time when the darkness was darkest, when the terror of being held against her will in a room full of psychotics with no way out was never far from her thoughts. She knows what it's like to be brutalized by a hospital's security staff. She knows what it's like to wake up every day without hope. And it was Gary who saved her.

COLONIAL GENERAL HOSPITAL, A.K.A. THE Colony, is located in Westchester, just north of LAX. The Colony's methods were as old as its cracked plaster walls. Heavy meds and lots of group therapy in brightly lit rooms were the norm. Melanie checked herself in with money promised by her aunt after she'd been arrested for being drunk and disorderly with possession of a controlled substance. She knew volunteering for rehab would paint her in a more penitent light and hopefully reduce the charges. She'd heard of conditional release but didn't think it applied to her.

She was so naïve.

The hospital was comprised of a single massive tower that stood thirteen stories tall. The windows on Melanie's room overlooked a freeway interchange, one of those futuristic-looking concrete marvels with overlapping exits and on-ramps—the last place she'd want to be in an earthquake. She'd been in the facility a month when they stopped giving her the meds she'd been taking since she arrived. No explanation. They just stopped. She spent an anxious night looking out the window, watching the cars go by without thinking about the people inside them.

The following day, they moved her to a different part of the facility. The vibe was very different in this ward. Though no one bothered explaining it to her, she'd been sent to detention because her financing had fallen through, and she had to stay there until she could pay. She had no one she could turn to. Her mom was dead and her dad had disappeared. Her aunt had pulled up stakes and left the country. Melanie was on her own.

Her new home was a large, crowded coed dormitory where the lights stayed on around the clock and the locks were on the other side of the doors. They didn't give her a bed to sleep in: just a blanket, a sheet riddled with cigarette burns, and a towel with a hole cut out of the middle that she could wear like a tunic, which some people on the ward did. This was The Colony. She'd never been in a rehab like this before—part prison, part homeless shelter. It was like a punk squat without the punks.

She found an unoccupied spot where the women congregated and arranged her bedding. She kept her eyes open and, after a few days, moved to a better location that had been vacated by a junkie who'd turned violent and had to be forcibly removed.

Melanie traded her wrist tab for a filthy pillow and some baby wipes. She stared at the ceiling for five quasi-sleepless nights. The ceiling was pocked with water stains. She stared at them until they formed patterns she could recreate from memory with her eyes closed. When she opened them again, she imagined turning her gaze into lasers that could cut the stains out of the ceiling like a saw. She pictured people on the floor above tumbling from the holes and she'd laugh until a voice out of the darkness hissed at her to shut the fuck up.

She was losing it.

What little rest she got came in snatches she couldn't measure. She was lost without her watch. The lack of sleep made her mean. Most detainees learned to leave her alone; those who didn't received their lesson in the form of a black eye or broken nose. She fought like a cat, wild and willing to sacrifice everything to leave her mark.

Then along came Applewhite.

He wasn't like the other corps. He was enormous, a giant with Slavic features who looked like he could take on a half-dozen men and enjoy doing it. A square-jawed, no-neck, gorilla-fisted brute who thrived on intimidation. He didn't carry a weapon—not even a submission stick, the electrified telescoping wands that all corps carried. Even the other corps were afraid of Applewhite.

He appeared on the ward at the end of her first week. Melanie watched him harass one of the other detainees, a Black woman in her early twenties who Melanie remembered from group therapy, which was already starting to feel like a lifetime ago. The woman had been kicked out of college for selling Oxies in her dorm room. Slender and slightly deranged, she wore a pair of ratty-looking bunny slippers twenty-four seven. Melanie recalled the sound they made when she shuffled from session to session, zonked out on mood stabilizers. Her name was Daphne.

Some of the women who'd been on the ward for a while befriended Daphne while she got her bearings. One day, Applewhite came to see Daphne, and when his teasing turned to tormenting, her friends scattered. He slapped Daphne in the face with one of his massive hands, and when Melanie tried to intervene, Daphne's "friends" held Melanie back while Applewhite had his way with her.

The way these women sold out Daphne was shocking to Melanie, but it shouldn't have been. It went against everything that recovery was supposed to be about. The bond shared by broken people committed to getting better was the miracle of recovery. There was no fellowship without it, but Melanie couldn't buy in after she saw how they turned on Daphne. Who would do such a thing?

Drunks. Addicts. Junkies. That's who.

Why did she have to keep learning this lesson over and over again?

Applewhite set his sights on Melanie next. On two consecutive nights, she fought him off. The first time she kicked him so hard she thought he'd lose his temper, but he laughed and taunted her with promises that he would return.

The second time she bit the fleshy part of his hand and he howled with fury. That night she lay awake, waiting for Applewhite to come back. Something had turned inside of her and she was powerless to stop it. She could feel herself moving to a place where she would have to test this new knowledge of the world. She was confident it would happen soon, maybe even that very night. She was drifting off to sleep when a voice came to her in the dark.

Open your hand.

It was a male voice, but it wasn't Applewhite's. It was soft but direct, like it had come from inside her own head. At first, she didn't believe it was real. Convinced her dreams were creeping into her consciousness, she did as she was told.

When he comes for you, the voice said, *give him this.*

A cold, dead weight filled her palm. She instinctively clenched her fist and grasped something solid yet light. She didn't need to look at it to know what it was, to know that it belonged there.

Do you understand what you have to do?

Melanie couldn't speak. She nodded at the ceiling, tears pouring down her cheeks. She buried herself in her blanket and held the knife to her chest. She could use it to make things better, imagine alternate outcomes, nourish thoughts about the future. She could slash her way to a place where fear ended and hope began. The knife gave her power and possibility. With the knife in her fist, she could finally sleep.

After three nights, Applewhite came back.

He seized her by the hair and yanked Melanie to her feet the way a child pulls a toy out of its box. He pulled her close and growled in her ear.

"Are you ready for me, slut?"

"Yes," Melanie whispered with the fullness of someone whose greatest desire is about to be fulfilled and plunged the knife into the brute's neck.

Applewhite twisted away with such violence it ripped the blade from her hands. He didn't scream or make a sound. He simply vanished.

Come, said the voice. A hand found hers and guided her through a maze of corridors and stairwells until they were free of the building.

Out on a median, the hospital tower looked like some great electric tombstone. The grass was damp and shockingly cold on her bare feet. Cars rushed by at impossible speeds. An empty potato chip bag tumbled in the gutter where it caught the light. Streetlamps glowed with otherworldly intensity. It was all so beautifully real she thought she was having a breakdown.

Don't stop, the man said, and they ran across the street, through several parking lots, and down a long, dark alley lined with chain-link fences and filled with dumpsters. They took shelter behind an abandoned gas station. A blue sedan with tinted windows pulled up. The man opened the door for her and Melanie finally saw his face. It was lined and creased and disfigured with ink. He had big bulging eyes and a gap-toothed smile.

"My name is Gary," he said. "Are you ready to make it stop?"

4

TRULUV

It's been three years, nine months, and twenty-four days since he'd chewed up three hundred milligrams of OxyContin, chased it with a pint of rum, and waited to die. Trevor woke up in a hospital in restraints, hooked up to all kind of tubes. For three days the lights burned through his eyelids while the voices of his deceased father and missing mother drifted through his head and he truly wished he was dead.

When he got out of the hospital, he was seventy-three thousand dollars in debt and remanded to court-ordered rehab, where he started plotting his next attempt. There he met Doyle, who enlisted him in his organization. Trevor wasn't a smash-the-state type like many of the others who were drawn to Make It Stop and groups like it. There seemed to be more of them every week. He spent a lot of time researching these groups and even attended a few meetings. But MIS was different. Though the work was dangerous and challenging, his life got better. Helping others helped him. He never relapsed.

Trevor has spent most of the day preparing a surprise for Melanie he's certain she will hate. When he's done, he puts his tab on hologram mode and waits for her to call.

Before his suicide attempt, Trevor wrote code for a pornographic movie studio that incorporated holograms into its portfolio of products. By then holos were everywhere: on the street, in restaurants, on public transportation. It was like a population explosion. You couldn't get away from them, but not everyone liked sharing space with holograms. Trevor hardly ever sees them in public anymore, but he and Melanie occasionally use them while speaking on their tabs. Trevor wonders if this practice created a false sense of intimacy between them. She's grown accustomed to spending time with his hologram, and now she wants more. Is that the problem?

Difficult to say. Recovery fosters bonds that form faster and with more intensity than regular relationships. Sometimes it's hard to know if the attraction one feels is legitimate or a product of the overwhelming realness of recovery.

When Trevor signed on with MIS three-and-a-half years ago, he started as a data analyst, although the title didn't really cover all that he did for the organization. He excelled at crafting cover stories for ops and then insinuating details about the personalities he constructed by hacking into the websites of local and state government agencies to establish a verifiable digital footprint. Two years ago, Doyle promoted him to case manager. This was right after one of Doyle's operatives relapsed and overdosed. Her death put a damper on things, but Trevor was excited to work with his first mentee, a wild new recruit named Melanie Marsh.

They'd gotten off to a rocky start, but after a few months they settled into a productive working relationship. She was close with Gary and seemed to get along well with Doyle. While she was an emotional person at her core, he always knew where he stood with her.

It must have been shocking for Melanie to see him and Viviana together. It shocked *him*. He had no idea Viviana had feelings for him. None. She was always nice to him, but she was nice to everyone, even Melanie, who made no secret of her contempt for her.

He was passing through the dojo when Viviana called out to him. He went to see what she wanted and she lunged at him, wrapping her arms around his shoulders and laying her head on his chest while her body shook. Trevor didn't know what to do. Was she crying? Or was this something else?

Eventually, reluctantly, Trevor put his arms around her. Viviana responded by pressing her body against his in a way that didn't seem appropriate to the situation but felt *amazing*. He felt like he ought to say something to her, but what? Viviana lifted her head off his chest and kissed him. And then Melanie walked in.

He'd been trying to figure out what to say to Melanie about it. He supposed he could tell her the truth: Viviana had ambushed him and he was as surprised as Melanie, but that could potentially make things worse. If he swore that he had no feelings for Viviana, it might encourage Melanie. If it meant that Melanie would stop flirting with him, it might be worth letting her think that something was going on between him and Viviana. Either way, Melanie would be hurt, which pains Trevor because he cares about Melanie, just not in the same way that she cares about him.

And what about Viviana? What made her come on so strongly? He doesn't know what to make of it. His feelings range from wanton what-ifs to a disavowal that he feels anything at all. His duty to MIS comes first. But there's no getting away from the fact that he's attracted to Viviana. That's the thing about desire—it doesn't require understanding.

Despite having thought about little else, he still doesn't know what he's going to say to Melanie about what happened in the dojo when his tab lights up and Melanie's hologram shimmers to life above his desk. A jagged seam runs up and down Melanie's holo—he's overdue for an upgrade.

"There you are," he says.

"Here I am."

Melanie's holo looks amazing. She's wearing some kind of slip or nightgown, though she's told him plenty of times that she sleeps in the nude.

"So, how deep in the shit am I?" Melanie asks.

"Pretty deep."

"Doyle thinks we're fucking."

Trevor takes a deep breath. "Yeah, he brought it up with me, too. I think we should talk about it."

"Oh, now you want to talk? Now that Viviana's on your jock—"

"It's not like that," Trevor says. "I'm your case manager, but I'm also your friend. As for what you saw down in the dojo—"

"I don't want to hear about it."

"We can talk about anything you want," Trevor says. "I feel like we haven't been especially honest with each other."

It's hard to hold someone's gaze via holo, the tech isn't that good, but there's no mistaking Melanie's intensity. "How long before I get back into Doyle's good graces?"

"That's up to you."

"Spare me, Trev."

"There isn't a timeline, but Doyle has a special project for you."

"I thought I was suspended?"

"This is something you can do on your own."

"Lay it on me," Melanie says.

"He wants you to start dating."

"What?"

"To work on your social skills. I've set up an account for you on a dating site so we can monitor your progress."

"Are you being serious right now? You want me to go on actual dates?"

"That's kind of the whole point of signing up for a dating site."

"Are you sure this wasn't your idea?"

"I'll be your case manager just like on any other assignment. I've created a new persona for you."

"I can't use Rachel Roark?"

"Negative."

"Why not?"

"Compromised."

"I liked Rachel," Melanie pouts. "I feel like I was just getting to know her."

"Well, she's gone now."

Trevor logs on to the account he's created for Melanie. No coding involved. He isn't worried about her cover story since most users employ aliases. He'll leave that to Melanie. All Trevor had to do was fill out her profile, but it had been massively time-consuming. The website wanted to know *everything*.

"What site did you sign me up for?" she asks. "Junkie Lovers? Stabby Bitches dot com?"

"This one is called TruLuv. I've built most of your profile already, but I'll need some more info to get you started."

"Like what?"

"The kind of relationship you're looking for, the type of partner you're attracted to, what you're, um, into…"

"I don't believe this."

"Mel…"

"I risk everything for MIS, and now you're pimping me out. *You* of all people."

Trevor suppresses a smile. Melanie's in-your-face attitude makes her exasperating to deal with, but in holo mode he finds her easier to handle. "Don't think like that."

"How should I think?"

"Like it's an assignment."

"An assignment with benefits." Melanie leans forward, bringing her bosom into view. Whatever she's wearing, it definitely isn't a dress.

"I'm here to help," Trevor says. "I'll leave the rest up to you."

"Could make for some hot and heavy debriefing sessions."

"Okay," Trevor says, his patience slipping away. "You've been through a lot. We'll do this after you've had time to take it all in."

"Oh, I'm ready. It's been years since I've *taken it all in*."

Trevor puts his head in his hands. She's getting to him, and he's letting her. "You're not making this easy," he says.

"*I'm* not making this easy?" Melanie shouts. "You want easy, talk to Viviana."

That does it. He's had enough of her button pushing. "I'll send you your account name and password," he says. "You can take it from there."

"That's it?"

"That's it."

Melanie crosses her arms and blows a strand of hair from the ruined mohawk out of her eyes. "When can I come back to MIS?" she asks.

"That depends."

"On what? How many guys I sleep with?"

Trevor tunes her out. "I'll be in touch to monitor your progress."

"Do you want video evidence?"

"Doyle will be reviewing my reports."

"Is that how you pervy fucks get off?"

She's being nasty now. He doesn't like it, but he refuses to take the bait. Instead, he offers an olive branch. "I'm really sorry about Gary."

Melanie looks at him for a long moment without saying anything and abruptly ends the call. Her hologram freezes, suspended in midair like a portrait made of light. It's the last time he will see her like this: part Rachel, part Melanie. Pride wounded, eager to prove the world wrong. She looks more sad than angry, but he's confident she'll bounce back. Soon she'll have a new look, a new attitude. She's already halfway there, ready to shed the old persona and shift into something new.

5

MESSAGE IN A DRAWER

CALIENTE CANTINA IS A COMPLEX of stucco structures webbed together with colorful strings of holiday lights and papel picado. The layout confuses Melanie. To the left, patrons cluster around a crowded bar. To the right, an ancient espresso machine hisses like a locomotive and a long line of people queue up to place orders. Does that mean there isn't any table service here? Should she get in line?

Melanie prides herself on her ability to navigate new places. Infiltrate a ten-story prison-hospital? No problem. But here she doesn't know where she's supposed to go. This isn't a restaurant, Melanie muses as she makes her way across the trellised threshold, it's a goddam compound.

She plows across the patio in her new heels. Waiters dash around with cold drinks. A beer sounds good. A frosty margarita even better. She knows not to trust these impulses. There had been times in her life when malt liquor energy drinks, other people's half-finished cocktails, and wine she'd found in a bottle dug out of a trash can (not her wine, not her trash can) had *sounded good*. She'd drunk from beers that had been ashed in, bottles that had been passed around a hobo fire, and a flask that she'd lost in her car for over a year and whose contents tasted like gasoline run through a rusty carburetor (she'd gone back for seconds, then thirds, and finally polished it off). All of these things had not only flown under the radar of common sense but had *appealed* to Melanie somehow.

Maybe she has low thresholds. Perhaps she is a poor discriminator. Whatever it is, it leaves her defenseless in the presence of a frosty mug, a chilled glass, a schooner crusted with salt and dripping with condensation. Booze porn. She'd better stop before she snatches a shot of tequila off a tray as a waiter waltzes by.

Everywhere she looks, people are feasting on baskets of warm chips and salsa. They've either come straight from the office or are dressed coffee shop casual. There are a handful of holograms sprinkled into the mix. She feels overdressed and out of place. Her shoes, dress, bra, underwear, and wig are all brand new. She's here to be noticed, but it's Wednesday. She fights off the urge to turn around and go home.

Inside, where she expects a hostess station, she finds an extravagant altar in an alcove. Candles flicker in the darkness, casting shadows on the statue of a buxom revolutionary with bandoliers and a rifle. Her face is painted white and black like a skeleton. The ground is carpeted with bright orange marigolds.

"Makes you wonder what she's fighting for," a voice says from behind her.

"Revenge," Melanie says without taking her eyes off the adelita.

"Interesting," replies a voice both cocksure and smug. "What makes you say that?"

"When a woman picks up a gun, a man is going to pay."

"You must be Sonja."

Sonja St. John is a social worker who volunteers at an animal shelter. When she read the profile that Trevor created for her, she assumed it was a joke, but here she is. Sonja, Melanie decided, uses her body like a weapon, so she bought a new outfit and chose a wig a shade of scarlet so bright that every man who lays eyes on her will feel the burn.

It definitely has the attention of the young man standing next to her. He has short red hair that is several shades lighter than hers, a cleft chin, and eyes that are set deep and close together. He's wearing the same green polo shirt he has on in his TruLuv profile photo. Cute. Sickening, even.

"Yes, and you're…" She blanks on the name. Tim or Tom. Jim or Josh. Something bland and monosyllabic.

"Tosh."

"Of course. Why don't you get us a table, Tosh?" she asks, not asking.

Tosh has the bearing of someone unaccustomed to being told what to do. An only child or manager-type. A box-store bureaucrat. Tosh blinks and does as he's told.

Melanie deliberately picked someone from TruLuv.com she knew she wouldn't like, and Tosh's demeanor pleases her because she's in no way attracted to him.

She wanders deeper into the cantina, where the tables are arranged around a fake fireplace. This part feels like a proper coffee shop. As she browses the racks of mugs and rows of prepackaged coffee and tea from faraway places, a young woman catches her attention. She seems distraught, or on the verge of being so, as she furiously scratches out a note on a small rectangle of paper. When she's finished, she sets her pen down, opens a small drawer in the table, places the note inside, and slides it shut.

This little ritual captivates Melanie, and when the woman looks up their eyes meet for a moment. She has a look of fragile satisfaction. She's accomplished what she came to do and can now enjoy her cup of tea. Melanie smiles and moves on, but she's dying to know what the note says.

"Oh, there you are," Tosh exclaims when she joins him at a table on the patio next to a gurgling fountain. His relief is apparent, and he promptly puts it back in its hiding place. Tosh is probably used to being stood up, but he looks like the kind of person who would sooner take a knife in the spleen than admit to the rejection that is written all over him.

"Did you think I'd taken a powder on you?" Melanie asks.

"Oh, no," he lies. Tosh is a terrible liar.

A stout Mexican waiter appears with menus. He introduces himself as Jorgé and asks them what they want to drink.

"I'm definitely having a cerveza," Tosh says. "Or shall we start with some shots?"

"I don't drink alcohol." Melanie is usually more circumspect about her sobriety with strangers, but Sonja doesn't give a damn. Sonja didn't come here to cut Tosh slack.

Melanie turns to the waiter and lays a newly manicured hand on his forearm, "Horchata, please."

"You got it," he says.

"Well," Tosh says after Jorgé leaves. "Here we are."

"Here we are," Melanie says.

"What do you do?" Tosh asks.

"I'm in between jobs," Melanie answers. "And you?"

Tosh launches into a long, boring description of his work at a mortgage company and his role in its recent string of successes. He goes on and on about how LA's lack of rental properties and resurgent real estate market has created opportunities for those willing to take on a bit of risk.

"Sounds dodgy," Melanie says.

Tosh scowls. Jorgé returns with their drinks, sets Tosh's bottle of beer on the table, and presents the horchata with fanfare. Jorgé asks if they've had time to look at the menu. Tosh orders a salad. Melanie goes for the nachos.

"Regular or Ultimo?" Jorgé asks.

"Definitely Ultimo."

Tosh raises an eyebrow. It's the first sincere gesture he's made all evening.

"Good choice," Jorgé says with a smile as he gathers the menus. Melanie is sad to see him go.

As Tosh sips his beer, he bubbles through his tab.

"Something urgent?" Melanie asks.

"It's nothing," he says and puts down his tab again.

"It's rude."

"It's work, actually."

"Well," Melanie says, "if you pick it up again, I'm throwing it in the fountain."

Tosh laughs and fidgets uncomfortably. "You wouldn't."

"I would, actually."

"It's brand new."

"Then you won't miss it."

While Melanie digs into the basket of chips, Tosh's eyes stray to the place where his tab sits on the table and darts away again when she catches him.

"Have some chips, Tosh. The salsa isn't bad."

Tosh cautiously dips a corner of a tortilla chip into the salsa and nibbles. "Spicy," he says with a grimace. He gulps down his beer like it contains the antidote.

Since he doesn't seem to be at all curious about her or the world outside his own pitiful sphere of low finance, their conversation is predictably one-sided. The date is going terribly but Melanie is completely calm, totally in control. She can do this.

She gives Tosh a reprieve and excuses herself to the women's room. Melanie makes her way inside and discovers another woman writing a note at the tiny table. When she's done writing, she furtively shoves the note inside the drawer. Apparently, this is a thing. A drawer full of secrets.

When the woman leaves, Melanie sits down and opens the narrow drawer. She finds a small pile of notes and begins to read:

> I just broke up with my boyfriend. Today would
> have been our one-year anniversary. We came here
> for our first date. I wish it wasn't over, but it is.

The second note is just as bleak.

I miss my mom. I didn't tell her how much I loved
her when she was alive and now she's gone. People
say everyone feels this way, but I don't know. I only
had one mom.

This isn't what Melanie expected, and she feels emotions well
up inside her. The next note brings her back to herself.

You bitches are all crazy!

The rest of the notes are blank. There is a pen in the drawer.
She picks it up and begins to write.

I wish Trevor

And then she stops. What did she wish from Trevor? And why
Trevor? Why not Doyle, who seems to be reconsidering her value
to the organization? Or Gary, who's scarcely left her thoughts since
he was killed? She doesn't know what to write. She doesn't know
what to think. How can she know what she doesn't know?

I wish Trevor would tell me how he really feels
about me.

There. She puts the notes back in the drawer and slams it shut.
She stands and looks around. Her cheeks feel flush, like she's been
caught playing with a Ouija board. Same kind of feeling. A bolt of
lightning. A deepening of the shadows. A queer certainty that the
world has changed somehow.

Melanie goes back to the patio where Tosh thumbs his tab.
The squeal of the iron chair leg on the concrete announces her return.

"You're back," he says and sets the tab down.

"You're still here," she replies and drills him with a fake smile.

His tab chirps, and he picks it up to read the message.

"I warned you," she says.

"That's right. You did," he says, ignoring her while he reads.

Melanie wonders what Tosh would do if she really threw his
tab in the fountain. He'd probably tell all his friends THAT BITCH

WAS CRAZY! Just not in person, as Tosh doesn't seem like the kind of guy who has a lot of friends. He'd send his colleagues and coworkers messages on his brand-new tab, which he could clearly afford. That seals the deal.

She snatches the tab from his hands and chucks it into the fountain where it makes a pleasing plunk. It glows with lurid intensity for a moment as it settles to the bottom of the fountain and then goes dark. Tosh jumps up and pulls his tab out of the water.

"What the fuck?" he shouts at the useless machine.

"I don't think they can hear you, sweetie." Sometimes she is so good at being a bitch she feels like she should get an award for it.

"You bitch!" he shouts.

Heads turn. Scene in a restaurant. Five-star entertainment.

"Apologize," Melanie says as she crosses her arms and leans back in her chair, "or I'll put *you* in the fountain next."

"In your dreams," Tosh sneers without bothering to look at her. Melanie stands and gets in his face so there is no chance he won't get the message.

"I warned you about your tab, and now I'm warning you."

Tosh looks from the device to Melanie and back to his tab again, as if the dead technology can give him the guidance he needs.

"I'm sorry," Tosh whispers.

"That's a good boy," Melanie says. "Now go home before I do something we both regret."

Tosh returns Melanie's gaze, a little scared, a little hurt. "I'm out of here," he announces, like it's his idea.

Melanie watches him go. She wanted him gone, and he left, doing exactly as instructed, but she hates the feeling of being abandoned. Those close enough to hear what went down are too embarrassed to look, and those seated out of earshot assume Melanie has gotten the short end of the deal. Isn't that always how it goes when a man leaves a woman? The woman is either pathetic or crazy, nothing in between.

As she sits down, she can feel the pity party descending on her, self-loathing being her go-to move in moments of emotional intensity. Her mother was the same way. The way of the lush. She'd learned it from her. Even though she knows getting all *woe is me* isn't going to change anything, she can't help but go there because that's where she lives.

Jorgé returns with a dinky salad and the largest platter of nachos she's ever seen. The look on his sweet dumb face turns to concern when he sees the empty chair.

"I'll take the bill when you get a chance, Jorgé."

Jorgé sets down the nachos and fishes the ticket from his apron pocket and leaves it on the table. "Anything else?"

"Can I ask you a question, Jorgé?"

"You can ask me anything," he says with a smile so sincere it breaks her heart a little.

"What did you think of my friend?"

Jorgé looks her in the eyes with startling intensity. The roles they'd been playing—waiter and customer—melt away.

"I think he must be an asshole to make a pretty lady like you upset."

"I'm not upset, Jorgé," she says as a tear plops into the nachos. "I promise you that."

"O-kay," he says, though he obviously doesn't believe her, which is genuinely upsetting.

"Really, I'm not," she says.

"Yes, ma'am."

Now she's ma'am. Why are men so infuriating?

She fishes a hundred-dollar bill from her wallet and sets it down on the table. She should leave it at that. Instead, she asks for a to-go box and offers one last assurance that she's fine. As more tears spill, Melanie curses herself for the ten thousandth time as her body invents yet another way to betray her.

TREVOR SITS IN THE BACK of a haze gray sprinter van parked on Vermont Avenue, listening in on Melanie's date through a pair of headphones while monitoring his tab. *Can I have a to-go box please?* he hears Melanie say. Trevor switches off the recording and places a call to Doyle. He answers on the first ring.

"How did it go?" Doyle asks.

"It went," Trevor answers.

"That bad?"

"She didn't assault anyone, so that's a plus."

"Oh?"

"Let's just say it was a very expensive date."

A loud banging on the side of the van interrupts the conversation.

"Shit, I gotta go."

Trevor ends the call and removes his headphones as the door slides open and Melanie hops in with a large paper bag. "Hungry? I brought nachos."

Trevor takes a deep breath and lets his nerves settle before he answers. "How did you know I was here?"

"Come on, Trev. This is why I work in the field and you do whatever it is you do. What did you hear?"

"Everything."

"So, you hacked into my tab?"

Trevor nods. "Technically, it's not your tab."

"Spare me. I've heard enough about tabs tonight."

"You should have heard what your date had to say about you while you were in the bathroom."

"So, how did I do? This wig cost a fortune."

"You look great." Trevor didn't mean to compliment Melanie's appearance. It just slipped out. "But…"

"But what?" Melanie asks, her voice sharp with suspicion.

"I want to show you something." Trevor scrolls through his tab and calls up Melanie's TruLuv account. A series of messages flash across the screen. All of them are from Tosh. *Sonja is a psycho! She dresses like a whore! That bitch owes me a grand!*

"Gross," Melanie says. "Delete that shit."

Trevor makes the messages go away but a new one pops up:

> Sonja's anger is out of control. She pretends to hold the world in contempt, but her dismissal of potential suitors is a preemptive strike to reject others before they can reject her.
>
> —Truthbot

"Get rid of that one, too."

"Can't. Tosh didn't write it."

"It does seem beyond his reading level."

"What's unique about TruLuv," Trevor explains, "is it looks at everything, from the things you say about yourself to what others say about you. It monitors the comments you make and the pictures you click on. It even has access to your messages, so be careful what you say."

Melanie opens up the nachos and digs in. "That's a little creepy, but so what?"

"TruLuv makes periodic assessments that are supposed to be uncannily accurate. At least that's what the testimonials say."

"So, I hold the world in contempt?"

"Well…"

"Fuck you."

"See?"

"Whatever, Trev. Get it off my page."

"The only way to change your truth is to change your behavior."

"That is *so* deep, Trev."

"You have to give TruLuv more input, more data to—"

"You mean more dates?"

"That's probably the fastest way."

"Un-fucking-believable," Melanie says, taking her anger out on the nachos.

"TruLuv determines which profiles you see, and which members see you, so…"

"Every maladjusted mouth breather in LA is going to be sending me messages."

"That's what happens when you play submarine with a guy's tab."

"I'm so over this." Melanie scoops a pile of meat and cheese into her mouth and chews noisily. Melanie is a messy eater and there are islands of salsa splattered all over the seats. Trevor tries not to let it bother him.

"Next time," he says, "maybe be a little less…"

"Less what?" Melanie asks.

"Aggressive."

"Aggressive is shoving these nachos in your face."

"Just give it a chance is all I'm saying."

"I am, Trev. I'm really trying."

"Really?" Trevor says. "Because this guy you picked doesn't seem like your type at all."

"Oh? What is my type?"

Trevor knows he's wandering into dangerous territory here. Agitating Melanie will only harden her position, so he softens his tone. "I don't know, Mel. Someone you don't threaten to throw into a fountain twenty minutes after you meet him."

Melanie thinks this over. "Okay. I'll go on another date."

"If you want, I can help with selecting—"

Melanie pulls open the van's sliding door. "Good night, Trevor!" She tosses her tab into the box of nachos and jumps out of the van.

"Good night, Mel," Trevor says. He fishes Melanie's tab out of the gooey pile. A clump of cheese sticks to the screen and he licks it off with his tongue.

DOYLE ARRIVES AT THE OFFICE of the Los Angeles County Coroner's Office just east of downtown and parks in one of the spaces reserved for staff. He arranged the visit through a friend of a former client. He's not planning on being here long.

The sky is all one color and pigeons coo at his feet on the sidewalk. The weather report predicts rain, and he hopes to be back on the road before it starts. A warm breeze carries a rumor of the ocean. Doyle savors it, knowing it will be much cooler inside.

The morning after he'd dumped Michael "Mick" Moriarity on a bench near the Silverlake Reservoir, he informed the target's parents that, after MIS had gotten their son out of Western Psych, he'd refused to cooperate and disappeared, a statement that contained the tiniest kernel of truth. His parents were upset, understandably so. This is the outcome they'd paid good money to avoid, but it's consistent with the kind of thing Mick would do. His parents had said it over and over again: "The boy is allergic to help."

An overdose is an overdose, but Doyle can't shake the image of Mick's poor parents, holding on to the slim shred of hope that their son will come home. No matter how Doyle twists the truth around in his mind, that is never going to happen. The least he can do is "look" for Mick, "find" him at the morgue, and put an end to their suffering.

Doyle enters the building and tells the middle-aged lady behind the glass he's come to identify a friend. She gives him a form to fill out and tells him to have a seat, that someone will be with him shortly. He barely has enough time to take in all of the boxes of tissues scattered about the waiting room when a trim, petite woman who looks to be in her forties comes through a door marked STAFF ONLY.

"I'm Sally Woo. You are…"

"Doyle. I'm here to ID a body."

"Are you police?"

Doyle shakes his head. Sally looks him over. He can see her trying to work out why a civilian who isn't next of kin is IDing a body.

"But you've done this before."

"Sadly, yes."

"Come with me."

Doyle follows Sally downstairs to the big cold room where they keep the John Does. She picks up a clipboard and consults a chart before moving toward a table near the sinks. She pauses to say something to one of the technicians and pulls back the plastic sheet covering the man he's come to see.

Doyle winces at the sight of the corpse. It's Mick all right. His face is blue, the whites of his eyes are yellow, and the rest of his skin has turned a shade of gray like the hull of a battleship. As Doyle processes what he's seeing, the sickeningly sweet smell of rot rises from the corpse. Doyle tries not to gag.

"Sorry," Sally says. "Should have warned you about that. These kannibals have an intense odor."

"Kannibals?" He fumbles in his pocket for a cough drop and pops it into his mouth. An old trick a cop taught him.

"Kannabliss users." Sally offers him a paper mask that Doyle waves off. "Though most of the time they just call it Bliss. Nasty stuff."

Doyle doesn't know what Sally is talking about. "My friend here was fond of pills," he says, just to say something. "Is that what this is?"

"Maybe. Won't know for sure unless we do a toxicology work-up, which hasn't been requested, but if I were a betting woman, I'd say this is a Bliss overdose, though I've seen a lot worse."

Maybe he's distracted by the stench coming off the corpse, but Sally's explanation makes no sense to Doyle. "I'm sorry. I'm not following."

Sally glances at her clipboard and moves to another table.

"Bliss is a party drug made by combining a synthetic cannabinoid with a synthetic opioid. Very easy to overdose—as your friend here discovered—and when they start shooting it up, this happens."

Sally pulls back the plastic sheet covering a body in much worse shape than Mick. Both of the man's arms are so swollen and black

Doyle thinks he's looking at a Black man's legs and not the arms of a Caucasian. One arm is significantly larger and darker than the other and gleams like an eggplant.

"Jesus," Doyle says.

"It's not pretty," Sally agrees and covers up the body again, but the smell remains, permeating the morgue. Doyle feels a sudden urge to get the fuck out of there but holds his ground.

"You see this a lot?" Doyle asks.

Sally shrugs. "More and more each week. It's becoming a problem."

Doyle is stunned—as much by Sally's nonchalance as by his own ignorance. Why weren't people talking about this and demanding something be done? How does he of all people not know about this drug?

"And the odor?"

"It's the Bliss. It's very distinctive. That's what gives addicts away. The next time you smell it, you'll know it immediately."

"It's powerfully unpleasant."

Sally laughs. "That's an understatement."

He sucks on the lozenge and accepts the clipboard Sally hands to him. She points to the blank space. Doyle nods and looks down at the chart. The space for the deceased's name is blank. Doyle writes down Michael's name and the names of his parents. He signs a name that matches the one on the fake ID Trevor made for him and adds the date, but before he hands the clipboard back to Sally, he scans the names above Mick's and finds GARY GRAY. Cause of death: HEART FAILURE. Status: CREMATED.

So much for Scary Gary.

Doyle hands the clipboard back to Sally. He knows he's sticking his neck out for a kid who probably didn't deserve it, but at this point he doesn't care.

"Do you want us to contact the next of kin, or would you like to do it?"

"I'll do it," he says, and Sally makes a note on the clipboard. "Can I ask you something?"

"You just did," Sally says.

Doyle takes the bottle of hydrocodone and hands it to Sally.

"Can you tell me if this is Bliss?"

Sally takes one look at the label on the bottle and her demeanor instantly changes. "Where did you get this?"

"I'm afraid I'm not at liberty to say," Doyle replies.

"If I were you," Sally says, narrowing her gaze, "I'd think twice about stepping onto county property with a narcotic you don't have a prescription for."

"I'll take that under advisement," Doyle says. He snatches the bottle from Sally and hightails it out of the morgue. Although rain has spattered the windshields of the cars in the parking lot, the clouds are already breaking up, daylight streaming through. The humid air traps the stink from the morgue clinging to his clothes.

Bliss. What a fucking world.

Doyle cranks the ignition on his car, but it won't start. He tries a second time and then a third before the engine turns over and rumbles to life. The air conditioner is broken, so he rolls down the window and jams the car into gear to get some air moving. He nearly backs into a Cadillac driven by a hunched over elderly woman in dark glasses who neither slows down nor turns to acknowledge him. Doyle curses, closes his eyes, and hums a bit of Brahms that always makes him feel better. He fumbles for a cigarette and finds the crushed pack floating in his pocket. Thank God. Doyle can't think of a single thing he wants more than a cigarette. He shakes the last one out of the pack and lights it.

6

BOMBS AWAY

ABIGAIL SITS ON THE FLOOR, curled up in Sonja St. John's wig, while Melanie does pull-ups on a bar in the doorway to her bathroom. She does each one the same. Her form is perfect. Her concentration? Not so much.

Melanie's tab buzzes, and she drops to the floor and climbs onto her bed, brushing aside the plastic packaging for her brand-new tab. The screen reads 99+ new notifications from TruLuv. Melanie is already adept at navigating the site. She bubbles through the screens at remarkable speed.

"Jock. No. Jock. No. Ex-con. Definitely no. Delete...delete... delete.... What the heck is this, Abigail?"

Melanie can't believe people voluntarily subject themselves to this kind of scrutiny. People actually do this for *fun*. A poll pops up on the screen. A poll about her.

IF SONJA WERE A BOMB, SHE'D BE A...

1 Suspicious Device: Potentially dangerous but likely a dud
2 Roadside Explosive: Ready to come apart at the seams
3 Bunker Buster: She'll blow you to smithereens
4 Nuclear Warhead: Total destruction

So far, the voting is evenly split between all four answers, and she doesn't know how she feels about this. She calls Trevor and barks at him as soon as he answers.

"What did you sign me up for?"

"Is there a problem?"

"Now they're making polls about me! I feel so...objectified." Abigail hops on the bed and regards the mess with disdain.

"At least your page is blowing up," Trevor says.

"Is that supposed to be funny?"

"Take it easy."

"So, which one am I?"

"I haven't made up my mind." Trevor seems to be in a lighthearted mood today and she doesn't care for it one bit.

"You're enjoying this, aren't you?"

"I didn't think I would, but I am."

Melanie clicks on the TruLuv message icon and another avalanche of requests arrives in her inbox.

"Incoming. Gotta run." Melanie ends the call and selects a message, which she reads aloud to Abigail. "Bomb squadder seeks challenge."

She opens the profile and studies a photo of an attractive man named Bill with short hair and a military bearing.

"Seems normal enough. What do you think, Abigail?"

Abigail meows her approval while Melanie types: *I pick. You pay.*

Bill responds immediately: *When and where?*

"Abigail, I think we have a winner."

MELANIE HAS CHOSEN A RESTAURANT closer to home so she'll feel more at ease with her surroundings.

She picks Evil Dave's Diner, a place that owes its popularity to its proprietor: a tattoo artist who'd made a name for himself on a reality TV show she'd binged during one of her many trips to rehab. People go to Evil Dave's Diner for the novelty but come back because the place is neither kitschy nor slick, modern nor retro. It's just a place that stays open late, pours a quality cup of coffee, and serves food that doesn't suck. In other words, a real diner—with one exception: Evil Dave's has an ice cream dish with a cult following.

Evil Dave's Black Sundae comprises sixteen scoops of handmade ice cream from dark Mexican chocolate and dusted with ground chili powder made from black peppers grown in Valle de Lucifero in Durango, Mexico, and harvested by a curandero in Echo Park. The chocolate devil sauce is a house secret Evil Dave obtained from a shaman who'd entrusted the tattooer with illustrating his body with elaborate symbols of ancient origin and shared the recipe with him on his deathbed, an event those close to Dave say changed his spiritual outlook. The sauce is reported to have hallucinatory qualities if taken in excess, which is impossible to avoid if fewer than six people polish off the sundae. The chocolate devil sauce is said to bestow the imbiber with a kind of second sight. The sundae is crowned not with a cherry, but a gummy eyeball filled with a translucent cream that leaves a sweet-but-not-too-sweet taste that baffles even veteran food critics.

A circle of devotees gathers for a "Black Mess" in the enclosed garden behind the diner every full moon to gorge on the powerful sundae and cultivate visions. Initiates are known to one another by a tattoo administered by Evil Dave himself, featuring an all-seeing eye atop an otherwise innocuous-looking sundae.

It takes Melanie less than ten minutes to walk to Evil Dave's. She arrives early and picks a booth that faces the door. She orders coffee and stops herself from fidgeting with the plastic stirrer.

Diners remind Melanie of being newly sober, which she supposes she is again after her latest relapse. Diners represent a safe place to go at night after counseling sessions and recovery meetings. They are brightly lit spaces where she can expend the excess energy she was accustomed to burning off in bars. Now here she is, back at square one in her recovery. She can't rule out the possibility that choosing a diner was an unwitting expression of a subconscious desire to do better this time, to not fuck this up. But since when has "Don't fuck this up, Mel" *not* been at the forefront of her thoughts?

Bill breezes through the door with a disarming smile. He looks the part of a military vet. He's better looking than his profile photo, which is a pleasant surprise.

She takes a deep breath—*no feelings*—and exhales—*only choices*.

"Hi, Sonja," Bill says as he slides into the seat across from her. The more she hears the name the more she likes it. Sonja is the name of a siren, a destroyer of men.

"Hi, Bill."

"You're a cheap date," Bill says as he looks around, taking in the diner's decor.

Melanie hooks an eyebrow.

"Let me rephrase that," Bill backtracks, holding up his hands in surrender. "I meant, when you said *you pay*—"

"I know what you meant."

Bill moves on, asking questions about her appetite, how her day has been. He is forthright and direct, unfazed by the discrepancy between Sonja's hypersexual profile and the person with whom he is talking. She likes that. She doesn't want Bill kissing her ass. At least not right away. She also likes that he ordered iced tea.

After the waiter leaves, Melanie turns the conversation to TruLuv.

"How long have you been on the site?"

"About a week."

"Any dates?"

"No. You're my first."

"So, no horror stories?"

"Not yet. It's hard to find people who actually want to go on dates. So many people are worried about what the Truthbot will say about them."

"Really?" Melanie says with laugh. "I haven't had that experience."

"It's different for guys. That's what attracted me to your profile. You obviously don't care what the bot says."

"Actually, I didn't know about the bot until after my first date."

"Would you have acted differently if you did?"

"No."

"There you go."

Their food arrives. A spinach salad for Melanie and a patty melt and an order of fries for Bill. He asks the waitress for a side of mayonnaise, slathers half of it on his burger, then dips his fries into what's left over.

"Wow, you're really into mayonnaise."

Bill laughs. "It reminds me of being a kid. What makes you happy?"

Melanie tries to think of something but comes up blank. She has happy memories. She must. So why can't she think of any of them?

"I don't know," she confesses.

"Oh, come on."

She tries to remember a time when she was one-thousand-percent, no-doubt-about-it happy, but searching for a memory has the opposite effect: it pushes her mind to times when she was miserable. Mom and Dad fighting. Dad leaving. Mom losing her shit. Relapse and rehab. Re-relapse and re-rehab. The day she'd learned her mother had died on a psychiatric ward. The afternoon she followed a man through a farmer's market, convinced it was her father. Applewhite. MIS gives her purpose, and there are people there who make all the bullshit worthwhile, like Scary Gary and Trevor, but look at her now. Is she better off than she was two years ago?

She supposes so, but is she happy?

Not even close. She doesn't know what happiness is anymore. She has a tendency to mix up happiness with the mindlessness of intoxication. Why can't she find satisfaction in the simple pleasures normal people seem to enjoy? What's wrong with her? What is she missing?

"Come on," Bill cajoles. "Everyone has a happy memory."

"Maybe I don't," Melanie says.

"Then we should change that." Bill smiles. She doesn't think he's being condescending. A little schmaltzy perhaps, but he's really trying. He's making an effort to connect. They're definitely *communicating*. It reminds her of sparring with Scary Gary and how she could let him know when to go harder or pull back without having to say anything. They'd shared an unspoken understanding she already missed. It dawns on Melanie that Bill might actually be a genuinely nice guy, which kind of blindsides her.

They finish their meals. Bill insists on ordering a sundae. Part of his happiness project. Melanie shrugs. She isn't a calorie counter. When she quit drinking, she developed a sweet tooth, which she barely manages to keep from blurting out to Bill. She doesn't want to talk about her sobriety because then he'll ask how long she's been sober, she'll tell him, and that will be that.

"What did you do in the military?" Melanie asks.

"I trained military personnel in the art of defusing ordinance."

"So, you really were on the bomb squad?"

"Training mostly."

"But the bombs were real?"

"The bombs were real."

"Will you teach me?"

"Teach you what?" Bill asks.

"How to defuse a bomb."

"I'm doing a pretty good job so far, aren't I?"

"I'm being serious," Melanie replies.

"So am I."

"Does that mean you're going to say nice things about me on my profile?"

"I'll tell you right now."

"You're changing the subject, but go for it."

"Sonja is an interesting—"

"Interesting? Next you're going to say I have a nice personality."

"Beat me to the punch."

"You're going to have to do better than that."

"Okay," Bill says. "How's this: *Sonja is an exciting, vivacious woman who hasn't had enough happiness in her life.*"

Melanie resists the urge to reach across the table and stroke Bill's cheek. She's spent how much time with this guy? An hour? And he has her down cold.

"I've upset you."

"It's fine," Melanie says.

"Let me rephrase that—"

"Never mind. Can you get the check, please?"

"I'm sorry," Bill says. "Let me—"

"There's nothing to be sorry about," Melanie snaps, "just get the fucking check."

Bill's voice stays calm, his gaze steady. "Of course."

Melanie presses the heels of her palms into her eyes until all she can see is black. She takes a deep breath. Then another. Bill leaves her alone. The military must have trained him for situations like this. All she needs is a moment and she'll be fine. Not fine, but normal. Not normal, but whatever the fuck she is these days.

She opens her eyes. The diner seems brighter, and all its light is focused on the monstrosity before her: Evil Dave's Black Sundae. A ginormous chocolate sundae served in a black champagne bucket.

"I don't fucking believe this."

Bill smiles, his relief apparent.

Melanie can't believe how big it is, and for a moment she wonders if she's hallucinating. The way the light reflects off the dark chocolate sauce creates a glare, a shimmering lozenge of white-hot light on the surface of the sundae, in which Melanie swears she sees something moving. She reaches out to touch it, to prove to herself it's real. She sticks her finger in the sundae and pulls out a shockingly gooey lump of chocolate sauce that spatters the tabletop like blood.

"Since we're being so brutally honest with each other," Melanie says after she tastes the chocolate—delicious, "tell me one true thing about yourself."

Bill raises his eyebrows and the effect is almost comical. Melanie wonders if he practices in front of a mirror. "Just one thing?" he asks.

"One thing," Melanie says, "absolutely true."

Bill's gaze hardens. "I'm a cop. I want to talk to you about Make It Stop."

TREVOR RECLINES ON THE FUTON mattress he put in the back of the sprinter van and listens to the Dodgers game while occasionally spying on Melanie through a telephoto lens app on his tab. After two days of reading TruLuv updates and messages from horny men, all he wants to do is listen to the baseball game. Viviana is training, Doyle is doing whatever Doyle does, and Melanie is eating what looks like the world's largest sundae.

The Los Angeles Exxon Dodgers are hosting the Raytheon Padres. He's pretty sure the Dodgers are losing but he doesn't care. That's not why he listens. The chirping of the organ, the murmur of the crowd, the cry of the umpire bellowing strikes—it all has a soothing effect on him; and most comforting of all is the Voice of Vin Scully, the deceased play-by-play announcer for the Dodgers.

Trevor loves the sound of his voice for what it isn't: smooth, velvety, unguent. Scully's voice is the opposite of all that. No golden tones on those pipes. More like a chocolate malt left out in the heat of a summer day. A vacuum cleaner salesman from the Bronx who doesn't want to be any trouble, ma'am, but sure could go for a glass of water.

The Voice of Vin reminds Trevor of his father, who used to listen to Dodgers games on the radio in the garage, where he smoked cigarettes and watched the cars go by. If his father could have figured out a way to squeeze a sofa into the garage, he probably would have slept out there, too—an arrangement that would have suited his mother just fine, though Trevor often wondered if this is really true or something she used to say out of exasperation. One of the million questions he will never be able to ask his mother, who walked out on the eve of his eleventh birthday.

Trevor's father died the day after Vin Scully passed away. His father was in the hospital with pneumonia. He was expected to make a full recovery but didn't. The last time Trevor saw his father alive he was watching the Dodgers play the Giants (they were still the San Francisco Giants then) on the television in his room at the hospital while sipping on a box of apple juice. The Dodgers were winning, so his father's spirits were up. Scully had retired a few seasons before and Trevor had no idea who was calling the game. He watched with his father until, just about midway through the seventh inning, a nurse told him it was time to go. Trevor couldn't remember what his father's last words to him had been. No pearls of wisdom or anything like that. Probably some anxious hope the bullpen would hold up. It didn't. The Giants had taken the lead by the time Trevor got to the parking lot and turned on the radio in his car.

When his father got the news the following morning that Vin Scully had passed in his sleep, he was distraught, then despondent, and then he gave up. "A little death," Trevor's grandmother had called it, which he thought was an odd thing to say about the passing of one's only son. She'd moved up to Daly City to be closer to her younger sister, and although they talked every once in a while, they were no longer close.

Trevor lost interest in the Dodgers after Scully's passing and he was not the only one who felt this way. Beloved by millions, baseball wasn't baseball without Scully, at least not in LA. So, the team brought him back.

Using video recognition software, the producers matched the play on the field with a database of Scully's essential calls and broadcast the most salient feature of the play. The audience hears the crack of the bat and Scully's voice proclaims, "Ground ball hit sharply to third," which the play-by-play team in the booth builds on to deliver the particulars. "Taylor makes the throw and Carswell is out at first."

"One away," Scully declares, and all is right with the universe again as far as Trevor and millions of other Angelenos are concerned.

Trevor opens the telephoto app and sees Melanie come barreling out of the diner with her date chasing after her and he doesn't look happy.

He grabs a miniature baseball bat emblazoned with the Dodgers logo and jumps out of the van. The mini bat is only as long as his forearm, but it will have to do.

Melanie must not have spotted him this time because she's running away from the van. Her date jogs after her. "Sonja, wait! I can explain!"

Melanie stops and turns to confront her pursuer. "Leave me alone!"

The man closes in, reaching for Melanie's arm. Trevor cracks him on the head with the bat. The man slumps to the ground, out cold.

"What are you doing?!" Melanie shouts. She shoves Trevor away and kneels by the man's side, which isn't the reaction he was expecting.

"He was harassing you!"

"He's a cop!"

"What?"

"He knows about Make It Stop!"

Stunned, Trevor tries to process what Melanie is telling him, but none of it makes sense. He feels as if their roles have been reversed. He typically interacts with Melanie before or after an op—never during one—and to see her in control of a situation that he's so thoroughly bungled is jarring.

"Go," Melanie says. "And don't tell Doyle."

"You know I can't promise that."

"Do you have the van?" Melanie asks.

"Yeah."

"Then get out of here."

Trevor doesn't want to go, but Melanie's date lets out a loud moan, which Trevor takes as a sign to leave. When he gets back to the van, the Dodgers game is still on. In fact, it's almost over. Two outs, two strikes.

"Here's the pitch," says the Voice of Vin who knows how many summers ago, a time when Trevor's father was still alive. It might even be from a game played before Trevor was born and every player who took to the diamond that day is now among the deceased, scoring the game from that great stadium in the sky where the grass is always green, the sky blue, and home runs travel to infinity.

"Way out in front. Strike three."

MELANIE PILOTS THE COP'S CAR home, a big brown sedan with all the bells and whistles. Bill, if that's even his real name, didn't want to tell her where he lived but it was a self-driving model and it didn't take a detective to figure out that his home address was programmed into the vehicle. She pressed the little house icon on the dashtab and off they went.

"Sonja," Bill begins, but Melanie cuts him off.

"Cut the shit. What's my real name?"

"Melanie. Melanie Marsh."

"How'd you ID me?"

"After the incident at Western Psych made the news," Bill says while rubbing his head, "I ran the hospital's security footage through facial recognition software."

"That's comforting."

"Well, you do make quite an impression."

"Meaning what?"

"I want to make you an offer."

"Arrest me now or arrest me later?"

"I'm a detective with the Narcotics Division," Bill says, "but this isn't a shakedown."

"What is it then?"

"It's about Kannabliss."

"You lost me."

"It's a designer drug that stimulates sexual desire. The drug provides a high that is intense but brief. However, the erotic charge lingers."

"So, the drug wears off but you still feel horny?"

"Something like that. We're not sure how the drug's aphrodisiacal elements affect the libido, but users have a tendency to fixate on the people around them, creating intense bonds. In this way the drug disguises its addictive qualities."

"Sounds…dangerous." She almost said "fun" before reminding herself that Bill is a cop and that all coppers are bastards.

"Extremely. It's stronger than fentanyl and responsible for hundreds of overdoses."

"Surprised I haven't heard of it."

"It hasn't been on the streets long. They call it Bliss."

"What does this have to do with…" Melanie can't bring herself to say Make It Stop.

"We have no idea who's making it or where it comes from. Synthetics are typically manufactured abroad and smuggled into the US, though we're not seeing this anywhere but LA."

"I don't know what you expect *me* to do about it," Melanie says.

"You're in a unique position to gather information about Bliss. You can get into places we can't."

"Not anymore," Melanie says. "I'm, uh, taking a break from those activities."

While Bill weighs this new information, the dashtab announces that they're approaching their destination: the Gaylord Apartments on Wilshire Boulevard. The car comes to a stop in front of the bar on the building's ground floor where she has had a wild night or two.

"I'm not asking you to do anything different than what you normally do," Bill says, "but if you see something, anything, that can help us get this off the streets, you'd be doing a great service to your community."

"Some would say I already do."

"Some would say what you do is illegal."

"Why does the LAPD suddenly care? I thought you were in favor of conditional release."

"Some are. I'm not."

"Maybe I should give LAPD a call and tell them about our conversation?"

"Maybe I should turn you over to Health Net Secure."

"You wouldn't do that."

"You're right, I wouldn't."

Bill's smile doesn't come easily, but when it does it's really something.

Melanie isn't sure what's happening here, but she likes it. "What can you tell me about Scary Gary?"

Bill's smile falls to pieces. "Gary Gray? The gentleman who was killed at Mojave Critical Care?"

"Gentleman," Melanie snorts. "He would have gotten a kick out of that."

"What about him?"

"He has a brother. Find him and I'll cooperate. But I'm not talking about Make It Stop. Not now. Not ever. If you want my help, you can't ask me about it again."

"Deal," Bill says, sticking out his hand. Melanie takes it but doesn't let go.

"How much of what you told me about yourself was bullshit?"

"None of it."

"Even the bomb squad?"

"All true."

"Come here."

Bill leans across the space that separates the two seats. Melanie comes in for a kiss, but her lips keep going as she pulls him toward her, and she can feel him tense up as she whispers in his ear.

"Boom."

7

BEASTS OF THE JUNGLE

Melanie is becoming obsessed with TruLuv. Trevor would say the compulsion has already taken hold, and Melanie would be hard-pressed to disagree. She's an addict with poor impulse control—of course she's hooked. What did he think was going to happen?

Melanie checks her TruLuv profile for at least the tenth time that morning, cycling through all the data dumped onto her account in a rigorous hierarchy: men who'd messaged her, men who'd commented on her profile, men who'd looked at her photos, men who popped up on her tracker. Men, men, men, and all of them looking at her.

It's hard to separate the real from the make believe. Compliments and rejections, as artificial and arbitrary as they are, work their deadly magic. Whenever there's a new message in her inbox or activity on her profile, a little red heart with the letters TL pops up on the screen. It's all so disgustingly cute.

There's *always* new stuff to look at, sort through, engage with, respond to. By the time she looks at the last match, there's a new round of messages, comments, and views to review, and her page is full of hearts. It's exhilarating. It's exhausting. Managing all the information has become a round-the-clock preoccupation. She wonders how people who have real jobs deal with the distraction.

The activity on her feed ramped up after her third date: dinner with a guy named Dan in a quasi-upscale chain restaurant with a menu that took twenty minutes to read. Dan was a nonunion carpenter who built things for the film and television industry. He was a large man with a big appetite and a face right out of a Norman Rockwell painting. He had goofy tattoos that took up a lot of real estate. Dan was undoubtedly tougher than he looked, but he would never be thought of as a tough guy. Case in point, after dinner they went to a movie, and Dan suggested a romantic comedy.

"I'm more of a car crashes and explosions kind of girl," she told him.

"Really?" Dan seemed genuinely disappointed.

Afterward, he tried to make out with her in the parking garage, the ground trembling beneath their feet as cars roared up and down the ramps. She liked the size of him. She felt so small in his arms. She looked up into his eyes as he narrowed the space between them but turned away at the last minute so his lips landed roughly on her cheek. He didn't push it and that was that.

By the time she got home and logged on to her TruLuv account, he'd already posted glowing reviews about their date. This resulted in more messages, more compliments, more requests. Even the Truthbot seemed pleased:

> Sonja is determined to put her past behind her.
> Her heart is a closed fist that is beginning to open.
>
> —Truthbot

She wonders if Bill is paying attention. Of course he is. He might even be paying closer attention than Trevor, which she finds exhilarating. She is surprisingly calm about this, considering what Bill could do to the organization and everyone in it. But if Bill can help MIS find Gary's brother and she can help assist with his investigation, everyone gets what they want. But does Bill want Melanie? Does Melanie want Bill?

She's not sure. She's definitely attracted to him. The majority of the people reaching out to her are undateable, but the interest is flattering. It's awakened something in her that's been dormant for a long time. Being the subject of so much desire arouses her. It's simple really: to be desired equates to feeling desirable, and that is making her horny.

She flirts shamelessly with the guys who reach out to her on TruLuv. When a hot guy asks if she'd like to see his NSFW pics she always says yes, and she always looks at them. Sometimes she does more than look. A lot more. And that leads to date number four.

Melanie selected a restaurant in an old train yard on San Fernando Road in Atwater Village. The space is kind of a letdown; most of the seating is outdoors. Women with thousand-dollar handbags sit at picnic tables and fuss over farm-to-table salads while starving artists in filthy jeans nibble on day-old rolls. The problem isn't the place, but her date, Lucas, whom she has badly misjudged. His profile had given Mclanie the impression he was a muscly surfer type, but he's an overdressed bouncer whose job at an upscale nightclub has poisoned his perception of himself.

They both order the same thing. He talks about beating people up at the club while they wait for their food. Melanie lies her way through her salad and dies a little on the inside. Here she is, reluctant to speak her mind because she's afraid of what this goon might say about her on TruLuv. Lucas studies his watch and rubs his face, the muscles in his forearms twitching. If he could just flex his muscles and not talk, she'd be more than entertained.

"Let's make a deal," she says.

"I'm all ears," Lucas says. It's like he *tries* to speak in clichés.

"This date isn't going anywhere. You know it and I know it. Let's keep it civil and say positive things about each other on TruLuv."

"You mean you and me?"

Melanie breaks it down into simple sentences, language he can understand. "You're hot, but we're not clicking."

Lucas nods as he comes to terms with what Melanie is saying, but it takes a moment for the implications to sink in: date over, time to go.

"I'll pay," she says, which speeds his exit. They exchange a chaste hug by the table. Melanie stays behind to settle the bill. She feels kind of down about the whole thing and doesn't stick around for long. Five minutes after Lucas leaves, she follows him out the door. She scans the street for a gray sprinter van but doesn't see it. As she approaches her car, someone slips out of the shadows.

"That was fast," Bill says. Her detective has been spying on her.

"Just get in." She slides behind the steering wheel and cranks the engine. As soon as Bill sits down, she pulls away from the restaurant like a getaway driver. She heads south and immediately hits traffic. She has no idea what day of the week it is.

"Are you stalking me?" Melanie asks.

Bill seems surprised by the question. "I wanted to see you."

"You're not exactly putting my mind at ease."

"I thought—"

"Unless you have something to tell me," Melanie interrupts, "I don't think it's a good idea for us to be seen together."

Bill nods, staring straight ahead. "You can let me out at the light," he says as they approach the intersection. Melanie pulls over at the bus stop where a group of young men stand in a loose circle, sharing smokes, trading jokes, hitting up passersby for change. Bill takes what looks like a pencil case from his jacket pocket.

"This is for you," he says.

"What is it?"

"Your friend."

Melanie stares at the case in confusion.

"These are his remains," Bill says.

Oh God, it's Gary. She takes the vinyl satchel and measures its heft. It's surprisingly light. Is this all of him, she wonders, or did they... It doesn't matter. She isn't going to open it. Not in the car. Probably not ever.

"You didn't have to do this," she says to Bill, but he is watching the bus stop, his cop instincts attuned to the action on the street. An immense feeling of gratitude washes over her, a mix of tenderness and affection that feels alarmingly alien.

"I thought you should have it," he says, still looking away.

"Thank you. It means a lot."

She thinks about kissing him, but he opens the door and slips out of the car. He turns and gives her a half-assed salute as he drifts down the street. Melanie pulls into the flow of traffic. The night air feels cool, but she keeps the windows rolled down and Gary in her lap.

HANSEN BARGES INTO A LARGE, windowless laboratory with Bethany on his heels. The sign on the door reads EXPLORATORY RESEARCH. It's early in the morning and he was up late with a "volunteer" in detention, but Bethany has dragged him here with news about the device that bitch from MIS left behind. All he can say is it better be good.

A dozen lab techs wearing white coats, latex gloves, and paper masks work at a bench. Hansen is the only one not wearing a mask—he hates those fucking things. A pair of techs, a man and a woman, peer at the device through a modified tab mounted on a stand.

"What have we got?" Hansen asks.

"GPS," the man says.

"When the device is activated," the woman adds, "it sends its location to a receiver."

"And you are?" Hansen asks.

"Grace Mickens, I work in the technology sector—"

"Thank you, Grace." Hansen wonders what she looks like naked, but it's hard to tell under that bulky lab coat.

"It's a distress signal," Grace says.

"Can we see who is receiving the signal?" Hansen asks.

Grace adjusts her eyeglasses, which inexplicably turns him on. "Yes, but—"

"What are we waiting for?" Hansen says. "Activate the bloody thing!"

"When we do that," Grace says, "the receiver will know it's been activated."

"We'll know where they are," Hansen says, catching on, "but—"

"They'll know we know," the man interrupts.

Hansen shoots him a withering look. He hates being interrupted. "We've got one shot at this, so we better make the most of it."

"Precisely," Grace says.

"Thank you, Grace. I knew you wouldn't disappoint me." He absolutely must find a way to get a look at what she's got under that coat. "Bethany?"

"Yes, sir?"

"I want Applewhite on this. Tell him to assemble a team."

Bethany nods, but is practically trembling, which means she has bad news.

"Spit it out," Hansen says.

"Michael Moriarity turned up in the system."

That's not bad news, Hansen thinks. "Then dispatch a team to collect him."

"He's dead, sir," Bethany says. "Arrived at the morgue DOA. His parents have already claimed the body."

An alarm sounds and two men in riot suits enter the lab and pull one of the techs away from the bench, and that sends Hansen over the edge.

"What did he do?" he demands.

"Theft," says one of the men in the riot suits. "His locker is full of contraband."

"Give me your stick," he says.

The man hands over his submission stick. It's one of the newer models. Quieter, holds a charge longer. Hansen prefers the old ones. "You turn it on by..."

"I know how to use the bloody stick!" Hansen shouts as he snatches it away. He extends the stick to its full length and cranks it up to the highest setting. He can feel the power surging through it. Three will knock a man down, four if he's got some mass on him. Anything over five is a cardiac risk. Ten is like an electric chair on a stick. Hansen strikes the lab tech with it, delivering a ferocious jolt that knocks him off his feet and fills the room with the smell of ozone, like the moment after a lightning strike.

That was enjoyable, Hansen thinks as he powers down the weapon and returns it to the security officer, but unsatisfying. Getting his hands on the woman who slipped away from him, now *that* will be a good time.

DOYLE LISTENS TO BÉLA BARTÓK's String Quartet No. 6 while working out in the dojo, but what he really wants is a cigarette. It's late, nearly midnight. Those who are required to be at HQ are watching a movie in the rec room. Doyle prefers the company of his two closest companions: music and exercise, exercise and music. The two constants in his chaotic life.

He heads to the garage and climbs into his car with two things on his mind: get some sleep and don't smoke. The car starts on the third try and he makes his way to the exit where he waves a key card in front of a sensor to get the gate to open. He waits on a brown sedan to clear the intersection and exits the garage.

Doyle drives along Ventura Boulevard, whistling the Bartók piece he'd been listening to in the dojo. He reaches for cigarettes in his shirt pocket that aren't there. He doesn't want to stop and buy another pack, but the car pulls into a liquor store's parking lot as if of its own volition. Doyle sighs, gets out of his car.

"Gimme a pack of Coca Cola Marlboros," he says to the cashier.

The cashier slides a box of cigarettes across the counter. "Do you want to register for Coca Cola Marlboro Rewards? All I need is a retina scan."

"Just the smokes, please."

Behind him, the TV screen mounted in the corner shows a burning building, smoke billowing from a skyscraper in what looks to be midtown Manhattan.

"They got Fox News," the cashier says.

About time, Doyle thinks but does not say. "Who did it?"

"Who cares?" the cashier says, distracted by a young couple who've entered the store. They are loud and obnoxious and can't keep their hands off each other. Doyle grimaces as he picks up an unusual odor from the couple, who are now lingering at the Fiery Cat display.

"Is one enough?" the man asks.

"Definitely not," the woman answers.

"Let's get them all!" he says.

They laugh like there's no tomorrow. They each grab a pair of bottles and get in line behind Doyle, who is borderline nauseated by the smell coming off the couple.

Doyle turns and confronts them. "Bliss?"

The party girl slinks behind her boyfriend. "Not cool, man," the boyfriend says.

"I don't know how much you took," Doyle says, "but it's too much."

"Leave us alone!" the party girl shouts.

"Where did you get it?"

"What are you, a cop?" the boyfriend asks.

"Let's get out of here," the girl says.

They set their bottles down on the counter and run out of the store. The cashier mad dogs Doyle. Outside, Doyle leans against his car while he gets a cigarette lit, hating himself a little bit for it, when a brown sedan cruises by at a suspiciously slow speed.

"Fucking hell." Doyle says and gets in his car.

"IT WAS NOT A SURGICAL strike," the pundit on the radio says.

"They never are with these people," says the other one.

"I'm telling you it's amateur hour with these guys—sorry, men and women."

"Right, they call themselves 'vigilantes,' but as far as I'm concerned, that's just another word for terrorists."

"When I think of the people in that building…"

Trevor scowls at the dashtab. He's sitting in the driver's seat of the sprinter van, listening to news reports about the Fox News bombing in New York. He hasn't heard a number yet, but the casualties are reportedly "catastrophic."

"We'll see about that," Trevor says. In the hours after an incident like this, the news is always wrong. He's seen enough of his own ops reported as mass casualty events when not a single drop of blood was shed to be more than a little suspicious. It's all part of the disinformation playbook. When the news reports can't get the most fundamental aspects of the story right, it calls everything else into question, and then the conspiracies begin. Every time there's a high-profile target, vigilante groups dominate the news, making life harder for small-time outfits like Make It Stop.

He's about to switch off the broadcast when Viviana buzzes his tab. He accepts the call, and her half-naked hologram fills the van, an image lifted out of his adolescent brain.

"I need you," she says.

"What's the matter?" he asks.

"I can't get out of this sports bra. Wanna help?"

"Shouldn't you be at MIS?" Trevor says, ignoring Viviana's come-on.

Viviana frowns. "I decided to swing by my apartment for a quick shower. Care to join me?" Viviana lives a mile from HQ. Whenever MIS relocates, she moves to a nearby apartment with a month-to-month lease.

"I'm on a stakeout," Trevor says. Actually, he's parked outside of Melanie's bungalow, but Viviana doesn't need to know that.

Viviana pouts. Even though she's just put herself through a workout, she looks incredible. Viviana is long, willowy, model gorgeous, but she's a demon in the dojo. It was Gary who'd come up with the nickname for the gym where the ops did their training. The name had stuck, but it didn't feel like a dojo until Viviana came along. She *owned* the place.

"You pay more attention to her than to me," Viviana says as she putters in her bathroom, pausing to scrutinize her reflection in the mirror—an unguarded moment that captivates Trevor.

"Are you coming?" she asks.

"I can't."

"You mean you won't."

"Viviana."

"Don't make me beg, Trevor."

"I'll be right there," he says and ends the call. Viviana's image freezes like an apparition in the shape of his desire.

IN A FIT OF MASTURBATORY discombobulation, Melanie messages a man named Drew whose profile features shirtless photos that show off his toned physique.

Gimme some of that, she types.

Soriano's tonight at 8, Drew replies almost immediately.

It's a date.

Don't be late.

Regret sets in almost immediately. Did he really say, *don't be late?* Who does he think he is? Melanie laughs it off while she gets ready. The restaurant isn't far, a few minutes away. She won't even have to get on the freeway. Now that's she's been on a few dates, she wants to take things a bit further. She wants to get laid.

Soriano's is one of those Italian joints where the servers take turns singing songs and playing the piano. Melanie wishes she'd known this before she agreed to the date. It would have been a deal-breaker, but she's here and she's determined to make the most of it.

"Over here!" Drew shouts from a table near the piano as she walks in the door. At least she thinks it's Drew. He doesn't look like his profile pics, but that isn't necessarily a bad thing. He's still very good looking, just older and swarthier.

"That's right. It's me. Feast your eyes, baby. You look beautiful, by the way."

"Thanks," Melanie says as she slides into her seat. "Have you been waiting long?"

"For you? All my life, baby. All my life. You and me are going to make beautiful babies together. That's right, baby. I said it. I say a lot of crazy shit. I'm one of those dagos that gives wops a bad name."

Was this guy for real?

"Here," he says, splashing wine into her glass. "I got lonely, so I ordered a bottle of wine. You allergic to shellfish? I got prawns coming. You know what prawns are, baby? Same as shrimp only uncircumcised."

"I don't drink alcohol."

Drew smiles an oily smile that seems strangely rehearsed. "You don't expect me to drink all this by myself, do you?"

"You're a big boy. I'm sure you can manage." Melanie narrows her lips and smiles, because one fake smile deserves another.

Drew's smile disappears and something cold and cruel takes its place.

The waiter intervenes. "Sorry I'm late, folks! I was warming up the pipes with some Old Blue Eyes. Can I start you two off with some breadsticks?"

It isn't really a question, and he sets the basket on the table.

"Stifle yourself," Drew says as he swirls the wine around his glass without taking his eyes off Melanie. "I'm talking to fire crotch here. I'm going to be real disappointed if the carpet doesn't match the drapes."

Melanie slugs back half the glass of wine Drew has poured for her...

"That's more like it. If it was good enough for Jesus, it's good enough for a stu—"

...and spits it in Drew's face.

With reflexes Melanie cannot help but be impressed with, Drew reaches across the table and slaps her face. It's a good open-palm slap that sounds like a fat kid doing a belly flop. Soriano's comes to a shocked standstill. The server looks like he's about to have a heart attack. But Melanie feels perfectly calm. The violence of the blow clears her mind and wipes away a week of sexual frustration.

"You've got something in your eye," Melanie stage whispers.

"Oh, yeah?" Drew says, cocking his head like the dumb animal he is.

Melanie launches across the table and jabs Drew in the eye with a breadstick—one of those hard, crusty jobs with sesame seeds—only she isn't at Soriano's anymore, she's back at The Colony, and the man she's knocked to the floor isn't some greasy shitbag with terrible taste in cologne but Applewhite. The breadstick disintegrates upon impact, keeping her from stabbing that fucker again and again and again.

While Drew rolls around on the ground and engages in wild histrionics that win him zero sympathy from the onlookers at Soriano's, Melanie slips out the door and walks down the street to where she'd parked her car to avoid paying for the valet. From an operational standpoint, it's the first smart move she's made all night.

When she reaches her apartment, she fumbles with her keys, lurches past Abigail, and barely makes it to the bathroom in time. She empties her stomach into the toilet and collapses onto the floor in tears. Her face still stings. It was just a slap, she reminds herself, but it feels like so much more. She'd let Applewhite get inside her head again, as if he'd enlisted Drew to remind her he would always be with her. She'd worked so hard to put him in the past, to lock him up in a place where he couldn't hurt her anymore, but here he is making himself at home in her head.

It wasn't even the slap, it was the certainty of his dominance, she realized. It was how Applewhite had terrorized her during those long sleepless nights at The Colony, waiting for him to materialize out of the darkness even though she knew he would come boldly, like some beast of the jungle, so everyone would know that he was claiming what he believed was rightfully his.

In her despair, Melanie wonders if it will always be like this. There aren't enough knives to stab Applewhite away. The memory will find her. It isn't the violence. Or it isn't *just* the violence. Not all violence is a violation. Not all violations are violent. She knows the difference. She is intimate with this pain. When she sparred with Gary, there was no shame in submitting when she lost. Win some, lose some, and—if you can—get up and do it again.

This is different. There are nights when Applewhite comes to Melanie in her dreams. The worst aren't the ones where he has his way with her, but the nights she lets it happen without a fight. These dreams make her realize no matter how many thousands of hours she trains, there's no defense against the damage he's already done. What use is training or staying sober when he knows what she's really like?

That's why he chose her. One look and he knew she was the kind of person for whom everything was negotiable. Nothing was exempt, not a cause, an ideal, or even a life—especially not her own—and that, more than anything, destroys her.

She checks her TruLuv account on her tab. She hadn't meant to do it. She didn't consciously say to herself, I'm going to do this thing that is the opposite of what I want. That's just what addicts do. A message from Bill appears in her notifications: *Gary's brother, Robert Gray, is at Evergreen Medical Center in Gardena. Good luck.*

Melanie's heart swells with gratitude. Thanks to Bill, she has Gary back. She's his caretaker now, and the best thing she can do for him is to get his brother out of Evergreen. She sees it as a kind of test. If she can't pull her shit together for herself, then she'll do it for Gary, and if she can't do it for him, then what's the point of even pretending she'll ever be anything but broken?

8

BOMBS MAKE SENSE

TREVOR WALKS WITH DOYLE ALONG a ragged stretch of sand in Playa del Rey, a beach south of the marina that sits directly under LAX's flight path. The sand is trucked in from somewhere else and the face of the slope is held together with iceplant and residue from the refinery farther down the shore. Even the seagulls look dodgy.

Doyle has summoned him to the beach for an early morning meeting. When he got the call, Trevor was certain Doyle had discovered he and Viviana were sleeping together. But now he isn't so sure. Doyle seems disheveled, borderline distraught, like he's been up all night. Doyle has always been a bit paranoid—it comes with the territory—but calling a face-to-face meeting on an empty stretch of beach socked in with fog like a couple of Cold War spies is highly irregular, even for him. Seeing Doyle like this unnerves Trevor. In order to believe everything is going to be okay at MIS, Doyle needs to act like it.

"I don't have to tell you Gary's death has taken a heavy toll on our organization," Doyle begins. "It's not an overstatement to say it's impacted every aspect of what we do, including safeguarding our secrecy and security."

"Did something happen?" Trevor asks.

Doyle stops and looks up and down the beach. If the wind and wave noises aren't enough to frustrate potential eavesdroppers, the jetliners cutting through the petrochemical murk will do the trick. Trevor wonders if paranoia is contagious, if it can be passed from person to person like a virus. He's pretty sure it is, especially in an underground organization like MIS.

"I'm afraid our operational integrity has been compromised. I was followed last night after leaving MIS."

"Are you sure?" Trevor asks, playing along.

"I think it was LAPD."

Trevor wonders if this is about Melanie's cop friend or part of a plot by HNS.

"I want you to wipe the servers and scramble all of our communication devices," Doyle continues. "I'll alert our ops to stay away from HQ until we've established a secure location. We're going to need some new tabs."

"Got it."

Doyle looks out beyond the horizon and seems to get lost there for a moment. There's a jogger headed north, a walker going south, some kook on a paddleboard splashing around offshore. Nothing sketchy or unusual.

"Before you dismantle the network, there's something I need you to do for me."

"What is it?" Trevor asks.

"I talked to Melanie last night. She says Gary's brother is at Evergreen Medical Center. An HNS stronghold."

"Well, that's good news."

"Is it? What if he's working for HNS?"

Trevor lets that sink in. "Are you saying Gary's brother might have ratted us out?"

"I didn't say that," Doyle answers. "But I'm not *not* saying it either. HNS has been racking up too many victories against us for it to be a coincidence."

"So, you think Gary told his brother about us?"

"If Gary's brother needs help, we're going to give it to him," Doyle says.

"We owe Gary that much," Trevor agrees.

"But if he's a threat to our mission," Doyle continues, "we neutralize him."

"Gary wouldn't have jeopardized—"

"They were brothers, Trevor. Junkie brothers."

Another passenger plane soars overhead before banking over the Pacific and turning east. Doyle slips off his running shoes and walks farther out onto the firmly packed sand along the shoreline, where the white foam kisses his feet.

"Who are we going to send after him?" Trevor asks.

"Who would you pick?"

Trevor doesn't relish the thought of sending *anyone* to Evergreen, which he now realizes is the point of this meeting. "I don't feel good about this. I used to feel like we could handle anything. Now..."

Doyle turns and looks Trevor in the eyes. "You didn't answer my question."

"Melanie," Trevor blurts without thinking. Viviana has been itching to go on another mission, but Trevor doesn't want her to go. Viviana can look after herself, but Trevor can't bear the thought of losing her. Not now.

"How is she doing with her...project?"

"Melanie?" Trevor says. "It's been an interesting opportunity for growth." The words are MIS boilerplate, a total cop-out, but what is he supposed to say?

"You'll be Viviana's case manager going forward," Doyle says.

He doesn't know, Trevor thinks. Doyle has been so distracted he hasn't noticed how hard Trevor has fallen for her, and she for him, which means he needs to tell him. Not later, but now.

"Viviana…" Another jet plane goes screaming across the sky. Trevor holds his tongue while he gathers his thoughts. What exactly are his feelings for Viviana? He doesn't know. She's like a drug, it suddenly dawns on him, a drug he isn't willing to give up, even if it means feeding Melanie to the wolves…

"You were saying?" Doyle asks.

"Viviana's good."

"One of our best. You want to tell her, or shall I?"

"I'll tell them both," Trevor says.

"Good. Have Melanie meet us at HQ. Tell her to be ready for anything."

"I can send Vinnie to pick her up."

Doyle shakes his head. "Vinnie's not with the organization anymore. He relapsed."

Damn, Trevor thinks. What a shame. Vinnie wasn't an op, but he had more days sober than anyone else at Make It Stop. He was an unrepentant jerk, but you don't have to like your comrades to be inspired by them. The sound of the surf is replaced by jet engines. The two men look skyward as an airplane rises above the gray waves, banks into the marine layer, and disappears.

A CLUSTER OF VEHICLES IDLES in a remote corner of the parking lot at Western Psychiatric: a black passenger van and two black SUVs. Hansen steers his Jaguar into the lot—self-driving cars are for pussies—and parks. Security officers pile out of the vehicles. Applewhite stands head and shoulders above the rest. Grace, he's delighted to see, is also here, but so is that annoying twat she works with.

"Applewhite," Hansen says as he steps out of the car, "is your team ready?"

The brute nods.

"Grand." Hansen turns to Grace. "And you?"

Grace opens her mouth, but the man talks over her. "We selected this site—"

Hansen cuts him off. "You are not to speak to me ever again. Do I make myself clear?"

The man begins to answer, realizes his error, and nods.

Hansen smiles at Grace. "Please continue."

"We picked this location in the hopes that whoever receives the alarm will assume the GPS was lost here at Western Psych and unintentionally activated. Hopefully, we can catch them off guard."

"Well, get on with it," Hansen says, "and send the bloody signal already."

Grace picks up the reassembled pin and activates the GPS. Everyone huddles around the tab it's hooked up to. A map of greater Los Angeles appears on the screen and a spot near the intersection of Wilshire and Sepulveda lights up.

"That's us," Grace says.

A second spot on the map appears: a location at the southeastern corner of the intersection of the 101 and the 405 freeways.

"The Sherman Oaks Galleria," Bethany says.

"The bloody mall?" Hansen asks.

"Yes, sir," Grace says.

Hansen turns to Applewhite and his crew. "What the fuck are you waiting for?"

MELANIE WALKS THROUGH THE EMPTY lobby. She was delighted to get Trevor's message to report to MIS HQ but is more than a little spooked by how quiet it is. There's no one in the lobby and the hallways are dark. Melanie searches the locker room, dojo, TV lounge, and briefing room, but there isn't a soul to be found.

It's not until she thinks to check the workroom that she finds Trevor, hunched over a tab, looking majorly stressed out. His desk is in disarray, and he's got a stack of tabs piled up next to the one he's working on.

"What's going on?" Melanie says, startling Trevor. She can't remember seeing him look so bedraggled. She, on the other hand, feels a thousand times better than the last time she was here.

"Give me your tab," he says.

"What for?"

"Shutting down all comms."

"It's not one of yours." She tosses it on the table anyway.

"We're going dark."

"Holy shit. What's happening?"

"We're losing. That's what's happening. HNS is all over us. Ops are getting killed. And Doyle thinks he was followed last night."

"I *was* followed," Doyle says as he enters the workroom. He's dressed in dark jeans and a tight-fitting T-shirt.

"Hey, chief," Melanie says.

"Did Trevor tell you about the assignment?" Doyle asks.

"Not yet," Melanie says, "but I'm assuming it's about Gary, right?"

"Let's go to my office and we'll talk about it, but we don't have much time."

An alarm—loud and piercingly shrill—sounds from Trevor's desktab. Melanie, Trevor, and Doyle freeze.

"What's that?" Melanie asks.

"Your mayday signal," Trevor answers.

"So that's what it sounds like," Melanie says. "Annoying."

Trevor turns off the alarm. "Did you trigger it?"

"Uh, no," Melanie says, running her fingers through her hair. "I lost it."

"You lost it?" Doyle demands.

"Yeah, at Western Psych. I guess I should have told you." Melanie hopes this doesn't fuck up her assignment, put her back on double secret probation.

"That's where the signal's coming from," Trevor confirms.

"Maybe someone found it and accidentally activated it," Melanie says, but isn't really sure if she believes that's what happened.

"Or maybe HNS is using it to determine our location," Trevor says.

They exchange looks as this possibility sinks in. Were Hansen and his goons on their way?

"We need to get out of here," Doyle says.

HE SHOULDN'T BE HERE, HANSEN thinks as the motorcade from Health Net Secure hauls ass toward the Valley. He should be back at the office, working the phones, reading reports— anything but this. He's got three or four offices he uses regularly, but there are many more. He could show up at any hospital in the network and commandeer the CEO's office. Send a surgeon out for sushi, terrorize the nurses, literally anything. Instead, he's following a pair of Escalades and a passenger van because if he doesn't he knows it will all go to hell. They've entered a new phase of this war, and he's not going to let a bunch of vigilante scum interfere with his plans. So instead of stuffing his face with yellowtail sashimi—the real deal, not that clone shit—Hansen drives while Bethany works her tab.

"How much longer?" Hansen asks.

Bethany hesitates. "Five minutes."

"You said that five minutes ago!" Hansen screams.

"Traffic," Bethany says.

"Fuck this." Hansen jerks the wheel and passes the HNS vehicles. Bethany braces herself as he weaves in and out traffic. When they approach the exit from the passing lane, Hansen whips across all five lanes of the freeway to hit the on-ramp with the rest of the vehicles following close behind. A waste of effort, maybe, but he feels better.

Hansen pulls up in front of the mall on Ventura Boulevard. As he pops out of the car, the rest of the HNS vehicles slide in behind the

Jaguar, taking up the entire bus lane. Hansen waves them on while a crowd of people waiting for the bus gawk at the sight of armed men piling out of the vehicles to storm the Sherman Oaks Galleria.

"What are you looking at?" Hansen shouts, but the bus riders, having nowhere to go and nothing to do, are unmoved by his aggression.

Melanie dumps all the tabs she can find into a large duffel bag while the boys get into an argument.

"Are the servers clean?" Doyle asks.

"They should be," Trevor says.

"*Should be* isn't going to cut it," Doyle snaps.

"Let me double check," Trevor says, but Doyle waves him off.

"I'll take care of it," Doyle says.

"With all due resp—" Trevor begins.

"You two go down to the garage and get us a fresh set of wheels."

"On it," Melanie says to blunt the tension in the room. It's not like Trevor to challenge Doyle like this—or, if it is, he's never done it in front of her before.

"I'll be there in five," Doyle says.

"Let's go," Melanie says to Trevor, but before they can leave, Doyle stops them.

"I'll take that," he says to Trevor, pointing at the tab broadcasting the mayday signal.

Trevor hands it over, but he doesn't look too happy about it. Trevor is still sulking when they get in the elevator.

"What's eating you?" Melanie asks.

"What's eating *me*? What's up with Doyle?"

"I don't know," Melanie says, "but now is not the time for this."

Trevor rolls his eyes. The elevator dings and the doors slide open. Melanie charges into the parking structure, but Trevor stumbles out of the gate. The strap to the duffel bag slips off his shoulder and half the tabs go skittering across the garage floor.

"I'll grab a vehicle." Melanie double-times across the massive garage. The place is a labyrinth. The end of one structure marks the beginning of a new one. She sprints toward a sign that reads VALET, but no one's at the station.

"Excuse me!" a voice calls out. Melanie turns and sees a rich prick standing half-in, half-out of a bright orange high-performance smart car. He looks middle aged but dresses like a teenager. There are a million men like this in LA and every one of them thinks he's a very big deal.

"Yeah?" Melanie says, sensing the solution to her problem has presented itself.

"I'm kind of in a hurry?" the prick says.

"I can help you with that." Melanie jogs over and makes a big production out of holding the door open for the man, but as soon has his ass clears the vehicle, Melanie slides into the driver's seat.

"I'm going to need a receipt," the man says, but Melanie is already speeding away, leaving the rich prick in the dust. By the time she circles back to the elevator, Trevor has cleaned up his mess. Melanie taps her horn to get his attention.

"Let's go!" she shouts.

"Subtle," Trevor says as he scrutinizes the car.

"Where's Doyle?" she asks.

Doyle emerges from the elevator.

"I left a little surprise for our friends," Doyle says.

"Can we please get out of here?" Melanie says, feeling anxious.

"Sure," Doyle says as he eyes the vehicle, "but I'm driving."

Melanie doesn't like it, but Doyle's in a good mood and she'd like to keep it that way. Melanie crawls over the gear shifter to sit in the passenger seat while Trevor climbs in the back.

"Seatbelts, boys and girls," Doyle says as he buckles in. "We're in for a bumpy ride!"

OUTSIDE THE SHERMAN OAKS GALLERIA, Hansen feels his tenuous hold on his composure begin to slip away while demanding updates from Bethany. For a brief moment, he exits his screaming body and sees his own screaming face. It's not pretty.

"I've lost them," Bethany says.

Hansen comes back to himself. He grabs Bethany by the shoulders and addresses her as calmly as possible. "If you don't tell me what's going on, something very bad is going to happen to you. Do you understand me?"

"I'm trying to reach Applewhite for an update, but I'm not having any luck...maybe they're in an elevator?"

Hansen is distracted by the high-pitched sound of an engine moving at great speed. He looks up and sees an orange blur go buzzing through the intersection. He knows without having to be told that MIS has slipped away.

But Bethany has news. She's finally gotten through. "Applewhite says there's no one up there."

"No shit!" Hansen shouts. "Get in the car!" Just as Bethany looks up from her tab a massive, double length MTS bus pulls in front of the line of HNS vehicles, blocking them in. The doors open and an irate driver gives Hansen hell.

"You can't park here!" he shouts, "This is a bus lane!"

"Move that piece of shit!" Hansen screams, his self-control a distant dream.

"This piece of shit is calling the police!"

Even if the driver wanted to move, there's already a long line of people boarding the bus. This is going to take a while, Hansen realizes. The bus driver shrugs as if to say, *that's what you get.*

Hansen looks up at the office tower and screams.

"SO, ABOUT THIS MISSION," MELANIE says to Doyle as they race down Ventura Boulevard in the smart car they've commandeered.

"Wait one," Doyle says as he glances at his watch, an old analog wind-up, and eases the vehicle over to the side of the road.

"What are you doing?" Trevor asks from the back seat.

"Rest stop."

"But HNS..."

"Just get out of the car," Doyle says.

Trevor glares at Melanie like she has something to do with the delay. Don't look at me, Melanie wants to say.

Doyle hops out of the car as soon as it stops moving, and immediately lights up a cigarette. Strange. Doyle quit smoking months ago. They're less than a mile from the Sherman Oaks Galleria, which Doyle now turns and faces. He looks at his watch and starts counting down.

"Three...two...one..."

A loud but muffled explosion rocks the office tower of the Sherman Oaks Galleria. All the north-facing windows on the fourth floor blow out at once.

"Whoa!" Melanie says.

Doyle smiles, delighted by the plume of smoke rising from the tower. Trevor stands next to him with a look of astonishment on his face.

"You blew up the Sherman Oaks Galleria?" he asks.

"Just the fourth floor," Doyle says with a wink that Melanie finds immensely reassuring. This is the leader she pledged to follow.

Doyle takes a long drag off his cigarette as though it's the sweetest thing he's ever tasted. He stubs out the cigarette on the hood of the car and puts it in his pocket.

"Shall we?"

9
MASTODONS AND MARIPOSAS

THE AIR FEELS HUMID, MAKING it easy to imagine what the La Brea Tar Pits must have been like a couple thousand years ago, when dire wolves and saber-toothed tigers battled it out under the warm Pleistocene sun. Melanie can feel the sweat gathering at her hairline as she, Trevor, and Doyle cut through the garden, presided over by a bronze replica of a giant sloth that looks like a massive turd.

They didn't talk much on the way over because Doyle was paranoid about being recorded inside the smart car. Now that they're outside in the open air, she's anxious to hear the details of the assignment Doyle has cooked up for her. Apparently, she's not the only one with questions.

"What did you find out about Melanie's intel?" Doyle asks Trevor.

"It checks out," Trevor says. "Gary's brother is at Evergreen."

"I told you!" Melanie punches Trevor in the arm to get him to lighten up, but he ignores her. "I'll get him out."

"What if the target doesn't want to leave?" Trevor asks.

"He's not a *target*." Melanie says. "He's Gary's brother!"

"Trevor's right," Doyle says. "He may have other reasons for being there."

"After today's stunt," Trevor says, "if anyone finds out she's MIS, she'll be in a tremendous amount of danger."

"Danger is what we do," Melanie says. It's such a cornball thing to say, but so is talking about her like she isn't here. Besides, who does Trevor think he's kidding? *All* assignments are dangerous.

"If you don't approve of my methods," Doyle says, "you can always go work for someone else."

Melanie doesn't know what's going on between Trevor and Doyle, but she's never seen them act so aggro. Is this about her? Or is there something else going on that she doesn't know about?

They approach the bubbling pit of tar-like seepage that fills the remnants of an ancient asphalt mine. Melanie has been here before. It's basically a giant sink clogged with prehistoric sludge that occasionally burps up bones. Three plaster mastodons are arranged around the lake in a tragic tableau: dad sinks into the muck, mom freaks out on the shore, and baby mastodon completely loses her shit. What makes her think of these three as a family? Oh, no reason…

"So, am I going to Evergreen or not?" Melanie asks.

"I've been thinking about your method," Doyle says to Melanie.

"Getting drunk before an assignment?" Trevor says. "I wouldn't exactly call it a *method*."

Doyle chooses his words with care. "In some situations, like the one we're in now, it could be beneficial."

"Now you're saying it's okay to relapse?" Melanie asks.

Doyle stops to take in the trio of mastodons. "I've been asking myself if I'd be willing to do what I'm about to ask you to do."

Melanie can sense how important this is to Doyle, and she's touched by his sincerity, but this is a no-brainer. She doesn't value her sobriety the same way Doyle does. She isn't even sure what sobriety means anymore. She's never more than a few minutes away from burning the whole thing down to the ground. The urge to fuck up her life is the strongest one she has.

"I've got what? A week of sobriety? It's not that big a deal."

Doyle shakes his head, lays those intense blue eyes on her. "For people like us, it's a very big deal."

"I understand," Melanie says. "Thank you."

"This is nice," Trevor says. "We should bond like this more often."

Melanie rolls her eyes. What a cynical crew they'd become. It wasn't always like this.

"You know that bottle of hydrocodone you lifted from Western Psych?" Doyle asks.

Here it comes, Melanie thinks. "Yeah?"

"It wasn't hydrocodone," Doyle says. "It was something called Bliss. That's why your target overdosed. HNS is planning something big, and I'm convinced Bliss has something to do with it."

"Which is why we should walk away from this mess right now," Trevor says. "It's not our fight."

"I can take care of myself, Trev," Melanie says, but she's starting to feel like they're all talking about different things.

"This has nothing to do with you," Trevor snaps at Melanie. "I don't like the thought of *anyone* going undercover right now."

"Not even Viviana?" Melanie says. "Things must be *really* bad."

Doyle hooks an eyebrow. Normally this would put a stop to the argument, but Trevor keeps it going. It wasn't like him to be so bold. "There's more to it than that," he says.

"I'll bet," Melanie replies.

"Look," Doyle says, "we're going to get you through this."

"With what resources?" Trevor asks. "We've got no head-quarters, no servers, no ops."

"With this," Doyle says, handing Melanie a California driver's license.

"Who's this?" she asks.

"The new you."

"Looks real."

"Because it is."

"Lindsay Moran?"

"She was one of us," Trevor says with a heavy sigh.

According to her California driver's license, Lindsay Moran has blue eyes and blonde hair. She lives in a studio apartment on Shell Street in Manhattan Beach. She stands five foot five and weighs one hundred thirty-five pounds. She's an organ donor.

"What happened to her?" Doyle and Trevor look at different parts of the tar pits. Melanie puts two-and-two together. "Oh."

"Yeah," Doyle says. "She OD'd."

"How are we going to process Melanie into Evergreen?" Trevor asks.

"We're not," Doyle says. "She's going to get arrested."

"Ooh," Melanie says, "that sounds like fun."

"I had a feeling you would say that."

WHEN DEREK HANSEN WAS SIXTEEN years old, he was beset by a mysterious illness. His parents had just moved from London to the United States, and he'd had trouble making friends. The only place he felt at ease was on the football pitch, which his stupid American classmates insisted on referring to as a "soccer field." One evening after practice, he felt especially sore and when he woke up the following morning, he was in excruciating pain that doctors determined was due to internal bleeding in his hip but were mystified as to the source of the injury. Hansen was admitted to the hospital, where he was subjected to numerous x-rays and tests that required the withdrawal of blood. The nurses doted on the blond-haired boy and Hansen relished the attention. There was one nurse who loved to tease him about his accent. She was younger, prettier, flirtier, and—as he would soon discover—dirtier than the others. One night when she came to draw his blood, he asked if he could put the needle in himself and she obliged. When the blood bag was full and Derek was bandaged up, the nurse produced another needle.

"Now do me," she whispered.

The nurse exposed her bum. When the needle went in, they both came.

The nurse got off on getting injected and she passed the kink on to him. In that sense, he had caught a disease, a rare and terrifying fetish that took root in his imagination and slowly began to bloom. Eventually, the bleeding in his hip subsided and Hansen was released from the hospital, and he went on to be a normal American teenager—with one exception. Though he got plenty of attention from girls, he discovered he couldn't achieve orgasm without imagining a sleek, silver needle plunging into flesh.

This filled him with great shame for many years until he stumbled upon the website Naughty Needles and discovered the wide world of medical fetishes. It seemed for every medical procedure there was a kink. While there were lots of videos created for those who fantasized about getting stuck by naughty nurses, there were plenty of scenarios for people like him who understood the purest pleasure could be derived from injecting others. On that day, Derek Hansen's career in medicine began.

Hansen climbs into his car and takes a deep breath. He's spent the last hour dealing with the police and the press and all he wants is to get out of this suit and let off a little steam. Bethany climbs into his car and settles in the passenger seat.

"I have something to show you," she says with a guarded smile.

"Tell me you have good news."

Bethany hands him a tab with a street map displayed on the screen. "Look."

Hansen is in no mood for riddles. If she wants a prize for a job well done, she's come to the wrong place. "Just tell me already."

"You're looking at the home address of Melanie Marsh, a.k.a. Rachel Roark."

The MIS agent. There was zero chance she'd go home. Not now. She's probably with Doyle and his motley band of reprobates, plotting their next move.

"She wouldn't be stupid enough to go home," Hansen says.

"Stupid? Probably not. But reckless? Maybe."

Hansen is already bored with the conversation and ready to move on. "Send Applewhite to check it out."

This isn't the reaction Bethany was hoping for, but she obediently types in his request.

"Luv?" Hansen interrupts.

Bethany looks up from her tab.

Hansen jerks his head at the bus stop. "Out."

It takes Bethany a moment to realize she's being asked to leave. When it does, she unfastens her seat belt and gets out of the car. Before she can ruin the moment by saying something asinine, Hansen drives away.

MELANIE SITS ON A BENCH by the tar pits staring at the mastodons, but her thoughts are a million memories away. She's in their apartment, the one with Mariposa Palms written in big, quasi-cursive lettering outside on the building's stucco walls. Anytime she had to give her address, she'd add Mariposa Palms in between the street address and the city. It made her feel special. Well, her family was special all right....

She remembers her last night at the Mariposa Palms like it was yesterday. She's standing in the kitchen, watching her mother sway before the stove while she cooks dinner. Her mother wears a silk dressing gown and clutches a wine glass in one hand and a spatula in the other. It's not clear what she's preparing, something with sauce from a jar, but she's got all the burners going and the main course is smoking on the stove.

Melanie knows something is wrong, but she doesn't know what to do, what to say. Her mother can sense her standing there. No matter how much wine she drinks, she always knows when Melanie is watching her.

"Set the table, sweetie. Dinner will be ready in a few minutes."

"I already did."

"Then what's the matter?"

"I think something's burning." Melanie knows the moment the words leave her lips this was the wrong thing to say.

Her mother whirls, threatening her with the spatula. She's not her mother anymore. She's Janet, the stranger who lives in their house and drinks too much.

"You think I don't know what I'm doing?!" Janet screams.

Smoke pours out of a pot on the stove, sending Janet into a fit of rage. She hurls her wine glass at the pot, and the entire stove top goes up in flames. She turns on Melanie again.

"Happy now? Dinner's ruined—thanks to you!"

Melanie stares transfixed as the flames run up the walls and across the counter, engulfing the kitchen. Janet pulls a pack of cigarettes out of her dressing gown as the flames spread and the smoke thickens. Melanie's father enters the kitchen carrying a fire extinguisher. He knocks Janet to the floor and blasts the stovetop, smothering the flames as they spread to other parts of the kitchen. Melanie can't see anything through the haze of powder and smoke, but she can hear her parents fighting. Curses. Sounds of struggle. Screams and shouts. Then, right on cue, sirens. The fire is new, but everything else is the same.

Melanie keeps screaming her mother's name until she answers her, which she finally does, calling out to her from the living room. She runs to her mother. She's crouched in a corner on the floor, her dressing gown is plastered with powder and her face is streaked with blood. Her father stands in the doorway, breathing heavily, fists clenched and full of rage. "Look what you made me do," he says. Melanie kneels at her mother's side. Her father turns and leaves.

"Dad!" she cries out, but he doesn't answer. He never answers. Not then, and not in her dreams. She chases after him and runs into the front yard in her bare feet. Her father climbs into his sedan, backs down the driveway, takes one last look at Melanie standing in the front yard in her nightgown, and drives away.

Melanie never sees him again.

The rest of the night is a blur. A pair of firemen carry her mother out of the Mariposa Palms on a stretcher. "Let it burn!" Janet shrieks. She says this over and over again before she starts to laugh, a sight made all the more terrible on account of her swollen, bloodied face. She looks like something out of a horror movie, and the performance earns her a trip to the hospital. Janet's laughter mixes with the sound of sirens from the police cars pulling up to the house. The policemen tell Melanie everything will be okay, but this is a lie. She will not be okay. Neither of them will be.

"Melanie?" the man asks.

She looks up at the man-sized silhouette standing over her. "Trevor?" she guesses.

It's not Trevor, but Bill. What's he doing here?

"Are you all right?"

"Yeah, sure." Melanie wipes her eyes. "This is where I do my crying."

Bill shifts uncomfortably.

"That was a joke." Melanie stands, takes Bill by the arm, and steers him away from the tar pits, which she would be happy to never see—or smell—again. "I have news."

"Oh?" Bill's face registers his surprise.

"I'm going undercover. Let's not talk here. Do you have your car?"

"Yes."

"Good. I need you to run me home so I can pick up a few things."

THE FIRST TIME APPLEWHITE KILLED a man he was sixteen years old. He and his friends had cooked up a plan to rob a record store. When the owner arrived to open up the store, they followed him inside.

The register was empty, of course, and when the owner told him the safe was empty, too, Applewhite shot him. His friends scattered but he stayed, transfixed by the site of the old man bleeding out on the floor. He has no idea how long he stood there and watched but when the cops came, it seemed like there were a million of them. His parents hired a lawyer who convinced the jury that the gun went off by mistake and he was sent to juvie. During his time in lock-up, he grew six inches and added sixty pounds of muscle. When Hansen found him, he was working in a slaughterhouse.

HNS has been good to Applewhite. It gives him everything he needs, and right now what he needs most is to find Melanie Marsh. Every time he looks in the mirror to shave or tries to lift his left arm above his head, he's reminded of her. The only thing that saved him the night she plunged the knife into his neck was he had the sense not to pull it out or else he would have bled to death on the spot.

He stands on the porch of Melanie Marsh's bungalow, peering through the window. There's not much to see: the place is tiny, a total shithole; but he'll need to search the bathroom, check the closet, look inside anything with a door on it. He pulls on a pair of latex gloves and tries the handle on the front door, which isn't locked and swings open, saving him the trouble of having to kick it down. As Applewhite steps across the threshold, a man calls out to him.

"Can I help you?"

Applewhite returns to the porch.

The neighbor stands at the boundary between the two yards. He looks like he could be trouble. Applewhite hopes so.

"This doesn't concern you," he says.

The neighbor doesn't like that. He crosses into Melanie's yard and steps onto the patio.

"That's where you're wrong."

Applewhite turns and sizes up the neighbor. He's big and brave, but no match for Applewhite. Then he sees it: a jagged scar on the right side of the man's neck.

"Fuck. Off."

The neighbor doesn't get the message. He comes at him, forcing Applewhite to put the man in a chokehold. The man strains for something tucked inside his boot—a knife, probably. He hates knives. Applewhite relaxes his hold on the man just enough for him to think he's won some kind of advantage, and when he shifts his weight, Applewhite snaps his neck.

A pair of HNS security officers waddle up the walkway to the bungalow. Applewhite instructs them to take the man to the van while he searches Melanie's apartment.

No furniture, clothes everywhere. He wonders if the place has already been ransacked or if she's just a slob. He spies a pair of photographs propped up against a plastic pouch on the windowsill. Both photos show the same two people: Melanie and the MIS op they iced in the desert. He's guessing the pouch contains what's left of him. He opens the zipper and peers inside. Yep. Cremains.

A sudden movement on the floor near the bathroom catches his attention. He assesses the threat. It's a cat. Applewhite loves cats.

He crosses the room and scoops it up in his hands. He lifts the cat to his face—so soft—and gently nuzzles the creature.

"What's your name, pretty kitty?"

The cat returns Applewhite's affection. "Meow."

"Aren't you sweet?"

No nametag. Of course.

"You're coming with me."

THE CLOUDS IN THE SKY light up pink and orange. Melanie remembers a time not that long ago when California sunsets thrilled her. They felt nothing short of miraculous. Not the sunsets themselves, but the vibe they conveyed when she was locked down in some shitty foster home or rehab facility. Now she's on the verge of going back to rehab and the sunset, though spectacular, doesn't move her in the slightest. Maybe she's depressed. She has every right to be.

"I'm going to Evergreen," she says to Bill from the passenger seat of his sedan. It's been a day of men driving her places.

"To get Robert out?"

"Yeah. Doyle thinks there might be a connection between HNS and Bliss."

Bill gives this some thought. "When are you going?"

"Tomorrow."

"I assume you're not going to use your real name."

"Nope," she says, "I'll be Lindsay Moran."

Bill nods.

"I'm going in through mandatory detox."

Shortly after conditional release was authorized for use in rehab facilities, LAPD started funneling people charged with being under the influence of alcohol or narcotics through mandatory detox. They maintained it was a way for substance abusers to get the help they needed, but it's a scam to entrap more people with conditional release.

"Make sure you get picked up in a community Evergreen serves."

"That's the plan. I'm going to party it up at the beach."

"That should do it, just…"

"What?"

"Be careful."

How many times has someone dropped her off on the doorstep of a death sentence and told her to be careful? Thanks for the public service announcement, pal.

"Why are you helping me?" Melanie asks.

"Easy," Bill says, "I like you."

"I like you, too," Melanie says, "but people don't put their livelihoods on the line just because they like someone."

"You'd be surprised," Bill deadpans.

"Regular people? Maybe. Cops? No."

"Cops aren't people?"

"Barely."

"That's good to know," Bill says, but he doesn't look the least bit perturbed. Melanie sees the sign for Buddy Liquor. Almost home.

"Turn here," she says, even though Bill's got the address programmed into his GPS. He turns and the car slows to a stop in front of her bungalow.

"Looks like you have visitors," Bill says.

Melanie's front door is wide open. She flies out of the car before the sedan comes to a stop. She sprints across the lawn and lunges into her apartment. Nothing seems out of place, though it's hard to tell. It's eerily quiet. Too quiet.

"Abigail?"

Melanie checks the bathroom and the closet. She moves on to the cabinets and drawers when Bill enters.

"She's not here."

"Who's not here?" Bill asks.

"My cat. Abby?" Melanie calls out.

"The door was open," Bill says. "She probably didn't get far." He seems preternaturally calm. Normally she would find this reassuring, but not today.

"I have to find her!"

"We need to go."

Something passes between them, an understanding that Bill is helping because he wants to, but without her cooperation that could change.

Maybe Abigail got scared and went to her second home. Melanie steps outside to look for her at Lou's. That seems like something she would do. Abby can be extremely obnoxious, but she isn't skittish, and she certainly isn't timid. She's kind of an asshole actually. Like Melanie.

Lou's front door is open and she slips inside. Lou's bungalow is identical to hers, but his feels cozier. There are books on the shelves, rugs on the floor, and the room is stuffed with furniture. Where did he get all this stuff? One wall is devoted to framed photographs of Lou's family: aunts and uncles, nephews and nieces.

"Abigail?" Melanie wails.

A pair of bowls sit on the kitchen floor. One is filled with water, the other cat food. If she opens the cupboard, she'll find more tins of food, bags of treats, even cat toys. Stuff Melanie is always running out to get.

"Abby?" she calls out one last time, but there's no one here but her.

"YOU'VE GOT TO BE KIDDING me!"

There's a part of Trevor that would love to be able to say to Viviana, "Ha-ha! Had you going there!" But that's not the case. He's sitting on the sofa in her nice, nondescript apartment, trying to dig himself out of a hole.

"Viviana, listen…"

"Who's the best op at MIS?" Viviana asks.

"You are," Trevor says, "but right now there is no MIS."

"Then why is Melanie going on a mission?"

"I'm not sure," Trevor lies.

Viviana crosses her arms. She's so beautiful he can barely look at her. "I thought she was in the doghouse."

"She is. Or was."

"Then what changed?" Viviana rages. "Why did she get the assignment instead of me?"

Trevor looks away.

"It was you, wasn't it?"

There's no wriggling off the hook this time. Trevor thought of himself as a cool customer, steady under fire, but Viviana can undo all that in an instant.

"You don't want this one," he says.

"You don't know what I want!" Viviana shouts.

"It's a suicide mission!" Trevor shouts back.

"Spare me."

"It wasn't my call to make," Trevor insists.

Viviana covers her face with her hands. Oh, shit. Is she crying? He moves to comfort her, but she pushes him away.

"I'm going for a run," she says as she barges out of the room and slams the door shut behind her. A second later, his tab buzzes. Trevor glances down at the crude display, expecting to see Viviana's number. It's Doyle's. Now what?

"I need you to do something for me," Doyle says.

"I'm afraid to ask."

"I want you to take Melanie to the drop-off point tomorrow."

"Why me?"

"Here's the address."

"Hold on."

Trevor goes into the kitchen and pulls open a drawer whose sole content is a Glock 19X. He closes the drawer and opens the one below it. He finds another gun. Another Glock. This time it's a Compact Crossover G45.

"Ready?" Doyle asks.

"Just give it to me," Trevor says as he slides the drawer shut.

FLIRTY & DIRTY. NAUGHTY NYMPH. Gutterslut.

These brand names aren't exactly sending a message of feminine positivity, Melanie thinks, as she selects a box of blonde hair dye and drops it into a basket that already includes black leggings, white canvas sneakers, and an oversized hoodie. Disposable clothes for her bender at the beach. She makes her way to the register and pays for her purchases.

Melanie walks back to her motel. Her room is on the ground floor. The mechanism lights up when she inserts her key. Melanie turns the handle and enters her room. The bed is big, the decor modern-ish, and the TV looks new. Could be worse.

She turns on the TV to combat the conversations buzzing through the walls and leaves it on an old black-and-white musical. She goes directly to the sink outside the bathroom, clicks on the light, and looks at her reflection in the mirror. Her hair hangs down on one side of her head. The sides are starting to fill out but are still very short. She can work with that. She checks her tab—no one's called—and sits down on the edge of the bed to read the instructions on the back of the box of hair dye.

A song and dance number breaks out on the TV screen. Her mother used to love these old movies. Sometimes they'd watch them together, but every so often she used the TV as a babysitter and she'd leave in the middle of the movie. Melanie could always tell when she had plans. She'd keep refilling her wine glass. After the fire, when Janet was let out of the hospital, they stayed in a series of motels for a while, and Janet went out all the time. Melanie begged her mother not to leave her until Janet snapped and threatened to hit her. Janet's hand had been badly burned and was heavily bandaged. She would have hurt herself more than Melanie if she actually went through with it, but it had frightened her. She was frightened all the time.

Melanie watches the dancers twirl their bodies to the music. She checks her tab again, not even sure what she expects. Nothing. She misses TruLuv. Misses Abigail even more. She doesn't even have a photo of her. She doesn't know if that's a good thing or a bad thing, but one thing is absolutely true: she can't take any more losses. She puts the tab in a drawer next to the Patriot Bible and goes to work on her hair.

I'm going to drink today. It's the first thought that crosses Melanie's mind when she wakes up the following morning.

I'm going to get absolutely shit-hammered. She gets dressed with a mixture of excitement and dread. When Melanie emerges from her room, she discovers a woman dressed just like her loitering in the motel parking lot: baggy sweatshirt, skintight leggings, cheap sneakers. While Melanie's clothes are brand new, this woman's outfit looks scuffed-up and slept-in. She smokes her cigarette with the impatience of a fugitive. Melanie guesses she's waiting for her fix to show up. The woman glares at Melanie, and not just with her eyes but her whole face, leaving Melanie no choice but to give it right back until they're locked into a full-on stare down.

A pickup truck rumbles into the parking lot and they both look away. Melanie can tell by the woman's reaction it's not for her. It's Trevor driving an older model she doesn't recognize. Melanie gets in, suppressing the urge to glare at the woman one last time as Trevor turns the truck around.

"Where to?" Trevor asks, doing a double take when he sees her blonde hair.

"Hermosa Beach," she says.

"You ready for this?"

Melanie shrugs. "Tell me about Lindsay."

Once upon a time, Trevor explains, Lindsay Moran was a good student who only partied to make up for the attention she didn't get from her mother. Her friends were a motley crew of college dropouts, beach burnouts, and trust fund fuck-ups. Men and women who sought to prolong the twilight of adolescence as far into adulthood as possible. Then things took a dark turn. She experimented with prostitution, was arrested a few times, and was on her third trip to rehab when Doyle recruited her into MIS.

"How'd that work out?"

"There's no such thing as an ideal candidate for MIS, but everyone liked Lindsay and she was making great progress when she, you know…"

Melanie knows. "How did Doyle take it?"

"Hard. He never said anything, but I think he considered shutting down MIS."

"What changed?"

"You showed up."

Melanie isn't interested in ancient history. Not today. Not with Abigail and Lou MIA. She's ready to start drinking. "Pull over," she says, pointing at a liquor store.

Trevor guides the truck into the lot. She goes inside to buy some beer and Trevor follows her into the store.

"I need to tell you something important."

"*This* is important." Melanie says as she plucks a tall boy of Hoppy Life from the beer cooler.

"It's Doyle," Trevor says. "There's something off about him."

"Funny, I feel the same way about you."

"I think there's something he's not telling us."

"What else is new?"

"I mean, deliberately keeping from us."

Melanie shrugs and walks to the cashier. There's no one in line and she sets a tall boy on the counter.

"You're really doing this?" Trevor asks, glaring at the can of beer.

"Yes, I'm really doing this." Melanie hands the cashier a five-dollar bill and leaves the change behind. Trevor follows her outside the store. Melanie cracks open the can and takes a long pull. She's appalled by how good it tastes.

"So, what's the big secret?" Melanie asks.

"Before I shut down Doyle's tab, I found all these encrypted messages."

"Who was it?"

"I don't know. But that whole stunt with the server? And blowing up the building? I think he's hiding something."

"Same old Trevor. Tall, dark, and neurotic."

"Maybe I shouldn't have said anything," Trevor says, "but Doyle's been acting weird ever since Gary—"

"We've *all* been acting weird," Melanie snaps. "You're supposed to act weird when someone you care about is murdered. You'd know that if you actually cared about anyone around here."

"That's a cheap shot," Trevor says. "You have no idea what it's been like since—"

"You're right, I don't have the slightest clue how you feel because you turn off your feelings whenever things go sideways. That may work for Viviana, but it's not how I operate."

"I wish it was just that."

"I'm done playing games, Trevor."

"All I'm saying is be extra careful in there."

Melanie sizes him up, but she isn't buying what he's selling. Not today, or ever again. "Shit," Melanie says. "I forgot to buy some gum. Will you get me some?"

Trevor nods and goes inside—just like she knew he would. Melanie makes a beeline for the truck and jumps in. She cranks the ignition and punches the gas. The truck fishtails out of the parking lot. By the time she reaches the freeway, Melanie's tab is buzzing. It's probably Trevor having a fit. She shuts it off and chucks it out the window.

10

RIOT AT THE BEACH

"Fiery Cat and Coke."

The bar is dark and gloomy. An incubator for bad decisions. Her kind of place. It's been a long time since she's gotten drunk in a place like this, and she intends to make the worst of it.

The bartender sets a pint glass on the bar. "Ten."

Melanie puts down a twenty. "Keep the change."

The bartender makes the money disappear. He doesn't nod or say "thanks" or even crack a smile. He doesn't look like he knows how.

"Is it always this dead in here?" she asks. It's got to be past five o'clock in the afternoon—happy hour—but the bar is mostly empty.

"We just opened," he says with a shrug. He's doing something super important with the pint glasses now. Soaking and stacking. Still no eye contact. His loss.

The sound of a cue ball clacking directs her attention to a pair of edgy-looking day laborers in heavy shoes and sweat-stained baseball caps. Melanie goes to investigate. They're playing a game of eight ball, stripes versus solids, on a warped table, the faded baize riddled with cigarette burns. A sign on the wall reads, NO FUCKING ON THE TABLE. They look like the kind of white, blue-collar guys who bet on sports and spend payday at the strip club. Their eyes blaze and their faces sag. They will have to do.

"Can I play?"

"Sure," says the less attractive but more outgoing of the two, who scoops up the balls and sweeps them into a plastic triangle. His name is Eric. His friend is Blaine. They have strong forearms and weak chins. They are tight with their feelings and loose with their cash. They are house painters, Eric tells her, but they're also framers, glazers, and roofers.

"Anything you need for twenty bucks an hour," Eric says.

"Eric?" Melanie interrupts. "Do I look like I care about any of that shit?"

Blaine laughs.

When the game is over, Eric fishes a joint out of his shirt pocket. "Care to step outside?"

As they head out the back door, Melanie rips a flyer off the wall for a punk rock band called The Furors. The show is for later that night at a country western joint called The Cattle Prod, farther down PCH. Perfect. She stuffs the flyer into her pocket as she surveys the parking lot. Chain link fence. Concrete wall. Ass-end of a dry cleaner on one side, a mini market on the other, all towered over by a parking structure to the south.

Blaine sparks the spliff and passes it to Melanie. She feels a tightening in her chest, a narrowing of her field of vision, as she takes in the smoke. How many hours has she spent in parking lots, backyards, and bathrooms, smoking with strangers who are only interested in getting in her pants? Hundreds? Thousands? Her whole life?

She passes the joint to Blaine, who holds it for way too long, telling one bullshit story after another. He is younger and a better physical specimen than Eric, but his big mouth is a turn-off. Blaine ends his rant with a story about a woman who's done him wrong. It's a story Melanie has heard many times before. Half of rehab is listening to stories of doomed romances from guys with commitment issues.

"Had a big score lined up," Blaine goes on. "Bigger than big. Could have set me up for a long-ass time."

"That's what he always says," Eric says to Melanie.

"That's cause it's true," Blaine insists.

"What happened?" Melanie asks.

"Bitch fucked it up. That's what happened, fucking bitch."

"Blaine?" Melanie asks. "Is that your name?"

Blaine nods.

"Shut your dick door."

Eric laughs so hard he nearly chokes on the joint. Blaine looks bewildered and sad. Melanie knows she needs to cool it. She doesn't know these dudes. They're ordinary guys. Predictable in their stupidity, but she has no idea what they are capable of. She needs to slow down. Take a deep breath. In with the positive, out with the paranoid.

The joint starts moving again. When it finally comes back to Melanie, she hits it and passes it on. She shoots a contrail of smoke into the air directly above her and waits for the cloud to settle. Blaine falls quiet and waves off the joint when it's his turn, and just like that it's back in Melanie's hands, this beautifully sculpted paper dart, this flaming arrow lighting up parts of her consciousness that've been kept dark for way too long.

Eric produces another joint, his face a question mark.

Melanie shoots that idea down. "How are we set in the go-fast department?"

Eric sizes her up, that "we" tumbling around his brain bucket. He looks to Blaine. Blaine stares at his shoes.

"Is there a problem?" Melanie asks.

"We, uh, have a connection," Eric says.

"Does he live nearby?" Melanie asks.

"She," Blaine says.

The connection is Blaine's ex-girlfriend, the bitch who supposedly did him dirty. They talk money and logistics and map out a plan in a haze of efficiency. It's not far, but they'll need to drive. Eric goes to get his truck.

"What's your girlfriend's name?" Melanie asks.

Blaine can barely get her name out. "Belle."

"She really did a number on you, huh?"

Blaine looks anywhere but at Melanie. Eric pulls up in his pickup truck, a big shiny penis extension of a rig, a rolling receptacle for fast food wrappers.

"Let's go, party people!"

Melanie hops into the back seat, Blaine rides shotgun, and off they go. Melanie wonders if she should ask if Eric's driver's license is any good but decides against it. If they get pulled over, they get pulled over. Melanie quizzes Blaine about his ex-girlfriend but he doesn't say much. Doesn't matter. They don't have far to go.

Eric catches Melanie's attention in the rear view as he drives. "You got cash?"

"Yeah," Melanie replies.

"Give it to me," he says, "and I'll get the stuff."

"No chance," Melanie says.

"I'm just saying it'll be easier if—"

"I'm not an idiot, Eric. Besides, I want to meet this woman who ruined your boyfriend."

Eric frowns and slows his rig as they approach a row of tiny studio apartments. "We're here."

"Fancy," Melanie says.

"Let's get this over with," Blaine says.

Blaine's ex is—surprise, surprise—pregnant, and a total fucking knockout, way too hot for a loser like Blaine. Amazing skin, beautiful hair, and perfectly sculpted eyebrows that frame gray eyes, crackling with intensity. Even with a bun in the oven and a ripped-up T-shirt, she's a stunner. What is it about guys like Blaine that make them incapable of seeing just how good they have it?

Does all that testosterone warp their minds? Damage the faculties that let them see things as they really are?

"Who's this?" Belle wants to know.

Blaine fumbles through an explanation that Melanie is the buyer he'd texted her about, but it's clear Belle thinks they're fucking.

"Okay, buyer."

"Do we need these losers?" Melanie asks, nodding her head at Eric and Blaine. Belle smiles and lets her in.

"Really?" Eric whines.

"Really," Belle says. That's all it takes to send the sad men away.

The apartment is miniscule, a narrow rectangle of a room with a kitchen on one end and a door that leads to the back patio on the other. There doesn't seem to be a bedroom or a bed for that matter. The ceiling is low and the walls are covered with tapestries redolent of incense. Or maybe the intoxicating aroma emanates from Belle herself. She sits cross-legged on the futon with a bottle of green juice in her lap and a box of tissues on the coffee table.

Belle pats a spot on the futon beside her. Melanie sits down nice and close. Belle does something dramatic with her hair, sweeping it forward and to the side so she can remove a chain from around her neck. She fits a little key inside the tiny padlock that secures the drawer in the coffee table where she keeps her stash. She is graceful and lovely. Melanie is enchanted by her every move, even though that bullshit lock wouldn't have slowed Melanie down for more than fifteen seconds.

Belle takes out a mirror, a razor blade, and a big bag of blow, and sets it all on the coffee table. While she chops up the rock and measures Melanie's cut, she talks about Blaine's many faults as a useful member of society. They do not discuss the baby. They do not discuss the future.

When Belle is finished, Melanie looks down and sees two long lines of coke Belle has shaped on the mirror.

"One for you and one for me," she says, "to be polite."

It makes Melanie a little sick to her stomach. Maybe she doesn't intend to keep the baby. It's none of her business. Melanie rolls up a twenty and pulls it tight. She bends over the mirror and zeroes in on the line. She vacuums it up with an ease she is delighted to discover hasn't deserted her. Just like riding a bike.

Belle asks Melanie how she feels but words can't approach the immensity flowering through every part of her. She feels grateful to be feeling this way again. It feels weird to use a word lifted from recovery to describe her high, but it fits. If it weren't for MIS, she wouldn't be doing blow with a beautiful pregnant coke dealer. Actually, Melanie isn't doing anything. Lindsay is the guilty party here.

"I should get going..."

"Ssshhh..." Belle drapes her hand on Melanie's wrist, tracing something there with her finger.

"I have something special for you."

Melanie looks up. A little scared. A little turned on. "Yeah?"

"Only for my best customers."

"Oh?"

"Would you like to try some Bliss?"

Fuck.

What Belle does with her body isn't Melanie's business, but the solicitation reminds her she's not here to destroy her life. Not yet. She's on a mission.

"No, thanks," she says and scooches away from Belle. It's only a few inches but it breaks the spell. Belle's eyes flash with anger, a burst of light around her pupils. Melanie has seen that look on every psycho chick she's ever met. Maybe Blaine was right about this one after all...

"Put the money on the table," Belle says. Her eyes don't look crazy anymore. Just sad. They've turned a light blue with a hint of purple, like a bruise. Melanie does as she's told.

"Have fun," Belle says as she hands the baggie to Melanie.

"I will."

"Don't come back."

"I won't."

Melanie leaves but looks back—she always looks back—and sees Belle reach for something on the coffee table, either the mirror or the tissues, she can't tell.

Standing on the stoop outside of Belle's studio with the baggie in her hand, a kid on a bicycle glares at her as he pedals past. He knows what she is, what she's about. Melanie slips the baggie in her pocket, huddles into her hoodie, and walks away. The line is a nice start, but she needs another one if she's going to kick things into high gear. Melanie makes her way to the beach where a trio of grommets mess around on their skateboards while listening to scuzzy punk rock. She plucks a tiny seashell out of the sand and angles toward a public bathroom. The walls inside the concrete bunker are dark, the floors wet, and sand clings to the corners. Melanie takes out her baggie and opens it. She absent-mindedly hums the song the punk rock kids were listening to while she uses the seashell to scoop out a bump of blow. She snorts it up with great gusto.

Oh, yeah. That's more like it.

She goes back for another bump just to be sure. She's so focused on what she's doing she doesn't notice the woman standing at the entrance to the bathroom. She doesn't say anything. She doesn't have to. Her mom vibes tell the story. She doesn't scold her or tell her to go away. She simply presses the button on the hand dryer, and Melanie scurries out of the bathroom, nearly running into a family thronged together outside. From their look of collective disgust, it's clear they all heard Melanie snorting like she was trying to suck a genie up her nose.

Melanie heads for the surf. She kicks off her shoes and plunges her feet into the cool, clean sand. Her mother used to love the beach. During one of the periods when she was actually trying to be a mom, they went to San Diego for a week and every day they went to the beach. They had towels and beach chairs and even an umbrella. The cooler was packed with ice, juice boxes, and egg salad sandwiches with the crusts cut off—Melanie's favorite. If she closes her eyes, she can see her mother lounging on the blanket with a zigzag pattern, drinking from a thermos through a straw. She's wearing a gauzy gown over her bathing suit, has her hair tied up with a scarf, dark sunglasses; the sunglasses were always dark.

"Can I help you?"

Melanie snaps out of it. She's wandered uncomfortably close to where a young mother has set up camp with her toddler daughter. They both stare at her with unnerving intensity.

"Sorry." Melanie turns around and heads to the pier. She's stunned by how dark it is already. What happened to the sunset? She feels disconnected, cut loose from every tether, and maybe this is her purpose in life: to wander the edge of the world for the rest of eternity. She could get down with that, but right now she's thirsty.

MELANIE PAUSES IN FRONT OF the refrigerated cooler inside the liquor store and considers her options. She's drunk beer, smoked pot, and snorted blow in her first few hours off the wagon. That's a pretty hard first act to top, but top it she will. She selects another tall boy of Hoppy Life.

"You want a bag?" the cashier asks.

"Don't bother," she says, cracking it open.

"You can't drink that in here."

"Wasn't planning on it," she says as she breezes through the door, but as soon as she's outside she takes a long desperate swallow and drinks most of it down in one go. Cocaine is an awful drug, but it makes drinking essential. She'd met people who did coke but didn't drink. She can't understand people like that. Doing coke without drinking is like fucking without climaxing. Sure, it can be done, but why?

She needs a ride. Cars jam the parking lot. She walks the line between two cars and tilts the can skyward, draining it. This brings on a feeling of intense déjà vu. An old white guy in the car to her left hangs his head out the window and tells her to get the hell out of the way. She grabs her crotch and tells him to suck it. He shakes his head and backs out of the space. The guy sitting on the passenger side of the next car over starts laughing.

"What's so funny?" Melanie asks.

"You, girl!" He's a good-looking Latino in his early twenties with thick arms and hair slicked back into a pompadour. Promising.

She tosses the empty can in his lap and tells him to get some more. He squints up at her for a moment, hops out of the car, and runs into the store. Melanie gets in the back. The driver is a kid who can't be more than sixteen.

"Where did you think you were headed tonight?" she asks.

The kid shrugs.

"You like to party? I only ride with people who party."

This time he doesn't respond. He doesn't need to. The poor kid is terrified.

The other guy buffaloes back to the car with a six-pack of Hoppy Life and flashes a squinty-eyed smile. She can see right away that they're brothers. His name is Oscar. Manny is the driver. The car, a beautifully restored Chevy Nova, belongs to their father, who is expecting them home in a few minutes. This is causing Manny some stress, Oscar none at all. Melanie assures them that what she has planned won't take long, which is a lie.

"Are you learning how to drive?" she asks Manny.

"I know how to drive," Manny says.

"Do you like to drive fast?"

"Yeah."

"Maybe you could show me," Melanie says, which makes Manny blush.

"Where are we going?" Oscar asks.

"The Cattle Prod."

Oscar frowns. "That's a cowboy bar."

"You know it?" Melanie asks Manny.

Manny nods. "It's on PCH."

Melanie slaps the back seat. "All right, Manny. Show me what you've got!" With her other hand, she curls her finger at Oscar and he climbs into the back seat. As the Nova lurches out of the parking lot with a muffled roar, Melanie takes out her baggie and they drink beer and key coke up their noses.

"What's your name?" Oscar asks.

"Oh, honey, let's not get into details."

"What's at the Cattle Prod?"

"Trouble."

"What kind of trouble?"

Melanie hands him the flyer.

"Oh, shit," he says with a complicated smile. "You weren't lying."

Oscar tells her The Furors are a punk rock band made up of Mexican-Americans who'd become victims of their own bad taste. After playing in relative obscurity at beach bars up and down the coast, they'd become a magnet for ex-cons in the white power movement who were attracted to the band's name. Even though The Furors wrote dumb, jokey songs peppered with Spanglish, they had an intense white power following, making life miserable for those who were offended by swastika tattoos and ethnic slurs and were averse to getting stomped on in parking lots.

"Are you sure that's where you want to go?" Oscar asks.

"Is it better to be brave and foolish, or shrewd and cowardly?"

"Brave," he answers.

"Good boy." Melanie scrapes up more blow from the bag.

While Oscar goes to town on the coke, Melanie finds Manny's eyes in the rearview mirror.

"Your friends aren't going to believe you when you tell them about this, are they?"

The poor kid shakes his head.

"They may not believe you," Melanie says, "but you'll never forget it."

"If you say so."

Melanie gets lost in Oscar's lips until Manny announces they've arrived.

"Do you have a knife," she asks Oscar.

He takes a blade out of his pocket and hands it to her. Melanie makes it disappear.

"Keep the engine running," she says to Manny, "but if you hear sirens, scram."

Manny nods.

Melanie turns her attention to Oscar. "Let's go start a riot."

THE CATTLE PROD IS PACKED with every kind of punk rocker. Every rowdy boy and reckless girl she's ever partied with is here. Not the actual people, per se, but the personas they project, the carefully constructed masks they wear because everybody goes undercover at the punk rock show. The sick-of-it-all sons and daughters of dildos and douchebags, each one uniquely unique: the big rockabilly guy in a tight shirt with fake pearl snaps and sleeves cuffed to show off his sailor tats even though he doesn't know how to swim; his wannabe chola girlfriend with intense eyebrows and hoop earrings so large they can almost be worn as necklaces; the wannabe chola girlfriend's girlfriend who was put on this earth to remind people she doesn't take shit from nobody; the girlfriend's broke-ass little speed freak cousin; the kid's grommet friends with fake IDs; the almost-famous, former professional skateboarder who makes a habit out of scoring coke off the most embarrassing people, like his drug dealer's gay boyfriend; the four skinheads the gay boyfriend has slept with; the three burly shirtless beardos who bodysurf off one another's slick bellies; the tattooed mother of two who loves to give head in the photo booth; the impossibly photogenic art school couple with multiple STDs; the crusty punk who is too old to be sleeping on the street and busking for change but it's the only lifestyle that suits his ambivalence toward personal hygiene; the hottie in the nurse's uniform; the zinester who knows she's wearing panties that say Wednesday even though it's Saturday; the balding dude who somehow manages to coerce every single hair on his head into impressive-looking liberty spikes; the sexy Latinas hot for '77-style English punker dunkers, every one of them in fictional romances with someone they shouldn't have fallen in love with in the first place; the woman wearing her daughter's cheerleading outfit (but not for long); the bruiser in a T-shirt that declares I PLAY MONGOLIAN BATTLE BALL on the front and PRAY FOR ME on the back; the woman writing a dissertation on masculine violence sucking face with a homeless gutter punk who may or may not be living in the garage of the house her ex-husband is still paying the mortgage on; the guy with the laugh that makes death tremble.

These are her people. She is them and they are her. Mad and sad and ready to raise hell for all eternity.

She sends Oscar to the bar for some top-shelf tequila. They take the shots like buccaneers, the liquor scorching a trail through her body. Doing shots is like leaping out of a burning building: relief mixed with terror because the closer you are to death the more alive you feel. Melanie has never been able to reconcile these feelings.

She tells Oscar to stay close and drags a fingernail across his muscular forearm, mostly for his benefit though she pretends it's for hers. He has a nice face, kissable lips, and an eagerness to please she likes. It's a shame she's about to ruin this boy.

She grabs his hand and plows through the crowd as The Furors take the stage. The crowd moves in two directions: the people in the back surge forward while those in front move off to the side, away from the menace the skinheads are making as they assert themselves at the foot of the stage as if defending their turf. We'll see about that, Melanie thinks as she pushes deeper into the pit.

The lead guitar and bass players adjust their microphones while the drummer fiddles with his kit. They turn knobs and stomp on pedals, testing notes that feed the tension felt by everyone who isn't in a white power movement. And what about the Nazis? What's going through their heads? Who fucking cares?

The vocalist announces they are down a Furor and the crowd screams and shouts. Melanie asks Oscar what's going on and he tells her the Furor's rhythm guitar player is MIA. Probably strung out somewhere. It happens.

The band begins to play: three chords, martial beats, falling-down-the-stairs progressions. Underneath the slashing guitars and fuzzed out melodies, the backline is disciplined and relentless. It's good music to get fucked up to. There is a kind of wildness to the performance, a message from the dark side. Plus, the singer is cute.

Melanie shoulders her way toward the stage between a pair of skinheads who aren't much taller than she is. Neo-Nazi action figures. One of them tries to elbow her in the face. She ducks the blow, clicks open Oscar's knife, and stabs him in the ass.

He bitch-screams, and it's on.

The second skinhead sees blood and wheels on her, but Oscar is there and he plants a fist in his face. Melanie ducks under the advance of the bald wall swimming into the pit, while those who are down go to town on the peckerwoods.

Melanie strides through the turmoil she's created. Screams of agony and ecstasy detonate all around her, punctuated by the sound of breaking glass. She puts the knife away. A skinhead girl comes at her and shows Melanie the brass knuckles she's wearing instead of just hauling off and hitting her, which Melanie appreciates as it gives her plenty of time to plant a foot in her face and knock her the fuck out.

She's just giving them what they want.

To fight and fuck and lose themselves in the music. You be the conqueror and I'll be the spoils. It bothers Melanie more than a little that in the midst of this animal savagery the thing she is most keenly aware of is the clarity of her own thinking. What is the point of creating all of this chaos if she can't enjoy it?

Melanie takes advantage of the confusion and plucks a bottle off the bar—good old Fiery Cat—and breaks through the back door and into the quiet night. The marine layer hangs in the air, turning the streetlamps into alien motherships, hovering above the parking lot. She knows without being told which van to go to, knows what she'll find before she even wrenches open the cargo doors to The Furors's dented shit can, and thrusts her head inside.

The smell almost makes her puke. Thick, stagnant, repulsive, like a thing unto itself that collaborates with her other senses to get its message across. The missing guitar player huddles in the shadows, draped in a Mexican blanket. He stirs slightly but only to turn his head away from the light. He wears filthy jeans and a sleeveless T-shirt. He wears makeup in a half-assed attempt to mask what is the gnarliest case of jaundice Melanie has ever seen. If anything, it makes him look worse. But cosmetics can't conceal the suppurating sores eating away at his flesh, transforming the crook of his elbow into a ragged hinge. Melanie thinks what amounts to a prayer: How could you let this happen?

The man abides her disgust. He lifts a corner of his lip, the sneer of a marionette, and cants his head ever so slightly at the needle and spoon that lay on a satin pillow, as if they are not in the back of some rolling gross polluter but in a pleasure house of unearthly delights. He doesn't say a word. He lets the narcotic communicate its intensity on its own behalf. Whatever Melanie had told herself she would or wouldn't do on this very fucked up day, she has not accounted for this.

He needs help, she thinks, but turns her back on the van with its awful smell and quietly slinks away.

Sirens. Shouts. Fuck yous.

The cops are coming.

The cops are here.

The Nova goes bouncing out of the parking lot, taillights disappearing in the fog that has descended on The Cattle Prod like a shroud. Good for you, kid. I knew you were smart. She doesn't think twice about Oscar. Melanie circles around to the front of the bar where the prowl cars are slanted in riot formation. The flashing lights do weird things in the fog. She thinks she sees a cop on a horse—a fucking horse. A bullhorn crackles to life. A voice tells Melanie to drop the bottle. She takes a long pull off the Fiery Cat as punks and skins pour out of the club behind her, scattering like roaches. Melanie takes aim and lobs the missile high into the air, where it sails up, up, up into the murk and disappears.

Melanie closes her eyes and waits for the world to shatter.

11
BLOOD DOESN'T LIE

Bill watches the officer who clubbed Melanie with a submission stick check her vital signs. He gets out of his sedan and walks over to the scene. The officer frisks her and comes up with a knife.

"I'll take that," Bill says.

The cop looks up at him. "And you are?"

Bill flashes his badge. "Detective William Carlos Williams Redondo."

The cop wonders if he's fucking with him. Bill's used to it, but gestures for the knife to speed this along. The officer sighs and hands it to him.

"Where you taking her?" Bill asks.

"Detox at Evergreen."

"No tab?"

"Probably sold it to score."

"What's she on?"

"About to check." The officer sticks her with a blood meter and reads the display. "Alcohol, cocaine, THC."

"Bliss?" Bill asks, afraid of the answer.

"We don't test for that."

Bill grunts.

Melanie stirs. "Abby," she says. "Where are you, baby?"

"You want to take over from here?" the officer asks.

"Nice try," Bill says as he walks away from the scene and disappears into the fog. "I'm not even here."

PART II
EVERGREEN

ONE WEEK LATER

12

REHAB FOR REAL

MELANIE IS SKEPTICAL.

She's skeptical of her group leader's cheerful optimism, the earnestness of the other addicts on her ward, the empathy the nurses ooze every time one of them asks if there's anything they can do. You can get out of my face with that fake bullshit, she thinks almost constantly during her first week at Evergreen, but then she grows skeptical of that, too.

She is skeptical of the florescent lights, the high-traffic carpet, the thrift store sofas. She's skeptical of the institutional coffee and sugary sheet cake doled out to celebrate milestones that are as insubstantial as the pink frosting she scrapes off the top but eats anyway. She's seen it so many times before, and she doesn't need to see it again. Besides, she isn't going to be here long.

She's skeptical of Lauren, who is too pretty to be so insecure. She's skeptical of Jeremy and his white-boy dreads and declarative tattoos. She's skeptical of Shanna's homelessness, of which she seems a little too proud. And she doesn't feel bad about any of it. The second you *stop* being skeptical around junkies, they've got you.

She's skeptical of the urge to underline passages in the material Shalanda passes out during group. She's skeptical of the compulsion to write her feelings down in the journal with Evergreen Medical

Center stamped on the cover. She's skeptical of the searching questions she poses to the constellation of glow-in-the-dark stickers a previous rehabee had affixed to the ceiling above her bed in the women's dormitory.

She's skeptical of the war stories people tell during group. She's skeptical of their highs. She's even more skeptical of their lows. She's skeptical of the words that tumble out of her own fool mouth when she *swore* she wasn't going to say anything. She's skeptical of the tears that spill down her cheeks after an intense share, the hugs that convulse her.

She's skeptical of her diminishing skepticism. What happened to the cynical chick that strolled in here mad-dogging anyone who tried to make eye contact with her?

She's skeptical of laughter. She's skeptical of sleep. She's skeptical of the pleasure she takes from pancakes drowning in syrup (and not just because she's skeptical of the syrup). She's skeptical of the hours that go by without thinking about Make It Stop.

She's skeptical of Trevor and all of his excuses. She's skeptical of Doyle and his bluster about the dangers of the assignment. She's skeptical of Bill's willingness to help.

But mostly she's skeptical about God.

After two nights in detox, Melanie was taken to a mandatory group session. Still exhausted from her rampage at the beach, she drilled holes in the floor with her eyes, arms crossed, giving off her best don't-fuck-with-me vibe when someone started talking about God. The guy spoke in a voice so tender she thought it had to be a put-on. This was precisely the kind of corndog shit she would have laughed at the last time she went to rehab for real. She looked up to see which one of these lame asses was getting heavy with the God trip, and there was this tall, skinny Native kid looking right through her sneering condemnation like she wasn't even there.

This was Morris. He wore big goofy glasses and a sawed-off leather jacket studded with so many buttons, patches, and spikes it looked like armor. He had long hair that he wore in a braid. When he talked during group, he got a dreamy, faraway look in his eyes that didn't seem to fix on anything.

Morris was always going on about God. Only he didn't say God. He said Creator. The first time she heard him say it something clicked in Melanie's brain or maybe someplace even deeper than that.

When Perry, the group discussion leader, pushed Morris to explain what he meant, Morris smiled and said, "The light behind the sun," and Melanie nearly keeled over. The word "God" came with too much baggage. And "higher power" was too accommodating to really mean anything. It was just so played out. But "the light behind the sun?" The bang at the beginning of time? The primal spark in the universe?

She could get down with that.

That night, when the lights clicked off in the dorm, the glow-in-the-dark stars on the ceiling lit up with unusual potency. She'd had stickers like these when she was a kid. She was fascinated with the sky, how dramatically it changed from day to night. After a rare sleepover at the house of a friend whose parents had set up a tent in the backyard, Melanie wanted to do the same thing when she got home: spend the night outside gazing up at the stars. Her mom was opposed to the idea but compromised by buying Melanie the stickers with her employee discount at the drug store where she sometimes worked. Melanie pestered her for weeks to put them up, and when her mom finally got around to doing it, she ignored the constellation map that came with the package and arranged the stars according to her own design. Melanie could still see her mother perched on a step ladder, wine glass in hand, mapping out the cosmos according to her own drunken whim. Melanie was too young to know the difference. But it worked. When the lights went off at night the stars ignited, pouring cosmic light into the room.

That's what Morris's words do for her: they let light into a very dark place.

She decides to keep an eye on him. See what he's all about. Even though she isn't going to be here long.

AFTER BREAKFAST, THEY SPLIT INTO groups. Girls with girls. Boys with boys. Shalanda leads the girls. Perry takes the boys. After these sessions, everyone eats lunch together, which is followed by some kind of activity. They all regroup for the main session, usually to resolve whatever drama has surfaced during the day, and then the evening is open for games, TV, whatever. There's usually a battle over the only television for the right to play vintage video games or watch a movie. The Internet is forbidden. Tabs aren't allowed. There are cameras in the rec room—one above the TV and another above the supply closet. They make Melanie nervous, so she sticks to the dorm as much as possible.

Most group meetings go something like this: the group leader starts the conversation with a topic like anger, forgiveness, jealously, or patience. The leader riffs on the topic, sharing his or her experience as an addict (Shalanda) or alcoholic (Perry), which is followed by a free-for-all of personal confessions. Most of these stories are about assigning blame, figuring out where the finger should be pointed.

Morris goes right to the issue, treating the topic as a leaping off point for a philosophical discussion. Morris is mostly optimistic, although he is big on oppression. He's always talking about humankind's need to dominate those who are less powerful, to control them through fear and intimidation so the oppressed become their own oppressors, prisoners of their own minds.

Tonight is different. A gangbanger from Long Beach named Josh calls Morris out. Josh fancies himself an intellectual because he'd read Eckhart Tolle in lock-up.

"That's a bunch of bullshit, man," Josh says. "First you fuck up, then you pay up. End of story."

"I see it differently," Morris says, looking right through Josh in that unnerving way of his. "Somewhere between 'fuck up' and 'pay up' you have to decide if you need to accept responsibility. Take an inventory of your own wrongdoings versus the systematic oppression designed to keep people like us down. People are always trying to put something on us that's not ours to take. It's about balancing the books."

"Damn," is all Josh has to say.

Watching these exchanges, Melanie tingles all over. What's up with this guy? How did this skinny little dude come by such wisdom?

Then she sees it. Nestled in the patches of his battle jacket is a pin with the logo for The Furors.

AFTER DINNER, MELANIE GOES TO the rec room, a large common area with a haunted institutional vibe. Patients sprawl on mismatched furniture clustered around the television. Bad things have happened here, but everyone carries on like they're chilling at home watching TV. She spies Morris sitting on the sofa and plops down beside him.

"What do *you* know about The Furors?" Melanie asks in a way that's intended to be confrontational.

"They're, uh, one of my favorite bands," Morris says.

"Me too. Saw them play in Hermosa last week."

"You were at the riot?" His excitement draws quizzical looks from Jeremy and Shanna, who are now officially, predictably, a couple. Rehab romance is for saps that haven't had their hearts stomped on enough. Melanie has heard Jeremy brag to Shanna about being a member of Make It Stop. It doesn't bother Melanie he's using MIS to get laid, but it annoys her that it seems to be working.

"You heard about that?" Melanie asks.

"It was all over the news. How was the show?"

Melanie shrugs. "They didn't play with a full lineup."

"I hear Scotty is using again."

"Yeah, he wasn't in good shape." Scotty must be the junkie she saw in the back of the van after the show. It's one of the last things she remembers about that night.

"They say he's a kannibal now."

"Kannibal?" Melanie asks.

"Someone who shoots up Kannabliss, though everyone calls it Bliss."

"Gross," Melanie says, disgusted by the revelation.

"Check it out." Morris nods at the television. Derek Hansen's face fills the TV screen. The camera pulls back to show him pushing an elderly Black man in a wheelchair while he delivers his spiel: *You'll never be left out in the cold with Health Net Secure!* What used to feel like propaganda registers as a taunt. You killed Gary, she thinks as she watches Hansen sell HNS to the masses. She wants to smash her fist into his face and wreck all that expensive dental work.

"What a bunch of bullshit," Melanie says.

"You know what I heard?" Melanie leans in so only she can hear. "The detention level is full of kannibals."

"Here at Evergreen?"

Morris nods. "They came through a couple weeks ago and took a bunch of people to detention. One of the counselors told me they're all kannibals now."

"No shit?"

Morris looks around the room to make sure no one's listening. Jeremy and Shanna are too wrapped up in each other to pay any attention to them. "We shouldn't be talking about this now."

"But we will later," Melanie says with a wink. She watches a smile spread across his face, and she knows she has him. "Smell you later," she says, springing up from the couch.

Melanie goes to the women's dorm and climbs into her bunk. Morris knows things that would be helpful to her arrangement with Bill, but she hopes he's exaggerating. After seeing what Bliss does to people, she isn't looking forward to dealing with it again. A dark thought occurs to her: What if Robert is a kannibal? What if Bliss is the reason he's here?

Melanie writes in her journal until a voice calls out from the doorway. "Yo, Lindsay."

Melanie freezes for a second, but it's just Josh. He shouldn't be here in the women's dorm. Melanie climbs out of her bunk and crosses the room in a flash.

"What do you want?"

"Take it easy," he says. "Morris asked me to give you something."

"What is it?"

Josh makes a performance out of handing over a sheet of notebook paper that's been folded in half. "It's a poem. You want me to read it for you?"

"No thanks, Josh. I got it."

"Okay, it's pretty good."

Melanie shuts the door and returns to her bunk. She opens the paper and reads by the light of the moon shining outside the window. It's a poem all right, a rhyming poem.

SONG FOR LINDSAY

I'll be your werewolf
If you'll be my moon
You make me an animal
Of four-legged doom
With these bloodthirsty claws
I'll rip the darkness apart
Because you are the goddess
That lights up my black metal heart
Owwooooooooo!

How sweet. Melanie drifts off to sleep with the poem in her hand. She dreams she is running in Griffith Park. She knows every curve of the trail by heart, but she isn't running for exercise or to avoid being seen. She's chasing someone. A large, well-built man. He is dark and hirsute and possibly naked, though it's hard to tell in the gloom. She doesn't know who he is or why she's after him, but she can't shake the feeling that if she doesn't catch him, something terrible will happen. Melanie kicks it up a notch. The cool, crisp air cycles through her lungs. As she gains on the man, his limbs lengthen, his torso thickens. He seems to be covered in fur. The man stumbles but keeps running on all fours. Melanie charges forward and tackles him. She rolls the brute over on its back and sees Applewhite's wild, smiling fangs.

THE ART INSTRUCTOR IS ONE of those eternally youthful-looking women whose age is impossible to guess. Perry and Shalanda stand between her and those assembled in the rec room, like zookeepers at the zoo. The rec room has been rearranged to accommodate an art therapy session. Several folding tables have been set up in the common area and are stacked with art supplies.

"All right, everybody," Perry shouts. "Listen up!"

Shalanda takes over from there. "We've got a special guest who has taken time out of her busy schedule to be here today. So, let's show Mrs. Manriquez the same respect you'd show the rest of the staff. Am I making myself clear?"

The patients murmur their assent as Mrs. Manriquez steps forward.

"Hi, guys! Call me Chelo. Today we're going to paint portraits. Everyone pair up with a partner."

Excitement ripples through the ward. Melanie points her finger at Morris and pulls the trigger. He takes the bullet and slumps into Josh whose, "Get off me, dude!" Melanie can hear over the ruckus.

Melanie has never seen the rec room—or any rec room— like this. These kids are *excited*. It isn't just Chelo's looks. They're pumped to be doing something other than talk at each other all day.

"This is more than a visual exercise," Chelo continues. "You will interview your partner and incorporate the things you learn about them into your portrait. Remember, a portrait doesn't have to be figurative."

"What does that mean?" Jeremy asks.

"When we think of a portrait, what usually comes to mind?"

"A person?" asks Lauren.

"A face?" offers Josh.

"That's right, those are good answers, but portraits can be many things. My husband," a groan circulates around the room as the boys react to the news, "loves to read. My portrait of him might be an image of him with his nose in a book, or it might be the book itself, or even a scene from the book. It can be symbolic, surreal, or abstract. Let the interview be your guide."

Perry looks at his watch. "You've got ten minutes for your interviews, homeboys and girls. Five minutes each."

Chaos descends on the rec room. Melanie and Morris head toward the back of the room. Morris is about to sit down when Melanie pushes him toward the closet where the art supplies are kept. Some joker has hung a sign below the camera that reads, THIS IS NOT A CAMERA. Melanie pulls Morris inside and shuts the door.

"I don't think we're supposed to be in here," Morris says.

"I *know* we're not supposed to be in here," Melanie replies.

"As long as that's out of the way..."

"I like your poem."

Morris blushes. "Thanks. Just some lyrics I wrote."

"You're a songwriter?"

"Yeah, I'm in a black metal band. Used to be anyway."

Morris tells her about his band, Rez Erection. She's having trouble imagining this nice, skinny kid in eyeliner and corpse paint.

"Yesterday you were telling me about Bliss," Melanie says, changing the subject. "They treat Bliss patients here?"

"Something like that."

Melanie senses Morris is being coy and she doesn't have time for that. "What happens down in detention?"

"Detention is a one-way trip," Morris answers. "When you get sent down, you don't come back."

"What's the Bliss connection?"

"You know when people can't pay their bills—"

"I know what conditional release is."

"Right. Well, here you can work off your debt by volunteering as a Bliss test subject."

"They give it to the patients?" Melanie can't believe what she's hearing. A loud knock on the door interrupts their conversation. Josh pops his head in with a panicked look on his face.

"Yo, they're looking for you."

"Just a minute," Melanie says.

"This is serious," Josh says, which alarms Morris.

"We better go."

Melanie has more questions, but when they emerge from the art supply closet, the vibe in the room has changed. There's an argument unfolding up front by the door. Chelo is yelling at a corp in charge of a security detachment.

"Excuse me," Chelo yells, "this is an art therapy session! You can't be in here!"

The corp shoves Chelo aside and points directly at Melanie. "That's her!"

All eyes swivel toward Melanie. She's been waiting for this moment since she arrived, but now that it's here she wishes she had a little more time.

"Run," Morris whispers and then he's off, but instead of running away from the security personnel, he goes right at them, whipping off his studded belt and swinging it over his head with his skinny arms.

"No!" Melanie shouts, but it's too late.

A corp clubs Morris in the head with a submission stick and he goes down. The rest of the room converges on the pile. Jeremy, Josh, Lauren, and Shanna all go on the attack. Morris disappears under the pile of bodies. Melanie tries to pull the corps off of him but it's impossible, like trying to roll a rock back up the hill after an avalanche. Shalanda backs into a corner like she's having a panic attack. More corps pour into the room, knocking Perry to the floor. Melanie never sees the blow that gets her. Just a flash of white and everything goes quiet as she crashes into the table where Chelo had set up her art supplies. There's red paint everywhere. Across the floor. On her sweatshirt. All over her hands. Someone wrenches her arms behind her back, and she realizes it would be better for Morris and Josh and Jeremy and Shanna if she gave up and let the darkness drag her down.

13

WELCOME HOME

THE MIS SPRINTER VAN SITS outside of Spicy Noodle House on Ventura Boulevard just west of Coldwater Canyon. Trevor sits in the back of the van, which is a lot messier than it was a week ago, slurping noodles out of a take-out container while watching Viviana work out through a feed on his laptab. He'd hacked into the cameras installed at her apartment complex, including the dingy little gym on the bottom floor where Viviana goes to exercise at least twice a day now that MIS has gone dark.

Even though Trevor is miles away from her apartment, he can feel her intensity through the video screen. She has a presence like no one he's ever met, and when they're apart, her absence registers as an ache. When they can't be together, he watches her.

Trevor has never gone this far, this fast with a partner before. It's all happened so quickly yet feels perfectly natural. Is this normal? Trevor doesn't know. He has no idea what normal is anymore. He suspects most people don't run surveillance on their significant other. He is in uncharted territory.

Viviana stops working out and stares at her reflection in the mirror as if waiting for something to be revealed. She seems tired, like her heart isn't in it, which is unusual. She is adept at focusing her attention and, like many people with exceptional gifts, she doesn't see herself as special so much as others as undisciplined. He wishes she would go upstairs and get some rest.

Trevor glances at his watch and decides to check on Melanie's patient status at Evergreen. He bubbles through his tab and explores the HNS server. He's written a short code that lets him browse its network. He selects Evergreen Medical Center and is about to access the patient directory when a call comes through his tab. He doesn't bother checking the number or even saying hello. It can only be one person.

"Let's go for a ride," Doyle says.

Trevor sits up, alarmed. "Where are you?"

"Right behind you."

Trevor pokes his head out of the van and spies an ancient, primer-splotched muscle car idling behind him. Trevor sighs and ends the call. He walks to Doyle's car and gets in. Doyle prefers older vehicles that haven't been equipped with smart car tech. He looks like he's been up for a few days.

"How did you find me?"

"It's Wednesday."

"And?" Trevor asks, growing impatient with this game Doyle thinks he's playing. "Wednesday is Spicy Noodle Day."

No argument there. Trevor loves Spicy Noodle Day. "You've been following me?"

"I came to tell you I canceled Lindsay's insurance."

"That means Melanie will be on her way to detention soon."

"If she's not there already."

"I wish we had better intel on Gary's brother."

"About that," Doyle says. "There's something I haven't told you."

Trevor braces for bad news. Doyle tells him how he knew Robert in the Marine Corps. They didn't serve together, but they crossed paths a couple times. A few years ago, Doyle ran into him at a VA drug rehab. Robert had acquired a taste for opiates overseas and was trying to get clean, but he was worried about his brother.

"He told me he could use some help," and you know how that story ends.

"Did Robert know Gary worked for MIS?"

"If you're asking me if it's possible Gary talked to Robert about us and Robert told HNS? I think it's more than possible. I think it's probable."

"Would he really do that?" Trevor asks.

"Of course, he would."

"Sell out his own brother?"

"Robert wouldn't see it that way," Doyle says. "If anything, he'd blame me."

He'd been angry at Melanie for stealing his truck on the way to the beach. Okay, it wasn't his truck—it was stolen—and he got it back, but he'd wasted an afternoon in the liquor store parking lot reading an actual newspaper about the Fox News bombers, who'd been apprehended and had been charged with a hate crime against a corporation, and its possible connection to the bombing at the Sherman Oaks Galleria. But how could he stay mad at Melanie when he'd sent her into a veritable death trap?

"We have to tell her."

Doyle shakes his head. "It's too late for that. It's not like we can go down to Evergreen and say, 'Sorry, we'd like our people back.' It doesn't work like that."

"You should have told her."

"I warned her the target could be hostile."

"Then I'm sure everything will be fine." Trevor doesn't even try to keep the sarcasm out of his voice.

"We have to trust her, Trev. Let her do her job."

"And if she doesn't?"

"We cut our losses and run. There's no Plan B, kid."

Trevor opens his mouth to speak but is at a loss for words. It isn't supposed to be like this, he thinks. MIS is supposed to be making a difference. If anything, it's getting worse. Trevor gets out of Doyle's car and slams the door in frustration. He walks back to the van, but Doyle doesn't let him off that easy. He pulls up alongside Trevor, gunning the engine until he looks his way.

"Give my best to Viviana!" he shouts and goes roaring down the boulevard.

DOYLE LOVES HIS NEW OLD car, but the air conditioning doesn't work, and now he's hot and thirsty and has a powerful headache. He pulls over in front of a terrible Irish bar called Flanagan's. He squints at the sign. I'll just have a glass of water, he thinks, and laughs and laughs and laughs.

Flanagan's is the worst Irish bar in the San Fernando Valley, maybe even in all of Southern California, but if you need a leg-breaker, a coke dealer, or an example of what late-stage liver failure looks like, Flanagan's is the place for you. Its only virtues are that it's dark and cool. It's a murky, manky place that smells of old beer and, on good days, disinfectant. Flanagan's serves beer by the can, wine by the box, and off-brand spirits. The only alcoholic beverage from Ireland on the premises is a terrible blended whiskey called Chadwick's Unadulterated, a whiskey so awful the regulars refuse to drink it even when it's on the house.

Flanagan's is an old-man bar in the morning, a place for dodgy deals in the afternoon, and a free-for-all at night. It's a haven for a certain kind of Irishman who lacks the proper papers to travel back and forth between the Auld Sod and the USA. Flanagan's doesn't go for the kitschy decor of Irish bars that try to replicate the look and feel of an authentic pub that exists mostly in the imaginations of homesick Paddies. What makes Flanagan's distinct from every other joint in the Valley is a massive movie poster of the John Wayne classic *The Quiet Man* that hangs behind the bar, a not-so-subtle reminder to the patrons to keep their traps shut about the things they see and hear.

Doyle is tired of the crusade, which is how he thinks of MIS these days: a well-intentioned but hopeless endeavor to fix a situation he's powerless to unfuck. A little over five years ago, his close friend, Ron, a retired Senior Chief Petty Officer Boatswain's Mate in the Navy, relapsed at a family barbecue and checked himself into rehab to jump-start his recovery. This development stunned Doyle because Ron had been instrumental in his own recovery nearly two decades earlier.

When Doyle was a young hell-raiser, he was sent to mandatory recovery meetings after getting arrested for crashing his pickup truck into a bollard on the pier. Whether it was because Ron was the first adult who didn't bark orders at him or treat him like an idiot, his message got through. Doyle gave up the bottle for good. The men stayed in touch and remained close. When Ron asked Doyle to come see him in rehab, Doyle visited him every day. After two weeks, Doyle went to the facility to take Ron home, but his friend was distraught.

"What's the matter, boats?" Doyle asked.

"They say I can't go," Ron answered.

"Was your rehab court-ordered?"

"Negative," Ron insisted.

"Then you can leave anytime you want," Doyle said.

"That's not what this says." Ron handed Doyle a conditional release form he'd signed when he was admitted. Doyle quickly scanned it, the phrase "indefinite forfeiture of liberty" jumping out at him. These were words anyone who'd run afoul of the Uniform Code of Military Justice knew intimately. It meant, "Your ass is ours until further notice."

Doyle put the form in his pocket and said, "Let's go."

He led Ron out of the visiting area under the pretense they were going to the gift shop and hightailed it out of the hospital.

Doyle didn't think anything of it until the next time he went to the meeting he occasionally attended with Ron, where an Air

Force officer who'd heard Ron's story enlisted Doyle's help in getting his daughter out of rehab. Doyle went to the facility and liberated her by hopping the fence in the "secure" smoking area. These were decidedly low-key operations, but they gave Doyle a thrill he hadn't felt since he'd left the Marines. He was driven by the conviction that going to rehab wasn't equivalent to enlisting in the armed forces—no one should have their freedom taken away for trying to get well.

Then his phone started ringing. Word got out that if you needed to get a friend or relative out of rehab, Doyle was the man to call. As time went on, his methods became more sophisticated, though "sophisticated" probably wasn't the right word for blowing up the lobby of a rehab facility disguised as a high-end wellness center in Palm Springs. That made the papers. Doyle went underground and Make It Stop was born.

In the beginning, many of his agents were people with military backgrounds, but they burned out quickly. The best operatives, Doyle learned, were those who weren't much different from the people they were trying to help. The media cast them as vigilantes, no better than the assassins who wiped out the senior leadership of the NRA two years ago or the hackers who targeted family members of the Supreme Court. Doyle swore he would never stop fighting conditional release, but HNS is more powerful than ever, MIS is on its last legs, and he is very, very tired.

"You don't have to do this," he says as he approaches the entrance to the bar. The faintest strain of music beckons him inside. Doyle opens the door and makes his way to the bar, giving his eyes time to adjust to the gloom. About half the seats at the bar are occupied. He settles on a stool. An Irish bartender with at least a decade on Doyle squares up on the other side.

"Welcome home."

"I've...been away," Doyle says.

"It's all right now," the bartender says. "What'll it be? Whiskey, is it?"

"Yes."

"Good man."

"That's debatable."

14

DAMAGED GOODS

Melanie can hear voices in the dark. The words sound like muffled collisions, boulders knocking together under the sea. She's in a place slightly less dark than the inside of her skull. She needs to regroup, regain some semblance of operational integrity, get her shit together.

Her name is Lindsay Moran.

She's somewhere inside Evergreen Medical Center.

Her assignment is to locate and liberate Scary Gary's brother, Robert Gray. Her secondary mission is to collect intel about the drug Bliss. After a week in rehab, she was taken off the ward and sent to detention. Is that where she is now? Her head throbs and her throat burns. She licks her lips and tastes blood.

The room floods with light. Melanie narrows her eyes against the glare as a man enters and shuts the door behind him.

"You are a shambles all right," the man says with an English accent. "How are you feeling?"

Melanie doesn't answer and he cuffs her across the cheek with the back of his hand. She screws her eyes shut to absorb the pain, which is astonishing, but the blow has a clarifying effect for which she is almost grateful. Time to stop fucking around.

"Answer the question," the man repeats.

"Fine," she says, feeling anything but.

"Open your eyes."

Melanie obeys—not out of a sense of duty but because the voice is so familiar—and sees Derek Hansen, CEO of Health Net Secure, standing before her.

"Do you know who I am?" Hansen asks.

Melanie shakes her head, plays dumb. The real question is whether he knows who she is.

"What's your name, luv?"

"Lindsay."

"Do you know where you are?"

"Evergreen," Melanie says, her confidence returning.

"Which is?"

"Drug and alcohol rehab."

"Very good," Hansen says while he snaps on a pair of black latex gloves and holds a syringe up to the light. "When was the last time you felt true bliss?"

"No..." She wants to scream, but it comes out like a whisper.

"That long? Well, congratulations, Lindsay. You've been volunteered for an exciting new drug trial here at Evergreen."

Melanie can't see what he's doing, but she can feel his hand running up and down her arm. She tries to move but can't. She's been shackled to some kind of table.

"Please," she says.

"You have no idea how lucky you are," Hansen says as he swabs her arm with a level of care and attention that takes her by surprise. "There's nothing like your first taste of Bliss."

Melanie doesn't feel lucky. She tenses up, but there's nothing she can do. She feels the needle go in. Her arm tingles and goes numb. The drug mingles with her blood, an immensity welling up inside her, a sweet purling wave that climbs up her body, a terrifying rush of pleasure that washes over her in dewy glissades.

"Now breathe," Hansen says.

Melanie and Hansen gasp as one. Good lord, what was that? The high deserts her almost immediately, a ghost of pleasure. She wants to feel it again. Not soon, not now, but right this instant. She bites her lip just to stop from crying out for more.

"Isn't that nice?" Hansen asks, his face strangely flush.

"Yes," Melanie says.

"Good girl."

His hands scurry across her body, unbuckling a complicated series of straps. She is too out of it to lift her arms or rub her wrists, but as each restraint falls away, she feels lighter, like she might levitate off the table.

Hansen brushes the hair out of her eyes and looks down at her with tenderness. "I have given you a gift. What happens next is up to you."

I hate you, Melanie thinks as he caresses her cheek, but instead of anger, desire solidifies inside her. She'd wanted freedom and now that she has it, she finds it isn't what she wants at all. She wants another shot, but Hansen leaves the room as abruptly as he entered it, and when the door slams shut everything goes dark.

"Hello?" Melanie calls out, but no one answers. She struggles to keep her eyes open. She's ready to give in when she hears a scuffling sound. She sits up in alarm.

"Who's there?"

Melanie… The voice is faint, like a whisper.

Melanie swings her legs around so her bare feet touch the carpeted floor. Carpet? In a hospital? Where the hell is she?

Soft light penetrates the gloom. Small and flickering. It gets brighter and brighter as it moves toward her.

"What do you want?" Melanie shouts.

A figure holding a candle approaches. As the light gets brighter, Melanie can make out more of the room and she realizes she's not in the hospital anymore. She's in a child's bedroom with stuffed animals on the bed and glow-in-the-dark stickers on the ceiling. This is her room. Her bed. Her stars.

So nice to see you here again, the figure says in a flat monotone without a touch of warmth. She's pale and white and wears a dingy nightgown.

"Who are you?" Melanie demands.

It's okay, darling. You're with me now...

There's something off about this place. The stuffed animals are filthy and the walls are streaked with mold.

As the woman moves closer to the bed, Melanie can see it's her mother, Janet, and she's in bad shape. There are dark circles under her eyes. Her head is ringed with electrodes and she drags a train of wires behind her.

"Mom?" Melanie cries out.

Her mother laughs, but there's no warmth in it. Janet's laugh has always been harsh. Cruel. Melanie tries to stand, but arms sheathed in black rubber reach out of the darkness and hold her down.

"Mommy!"

The arms are attached to a pair of hulking figures who hold her up as the bed, and then the entire room, drops away into darkness and all that's left is the sound of that scornful laugh.

THE ELEVATOR JUDDERS AND MELANIE steadies herself by clutching the sleeve of the corp standing next to her. There are two of them, one on each side. They are big and solid and decked out in some serious-looking gear. Melanie tries to peer through the darkened visor of the corp holding her up, but it's like looking into a storm cloud. Where did they come from? How did she get here?

The elevator car has padded walls and a corrugated steel floor that don't click with her inventory of memories. She can't tell if the elevator is going up or down or even moving at all, though of course it is. What else would it be doing?

She's missing time. She's blacked out in some awkward places before—on the bus, in the bathroom, under a man whose lovemaking skills existed in his imagination but not where it mattered—but she'd never passed out while *standing up*. Another new low.

The elevator dings.

"You ready?" one of the corps asks.

"Ready for what?" she tries to say but all that comes out is, "Mmmrrrwwwuuuhhh?"

"She's blissed out," the other corp says.

"Totally."

They laugh and her head pulses to the rhythm of her heartbeat as it thunders through her, louder than she's ever heard it before, so loud she swears the corps can hear it, too. How does one turn down the volume of a heartbeat?

The doors clang open and the car fills with a terrible odor that makes her stomach tumble. The stench is ancient and foul like a pool of sewer muck stirred up and cooked in a pot. It pushes into her nostrils and makes her eyes water. She suppresses the urge to gag.

Motors click on inside the corps' riot suits. Some kind of ventilation mechanism. One of them flicks a switch on the elevator's control panel and light floods the area in front of the open door, revealing a crush of half-naked bodies. *That's* what's making the smell? And this is a hospital?

The corp waves a submission stick that crackles with blue sparks. The crowd rolls back and clears out of the way. He motions for Melanie to move out of the car. Before she can say, "No thanks, I'm good," the second corp plants his foot in her backside and kicks her out of the elevator.

Melanie stumbles forward and falls onto her hands and knees, which are filthy and red. What happened to her pants? The rest of the data clicks into place: she isn't wearing any clothes. She's naked.

She springs to her feet and immediately regrets it. The floor wobbles underneath her and she steadies herself with her hands.

She feels dizzy and sick. She turns back toward the elevator and is smacked in the face with a bundle of clothing: blue coveralls and a gray towel. The corp offers a mock salute as the doors begin to close.

The crowd moves in on the elevator, rushing past her like she isn't even there. They're all kannibals, Melanie realizes, every single one of them.

"Wait!" they cry out. "Hold the door!"

The corps back into the elevator, ignoring their pleas. An alarm sounds as the doors close. One of the junkies, a broken-looking Asian man, makes a break for the elevator. No shirt, no shoes, and circles under his eyes that look like they're eating into his face. There's something wrong with his hands, which he holds in front of him like a praying mantis. His fingers are gnarled, monstrous-looking. He smells like he's already started to rot, like he's dead and doesn't know it.

The man lunges toward the elevator car. One of the corps clubs the man's outstretched arm with his submission stick. The blow shatters the bones with a sickening snap and delivers a ferocious shock that knocks him to the ground.

Melanie kneels at his side, tries to look into eyes screwed shut against the pain. "Are you all right?" she asks. A stupid question, but the words come out of her mouth the way they're supposed to.

The man picks himself up off the floor and staggers into the dark, clutching his shattered arm to his chest like a broken toy.

Melanie shakes out the coveralls and steps into them, nearly falling over in the process. She zips up and her surroundings close in: dirty linoleum floor, unfinished ceiling, dingy cinder block walls. The place has an institutional feel, like a prison laundry or school cafeteria. There's sadness in its bones. Every sofa, bench, or chair has a body on it. It's massively overcrowded. People everywhere. Way too many people.

A voice cuts through the buzz: "Hey, you!"

Melanie can't see where the voice is coming from, though it feels like she's being watched.

A white girl comes at her with a smile painted on her face. She's the same height as Melanie but thinner. She has the face of a toy doll. The kind of face Melanie likes to break.

"I need to talk to you" the doll-faced woman says as she approaches.

Melanie tenses up, gets her hands ready.

"Easy, now. I'm not running up on you. Just trying to help a girl out."

"Then find one and help her," Melanie says.

"I get it," the woman continues, keeping her distance. "First day is a bitch. But you should know, the second I leave someone else is going to swoop in on you."

"Welcome to try," Melanie says, trying to sound harder than she feels.

"Let me help you." The woman is next to her now, pulling a packet of wet wipes from her pocket. "No obligation."

Melanie laughs. There's *always* an obligation. Obligation is the lifeblood of rehab; but would it be so bad to be obligated to this woman?

She wants something from Melanie and it feels good to be wanted. A spark flares up inside her as she starts cleaning Melanie's hands with the wipe.

"How do you feel?" the woman asks.

Horny, Melanie nearly blurts. She can feel her temperature rise as the woman runs the cool, clean cloth over her skin. Melanie leans into the doll-faced woman. Her body feels unbelievably soft. Each point of contact between them its own pleasure center. Melanie is more than okay with this. She's copasetic with anything this woman wants to do to her.

"My, you're a shambles," she says with a giggle.

Shambles. The word rumbles through her like the vibrations of a bass cabinet. That's what Hansen had said to her before he drugged her. It's like a key has turned some secret chamber and a deluge of emotions surges through her, feelings not available to Lindsay or Sonja or Rachel but one hundred percent clear to Melanie. They remind her who she is and what she's doing here.

"What's your name?" Melanie asks.

The doll-faced woman looks up at her with big round eyes. "Bethany. What's yours?"

"Lindsay. Ever heard of me?"

"Should I have?" Bethany asks, a look of concern creeping into her pretty face, too late.

Melanie head butts Bethany in the nose. Bethany falls back, blood gushing out of her busted face. Didn't see *that* coming. Bethany touches her nose and studies the blood. Never assess the damage before you neutralize the threat, sweetie. Scary Gary taught her that. God, she misses that asshole.

"We can keep this up," Melanie says, "or you can back the fuck off."

"Fuck you, bitch!"

Bethany flicks open a switchblade. A pink switchblade. How cute.

Melanie sweeps Bethany's legs and knocks her off her feet. Bethany slashes at Melanie with the knife she doesn't know how to use. Melanie whirls out of harm's way and clocks her with a kick. It's a solid strike—Bethany is out before she hits the floor—but Melanie can't maintain her balance and falls on top of her.

A hand reaches down, not to steady her, but to snatch the switchblade away. "Hey!" she starts to say, but the words never make it out of her mouth. The blade disappears, the room spins. Melanie rolls over onto her back and watches the ceiling get smaller and smaller as it drifts farther and farther away: a white rectangle, a fuzzy lozenge, a tiny speck of light in an ocean of darkness.

15

SHAMBLES

Up is down, wrong is right, and Doyle is playing golf with Hansen.

When Trevor discovered that his boss had agreed to meet with Hansen, he assumed it had to be some kind of setup, that either he or Hansen would use the opportunity to take the other out. Trevor knew Doyle grudgingly respected Hansen's commitment to usurping the LAPD's monopoly on violence by creating a force of his own. Doyle believed that Hansen was a worthy adversary—some kind of Marine Corps warriors code bullshit. At least that's what Trevor thought until he discovered encrypted messages on Doyle's tab that were sent from HNS hospitals. That kicked Trevor's paranoia up a few notches. The last thing he expected was for the two men to meet at Rampart Park Putt-Putt on Sepulveda Boulevard in Sherman Oaks like a couple of sixteen-year-olds on a date. Has Doyle betrayed them?

Trevor is about to find out. He sits hunched over his tab in the back of the sprinter van in the putt-putt parking lot. He's wearing a pair of headphones and straining to listen to Doyle. He'd modified Doyle's tab so it relays all its data back to Trevor. As long as Doyle has his tab on him, Trevor can pinpoint his location and hear everything he says. If this meeting confirms Trevor's suspicion that

Hansen and Doyle are in cahoots, he'll drive to Viviana's apartment, pick her up, and get the fuck out of LA.

"Up for a round?" Doyle says.

"Are you joking?" Hansen replies. His accent is unmistakable.

"You've never been here before?"

"Most assuredly not."

"Try it. You'll like it."

"I'll walk with you," Hansen grumbles, "but I'm not playing."

"Suit yourself."

What is Doyle trying to pull? The old man always has at least one trick up his sleeve—he knew about his liaison with Viviana after all—but is there a conspiracy afoot?

DOYLE STUDIES HIS SHOT. THE course features a long ramp with an obstacle in the middle of the throughway. If he hits the Egyptian pyramid blocking the hole, it will deflect the ball into one of the dead ends that slope away from the center. Hit the ball too softly, and it rolls back. The key is to hit the ball hard, but not *too* hard. Focus. Don't let this bastard see you sweat.

Doyle squares up and gives it a good smack that sends the ball barreling up the ramp. A solid stroke. He's perfectly set up for a birdie.

"Well?" Hansen asks.

"I need more time," Doyle replies.

"We've been through this already," Hansen says. "I've been very flexible with you, but I'm afraid I can't wait any longer."

"You mean won't," Doyle says as he lines up his next shot.

"What kind of fool do you take me for, Doyle?"

"The kind that stands in the sun without a hat."

It's an exceptionally warm day. Dry, no wind. Earthquake weather. One of those long, shadowless afternoons when the sunlight seems to come from everywhere.

"Listen to me—"

Doyle takes aim and sinks his ball in the cup. "Birdie."

"I beg your pardon?"

"I just made a birdie. If you aren't going to play, at least you can keep score."

Hansen's face, already splotchy from the heat, contorts into a grimace. So far, Doyle's bluff appears to be working. Blowing up HQ had the unintended effect of rattling Hansen. Showing up at the scene of the explosion with a squad of security officers must have generated all kinds of heat for HNS—especially considering the media attention after the Fox News bombing. He'd been trying to cut a deal with Doyle for months, but now he's desperate. If Hansen knew that MIS is running on fumes and has just one operative in the field, he might waste Doyle right now. The press would love that: VIGILANTE SLAIN ON PUTT-PUTT GOLF COURSE.

"Here's what I'm going to do," Hansen says. "I'm going to expand my already generous offer in the interest of expediting it."

Doyle studies the course. "I'm listening."

"I'll add a second phase to our agreement. In Phase I, you concede all hospitals in our network to HNS, and I will permit you to do what you do in detox and rehab facilities outside of it. In Phase II, your jurisdiction expands to include all rehab facilities in and out of our network."

This gets Doyle's attention.

"Throughout California?"

"Anywhere you care to set up shop."

"Why would you do that?"

"Come on, Doyle. You can see where this is going."

Doyle slaps the ball down the fairway. Not bad, but the next obstacle is an ancient windmill. At one point, a motor turned the mill and the fans on the windmill spun. Players had to shoot the ball under the platform at the base of the windmill and between the arms of the spinning fans. Now, the platform sags and the whole thing looks like it will collapse under the slightest pressure. It would only take a pinch of ANFO to turn the structure into a pile of dust.

"Enlighten me."

"It's only a matter of time before conditional release expands to other aspects of patient care," Hansen says. "When that happens, I will allow your organization to conduct operations wherever you choose without interference from my security apparatus, provided you stick to your area of expertise."

"You mean rehab."

"Precisely. We can coordinate operations to minimize conflict and casualties. And, of course, you would enjoy a monopoly for your services so you can charge higher fees as conditional release gets more entrenched in the American health care system."

Doyle strikes the ball, sending it through the windmill and up a steep incline to the putting surface.

"Nice shot," Hansen says.

"Thanks. Sure you don't want to give it a try?"

"Some other time."

"You were saying?"

"Right," Hansen continues. "You will be able to expand your organization, set up shop in a permanent location, and do the good work you do for much more money and far less risk. While my grand experiment in social services and health care continues without any undue interference. It will be a golden age for both of us."

"You seem pretty confident about your network's expansion."

"Health care is facing a crisis the likes of which it's never seen before."

"A crisis you created."

"A crisis HNS is uniquely suited to deal with. You can either capitalize on it or be counted among the casualties."

"I appreciate the offer," Doyle says, "but like I said, I'm going to need more time."

"Time for what?" Hansen snaps.

"To bring my agents in from the field for one. I can't have my people at risk."

"What if I told you it's too late for those people?"

"Then you and I have nothing to talk about."

Hansen sniffs. "Are you drunk? How long before I see you in one of my facilities, Doyle?"

Doyle leans on his putter like it's a cane and gives Hansen his full attention. The Englishman's got a good sunburn going and is sweating profusely.

"Why are you doing this?"

Doyle expected Hansen to blow a gasket, to rant and rave about his superior firepower, but his response is much more nuanced. "We're disruptors. We both disrupt the established order of things. People like us are rare, so why not work together?"

"Because you're a psychopath?"

Hansen closes his eye for moment. He really is trying to keep his cool. "I understand you, Doyle. Better than you understand yourself. They call you a vigilante, a terrorist, but you don't want to destroy the system. You want to fix it, make it better. We're the same, Doyle. Two side of the same coin. Someday you'll regret you didn't see it sooner."

"Maybe, but not today."

"I'm genuinely sorry it has to be like this," Hansen says, "but you just signed your death warrant."

Hansen walks off the course and Doyle watches him go. He hauls a pint of Fiery Cat out of his pocket, unscrews the cap, and takes a pull.

Good Lord. How does Melanie drink this stuff?

TREVOR IS READY TO PUT LA in his rearview mirror. There are some things he will miss. The camaraderie of MIS, the Dodgers, Spicy Noodle House, but that's about it. He certainly won't miss being jerked around and lied to. He won't miss Doyle's head games. He won't miss Doyle period. After what he just heard, he knows Make It Stop is finished. As far as he's concerned, the outcome of Doyle's meeting with Hansen doesn't matter. Just the fact that Doyle would even consider Hansen's proposal is enough for him to call it quits. He's made up his mind. All he needs to do is collect Viviana and get out of dodge.

He pulls up to Viviana's apartment building and calls her on his tab. She's not going to like it. She's going to want an explanation and he's not sure what he should tell her. The truth?

Eventually. But right now, it's time to run.

The tab rings and rings and rings. Viviana isn't answering. Trevor makes his way through the security gate, goes through the complex, and up the stairs to her apartment. The door's unlocked. He pushes his way inside. Something feels off to him, something he can't quite place, an empty quality that makes his heart race.

"Viviana?"

He tries the bathroom, but she's not there. Nothing seems out of the ordinary. In fact, it seems a little too orderly. Same deal in the bedroom. The furniture's there, but Viviana's possessions are all gone. There's nothing in the drawers. No clothing in the closet. Not a speck of Viviana's presence to be found.

Trevor returns to the kitchen in the hopes of finding a note telling Trevor where she is, where they can meet, but there's no note, no explanation, nothing. He slides open the drawers in the kitchen where last week he found the pair of guns. The first drawer is empty, telling him what he already knows. The second drawer contains all the wireless cameras he'd installed.

Shit.

Trevor drifts over to the couch and collapses into it. Later, he will recall all of the things he said to her during their tender moments over the course of the last few weeks together and feel like a first-class fool. A confusing cocktail of anger, betrayal, and lust will hijack his thinking and confuse his emotions, but all that lies ahead of him.

Right now, as the fantasy of his feelings for Viviana dissolves, an all-consuming emptiness takes hold. It's a feeling he'd spent the better part of his youth trying to avoid and now it's back. He tells himself he'll be fine. But it's no use. When everything in your life is a lie, why should this moment be any different?

HANSEN STEPS INTO A WELL-LIT room on one of the upper floors of Evergreen Medical Center that he rarely visits. Bethany lies on a gurney holding an ice bag to her head while a nurse practitioner takes her blood pressure. Hansen makes eye contact with the guy. He gets the message and leaves.

"Well, aren't we a shambles," Hansen says.

Bethany tries to smile, but her face looks like hamburger.

"Are you all right?" Hansen asks, trying to keep the disgust out of his voice.

"I'm fine," Bethany says.

Hansen takes the plastic case out of his pocket. "Are you sure there isn't something I can do for you?"

Bethany stiffens. "I'm good."

Hansen suspects they've already got her on some kind of sedative. You'll get what's coming to you eventually, he thinks.

"I asked you to keep an eye on Lindsay, but she seems to have done a number on you."

"Lindsay?" Bethany laughs. "That may be her cover, but the woman I tangoed with is Melanie Marsh."

"Melanie Marsh is here at Evergreen?"

"You don't get it" Bethany says with mocking disdain. "Lindsay and Melanie are the same person."

Hansen doesn't care for Bethany's tone. He takes the syringe out of the case and without bothering with the pretense of an injection that will give him a great deal of pleasure, he jams the needle into her neck. Bethany puts up a struggle, but the Bliss quickly takes hold and she slumps on the gurney as her eyes roll back into her head. The whole thing is a waste. Hansen isn't even turned on. As he leaves the hospital room, he raises Applewhite on his tab.

"I need you at Evergreen," Hansen says. "She's here."

16

BLISS

Melanie's at a party with Scotty from The Furors. She knows she's dreaming because he isn't a kannibal and The Furors are famous. They are in some dank little beach bar with a killer jukebox, doing shots of Fiery Cat. Melanie seldom drinks in her dreams. There's always something holding her back, her head swirling with recriminations, but not in this dream. With Scotty she's loud, boisterous, out of control. They sing songs and take shots and make out in front of everyone. They're stumbling out of the bar when someone lunges at them and stabs Scotty in the heart. The attacker melts away in the marine layer. Scotty collapses in the street. There's blood everywhere, but when Melanie kneels to try to stop the bleeding, she can't find the wound. The EMTs come and—mistaking Melanie for the victim—strap her to a gurney and take her away. Melanie insists there's nothing wrong with her. A nurse with long, dark hair tells her everything's going to be fine. The back of the ambulance is lit like a bordello that pulses to the rhythm of a siren that gets slower and slower. The nurse climbs onto the gurney, crouches between Melanie's legs, caresses her thighs. "Doesn't that feel niiiiiice?" the nurse drawls. Melanie can't get the words out, but it does. It feels more than nice. It feels like nothing else could ever matter and she never wants it to stop. The nurse lowers her head between Melanie's legs. She braces herself for pleasure but is jerked back to consciousness when her desire turns into pain that arrives with the sharpness of a bite.

MELANIE COMES TO ON A thin bedroll in a makeshift shelter made out of canvas and plastic. Smoke drifts from a stick of incense. At the foot of the bedroll, a young Asian woman files her nails. Long and dark and lean, a hundred pounds if she's lucky.

"You're awake," she says.

"Barely," Melanie croaks.

"You don't remember me, do you?"

Melanie shakes her head. All she can recall is a woman with the head of a doll, but that doesn't seem right...

"I'm Kim."

"M-Lindsay."

"Mindy?"

Shit. "Lindsay."

Kim fixes her with a curious look. "Okay."

"How long have I been out?"

"A while. Do you know where you are?"

Melanie nods.

"I saw you when you stepped off the elevator," Kim continues. "Someone tried to pick a fight with you. Do you remember that?"

Melanie doesn't. "Did I kick his ass?"

"The ass belonged to a woman. You handled yourself pretty well, all things considered."

"What do you mean?"

Kim draws her long, slender legs under her, which gives Melanie a moment to collect herself. She's full of strange yearnings and she doesn't know what to do with them.

"They dosed you," Kim says. "They dose everybody now. Everyone gets a taste."

"Taste of what?" Melanie asks, because she needs to hear it from Kim.

"Where you been, girl? Bliss."

"Can I ask you something?" Melanie says.

"Sure."

"Did we, um…"

"No."

"What I mean is…"

"I know what you mean. You had paint all over you, so I cleaned you up with these." Kim holds up a container of baby wipes. "You really enjoyed that."

"Oh, my god." Melanie covers her eyes. Her shame is bottomless.

"It's not your fault. It's the Bliss"

"What do you mean?"

"You really don't know?"

Melanie shakes her head, too mortified to speak.

Kim gets up onto her knees and crawls over to Melanie. "Scoot over." Melanie slides her body to the edge of the bedroll and Kim joins her.

"Bliss kicks desire into overdrive," Kim says. "That's what you're feeling right now."

"But last night I—"

"It's the drug," Kim explains. "It was developed as a sex aid to get people to open up about their desires."

"Well, it works."

"A little too well."

"But it felt so…"

"Real?"

Melanie nods.

"You have to be really careful. Bliss messes up your pleasure center, makes your memories unreliable. You're not going to be able to trust them for a while."

Melanie rolls over on her side and buries her head in her hands. She is sad and tired and probably going to cry.

"I don't want to be a kannibal."

"It's going to be rough for a few days," Kim says, "but we'll watch over you until the Bliss is out of your system. It's really important you don't do any more."

Kim leans over and rummages through a plastic crate. She pulls out a bottle of water that's missing a label. "Drink this."

Melanie sits up and twists off the cap, tries to pull herself together. Her shitty mood doesn't change the fact she's here for a reason. Melanie glugs down the water.

"Better?"

Melanie nods. Looking around, it dawns on her that Kim's sanctuary is inside of a much larger space, like a tent inside a warehouse. "Where are we?"

"My humble abode. We'll see if we can find a space for you."

"Who is we?"

"Those of us who take our rehabilitation seriously."

"You organize this yourself?"

"Oh, no. We have a leader."

"Like a spiritual leader?"

"Something like that. Would you like to meet him?"

"I guess."

"Good," Kim says, her face brightening. "Because he'd like to meet you."

Melanie feels like she knows what's coming next, like she knows the answer to the question before she even asks it, but she can no more stop herself from asking than she can will herself not to breathe.

"What's his name?" she hears herself say, and when the answer comes it seems to travel from a long way away.

"Robert. Robert Gray. He runs the show around here."

MELANIE FOLLOWS KIM THROUGH A shantytown of shelters, some more elaborate than others. Everyone they pass stares at Melanie, sizing her up.

Kim takes her by the arm and leads her deeper into the labyrinth. Kim nods at some of the people but most of them she ignores. Melanie follows, tentative and unsure. She hates the feeling of eyes lingering over her and not being able to do anything about it. They know what I am, she thinks. They can smell it on me.

They pass a group of men bent over a woman lying prone on the floor.

"What's going on?" Melanie asks.

"Don't look," Kim warns.

Melanie doesn't listen and sees hands pulling at gray flesh. She starts to say something, but Kim pulls her along.

"That woman…" Melanie protests.

"It's not what you think."

Melanie turns and sees what Kim had seen: filthy hands, a needle, a patch of lunar skin. The look on the woman's face as urgent and intensely focused as if she were giving birth. Melanie knows she's never wanted anything like that before, but whatever is driving that woman's need is inside of her now, too.

"I think I'm going to be sick," Melanie says.

"I told you not to look."

In the far corner of the ward, a wall of plastic sheeting serves as a crude barrier. A pair of burly men stand sentry at a gap. These are the healthiest looking people Melanie's seen on the ward. They wear medical masks and matching black tracksuits.

"Who's this?" one of them asks.

"Noob," Kim says. "I'm taking her to a meeting."

"Welcome to Next Step," the other one says.

The two men step aside to let them pass. The floors are clean here, there are plenty of chairs, and the people are fully clothed. It's got all the charm of a church basement. Melanie's heard about places like this—inmate-run rehab centers—but she's never actually seen one. Kim guides Melanie to a pair of empty seats.

"Let's sit."

Melanie collapses into the chair. She's done nothing but sleep for who knows how long but she can barely keep her eyes open. She feels like she's on the verge of shutting down again. Kim senses her fatigue and leans into her to help keep Melanie upright.

"Why are you helping me?" Melanie asks.

"Because this is what we're here for. Some of us still honor that."

A middle-aged white guy with long gray hair to his shoulders and a white beard passes out cups of coffee from a tray.

"That's…" Melanie almost says "Gary's brother" but stops herself.

"Robert," Kim says. At the sound of his name, Robert stops and turns toward them. It's like looking at an older version of Gary. They have similar builds, but Gary was much leaner. Robert wears a faded green golf shirt, stained khaki pants, and no shoes. He looks like a bank manager on a deserted island. He's standing in front of her now. The coffee smells like heaven.

"May I?" Melanie asks.

"Of course," Robert replies.

Melanie grabs a cup and takes a sip. Robert winks at Kim and walks on. The coffee isn't particularly hot or strong, but she has to restrain herself from drinking it all at once.

When Robert's tray is empty, he moves to the center of the circle. He takes out a pack of cigarettes, lights one, and passes the pack. Robert takes a drag off his cigarette and blows out the smoke in dramatic fashion as he takes command of his room, for that's what it is now.

"The only good thing about this place is you can smoke anywhere you want."

The group titters. Robert continues.

"When they pulled me out of rehab and sent me down here, I thought, this is a death sentence. I'm gonna die here."

Robert pauses to take another drag and smiles as if something hilarious just occurred to him. "The mind of an addict warps the will to suit its needs. So instead of fuck *that*, it's fuck *this*. If I'm stuck here, I might as well party, right? What's the use of staying clean if I can't leave? Might as well just Bliss out."

Robert's spiel is punctuated by the occasional, "That's right!" "Uh-huh!" "Tell it, brother!" from members of the audience. Melanie finds it tiresome.

"With that kind of mentality," he continues, "you're a kannibal before you take your first shot. That's not how we do things at Next Step. What's the use of staying sober in a terrible place like this? Because it's good spiritual practice. Because being clean begins and ends not with the body but the mind. Because there's a better place waiting for all of us."

Robert claps his hands together and stares up at the heavens, as if the great reward is near. Melanie makes eye contact with Kim and rolls her eyes. Kim stifles a giggle.

"I'm not gonna lie," Robert continues. "This place is a real shit show. That's why we have to be rigorous in our resolve because it's all we have. That and each other. Because the care you came to Evergreen to get ended the second they sent you down here, but this is where your Next Step begins."

Robert bows his head and clasps his hands together, not so he can be alone with his thoughts, but so the assembly of addicts can be alone with theirs. In spite of being fully aware that Robert's spiel is a pitch he uses to bring people into the cult of the clean, Melanie takes comfort in the fact that in the middle of all this madness people are still trying to stay sober. Isn't that what it's all about, broken people helping broken people, trying to get better, no matter the odds, regardless of how low they've fallen? She hopes that message *never* stops getting through, especially now when she has Bliss coiled up inside her, waiting to fuck up her life forever.

Suddenly Robert is standing over them with an intense smile plastered on his face.

"Are you two talking about me?"

"This is Lindsay," Kim says, "the new girl I was telling you about."

Kim seems weirdly shy. There's something going on between these two. Melanie is sure of it.

"I'm very sorry it has to be under these circumstances," Robert says, "but I'm pleased as hell to meet you."

"Ditto, kiddo," Melanie blurts out. It was something Scary Gary used to say, but Robert doesn't react. Robert has his brother's intensity: bulging eyes and flared nostrils. But he has something else too: the fervor of a zealot. There are a few in every rehab. Smooth-talking addicts with rough and tumble pasts who have a way of letting you know everything is going to be okay—until you sleep with them or give them money. Then they turn on you. Knowing this about Robert gives Melanie confidence.

"I like your style, noobs," Robert says. "I hear you handled yourself like a pro out there."

"Thanks."

"We can always use people like you."

"Not interested."

Robert beams, a big beatific I'm-going-to-stop-talking-now-because-we-both-know-words-are-bullshit smile. "That's fine," he says. "The only thing we ask is you stay clean. If you can do that, you're always welcome at Next Step."

"I don't mean to be rude," Melanie says, "but I'm not really down with the whole group therapy thing."

"Oh?" Robert's features darken but he manages to keep smiling despite the hostility creeping into his tone. "Then why are you here?"

"To deliver a message."

"A message from whom?"

"Your brother."

Something shifts in Robert's eyes, an uneasiness that wasn't there a moment ago.

"My brother?"

"Gary," Melanie says.

"And what does Gary have to say for himself?"

"I'm not sure if this is the right time," Melanie says.

"There are no secrets here—right, Kim?" There's a hard edge to Robert's voice that Melanie hasn't heard before, but which Kim clearly has, judging from her reaction. Kim is staring at the floor like there's something really interesting down there.

"What is my brother up to these days?" Robert asks.

"Nothing," Melanie says. "He's dead."

REHABEES SIT HUDDLED TOGETHER ON the floor with stuff for sale spread out on dingy towels: toothbrushes, batteries, combs, a sad-looking dildo. An old man with a crown of white hair begins his spiel.

"I got wipes! You need some wipes?"

Melanie thinks she should get some for Kim since she's been so generous with hers, but Robert shoves the man aside.

"Excuse us, friend."

"Actually, I could use some wipes," Melanie says.

"I'll get you some."

Robert isn't the helpless junkie that Gary had told her about. Of course, people change—recovery hinges on this principle—but Melanie believes Make It Stop is essential because most of the time people *don't* change.

"So," Robert begins. "Gary."

"Do you know what your brother's been up to?" Melanie asks.

"I know he was involved in recovery work. Is that how you knew him?"

Melanie nods. "We used to work together."

This stops Robert in his tracks. He turns and faces Melanie, and in that moment, she can see how upset he is. His eyes are starred with the tears he refuses to shed.

"You work for Doyle?" he asks.

"Sometimes," Melanie says, which is mostly true, but if Robert knows Doyle, then he knows about MIS and if he knows about MIS, there's no point in holding back.

"How did my brother die?"

"He was on an operation. In a place like this."

"You mean an HNS facility?"

"Yeah." Melanie knows she needs to be careful here. This man may be Gary's brother, but he isn't Gary.

"I warned him this would happen," Robert says. "Too many people know about Make It Stop."

"He told you about us?"

"No, but it was obvious he was mixed up with Doyle."

"And now you work for HNS."

"I don't work for anyone. This is...temporary."

"A regular good Samaritan," Melanie says.

"I thought that was *your* job."

"Your brother was my friend. I was in a bad place, and he helped me out of it."

"That's what he did."

They reach a part of the ward Melanie recognizes: the elevators. Rehabees wait for the next arrival. The door opens and a hulking figure with an egg-shaped head, deep-set eyes, and a cruel mouth she'd recognize anywhere appears as if from a nightmare.

"Applewhite," she whispers, as if saying the name aloud will break the spell.

"What's that?" Robert asks.

"I need some air."

"Good luck with that."

Melanie clutches Robert's forearms, turns away from Applewhite. "I need to lie down."

Robert looks concerned for half a second before his sleazy smile returns. "You want to rest in my office? I've got a sofa, something to drink, anything you want…"

"No," Melanie says, pushing him away and pretending to be more out of it than she actually feels. She wants to get as far away from here as possible. "I think I'll go back to Kim's."

"I'll check on you later," Robert says, but she's already on her way. She risks one last look at Applewhite. He and a pair of corps decked out in riot gear push through a cluster of rehabees, telling them to disperse. He does it with an urgency that suggests he's looking for someone. He's looking for her.

Melanie returns to where rehabees barter for food, clothes, drugs, whatever. The old man who'd accosted her a few minutes ago is nowhere in sight. The ammoniac piss-reek of Bliss is more powerful here and even in her agitated state it triggers something deep inside her. She tries to shrug it off but the urge to score is strong. She slows down a bit, just to get her bearings, and a kannibal sitting cross-legged on the ground pulls at her hand. She whirls on the man, ready to deliver some punishment, but something stops her.

"Lindzzz…" the man hisses.

"Oh, my god," Melanie gasps. He's missing his glasses and his hair is loose, but the black and yellow Furors pin on his sleeveless denim jacket is a dead giveaway. The sweet kid who'd pledged his black metal heart to her is sitting on the floor, disheveled and disoriented.

"Morris?"

"Hey," Morris says with a smile, but it's not a pretty sight. One eye is a field of broken capillaries; the other is swollen shut. Scabs clot his lips. Bruises dot his long, skinny arms, and his skin is so gray it looks dusted with ash.

"Is that really you?"

"In the flesh!" Morris barks with laughter. He's so high he can barely keep his one good eye open.

"What happened to you?"

"Don't worry about that. Come sit with me, sister. I wanna show you something…"

Melanie hesitates—she really should be getting back to Kim— but sits down next to Morris anyway. "What is it?"

Morris takes a baggie of Bliss out of his pocket. "What do you think it is?"

"Oh, god."

"You wanna taste?"

No, Melanie thinks, but the refusal doesn't make it to her lips. It floats in her mind while other ideas take shape. What she wants. What she needs. There's no denying these feelings, not when it makes her blood jump and her brain hum like a machine slowly coming back to life after a long time in the dark.

"I can't."

"You mean won't."

"I shouldn't."

"But you want to."

The thing is she really doesn't, but the smell floats up to her, seductive and sweet. How could something that was so repugnant to her have the complete opposite effect on her now?

It doesn't make sense. Morris is a mess, but not like some of the others she's seen on the ward. She doesn't want to do Bliss with him. She wants to help him, find a way to get him out of this awful place. But instead of telling him these things, she says, "We have to do this quickly."

Just as the words leave her mouth, a foot lands in Morris's face and he goes flying onto his back like a bug. One of the corps flips him onto his stomach while the other one kneels on his neck and binds his hands with zip ties.

"Did you get the stuff?" one corp asks the other.

"I got it."

Melanie scurries away and melts into the crowd before Applewhite comes over to investigate.

"I'm so sorry," Melanie whispers again and again—because she wasn't able to help her friend or because he didn't get her high, she doesn't know.

Melanie ducks into the maze and finds her way back to Kim's cocoon and peers through the slit that passes for a door. Kim's slender body is hunched over something on the floor, engaged in some mysterious task. Probably doing her nails, she thinks. Melanie quietly slips inside so as not to disturb Kim and immediately realizes her mistake. Spread out on the floor before her is a baggie, a mirror, and a razor—the accouterments of a bad good time. Kim finishes snorting the line she'd inhaled through a rolled-up dollar bill. She lifts her head and locks eyes with Melanie, smoldering with something between resentment and rage.

"I can leave if…" Melanie begins before Kim cuts her off.

"It's not Bliss," Kim says as she stows her stash, "if that's what you're wondering."

"I wasn't," Melanie says. She has a feeling she'd have known if it was Bliss.

"I told you I don't mess around with that shit."

Melanie doesn't say anything. She doesn't have to. She wants Kim to tell her it's nothing, no big deal, even if it's a lie—*especially* if it's a lie.

"It's just a little go-fast," Kim says. "Helps the time go by."

An image of Applewhite combing through the catacombs intrudes. Did Robert notice how freaked out she was? Were they on their way here now?

"What's your deal with Robert?"

"Robert's scum," Kim replies, "but he likes you."

"I'm not like that," Melanie says.

"That's what I thought when I got here."

"Maybe I'm not like you," Melanie says to the woman who's been nothing but nice to her.

"Being friendly with Robert has its benefits. If he likes you, he can get you things."

"Even Bliss?"

"Especially Bliss," Kim says. "As much as you want."

"Where does it come from?"

"The Colony."

Melanie stiffens.

"You've been there?" Kim asks.

Melanie nods. That's where she stabbed Applewhite, where Scary Gary saved her, where one life ended and another began.

"They make Bliss in a lab there and distribute it to other HNS hospitals. Robert is in charge of distribution here at Evergreen."

"They get patients hooked on it and then they send them to detention for being addicts?" Melanie asks.

"They start the bullshit and then they make it stop."

Melanie winces at Kim's choice of words. "I really need to get out of here."

Kim stares at her for an uncomfortably long time. "I'm coming with you."

"What about Robert?" Melanie asks.

"I'll take care of Robert," Kim says.

"He spends most of his time in his office," Kim explains while they put on lipstick and eyeliner. "There's a door in his office that leads directly to the parking garage, but you need a key card to open it. His truck is parked right outside the door. He only uses it when he makes his runs, so he keeps the card and his key in a drawer in his desk. All we need to do is distract him."

"Security?" Melanie asks.

Kim looks away from her reflection in a handheld mirror—the same one she used to chop up a line a few minutes ago. "I've never seen any."

"Do you go out with him a lot?"

"When I feel like it," Kim says with a shrug that tells Melanie to drop it, so she does. Kim is wearing a white crop top and gray yoga pants. Melanie sports a red camisole and black leggings. It feels good to wear something that isn't a baggy sweatshirt.

"You look great," they both say, and they laugh together.

Heads turn as they make their way through Next Step, but once it becomes clear where they're headed, the gawkers look away. Kim leads her to a door at the end of the hallway. A window to Robert's office has been taped up with cardboard. Kim presses her ear to the door and urges Melanie to do the same. She can hear moaning sounds, muffled music. What is going on in there?

Kim moves her hand like a man jerking off and Melanie has to clamp her hand over her mouth to keep from laughing.

"Ready?" Kim whispers.

Melanie nods.

Kim raps on the door.

"Just a minute!" Robert shouts from inside.

Kim pushes the door open and they barge in. The office is an old security station with a futon crammed into one corner and a television in another. The screen plays girl-on-girl porn. Robert sits behind a desk covered with bindles of Bliss, fumbling with his pants, but his embarrassment gives way to arousal when he sees what Melanie and Kim are wearing.

"Well, well, well," he says. "To what do I owe the honor of this visit?"

"Lindsay and I were talking," Kim says, "and she has some questions."

"About?" Robert asks, thoroughly delighted with this development.

"Your talk earlier," Melanie says.

Robert turns from Kim to Melanie and fixes his gaze on her while Kim continues.

"I said, 'Why don't we ask Robert?' And here we are."

"Well, you came to the right place. Please, sit." Robert gestures at the futon and jumps out of his chair to clear it off. Melanie and Kim sit down, and Robert squeezes in between them, though he's still fixated on Melanie.

"What can I help you with?"

"You know what you said about broken people helping broken people?" Melanie asks.

"Yes, I do. Unfortunately, that's something I know a lot about."

"What if you're all the way broken?"

"What do you mean?" Robert asks.

"Like a car that's been totaled," Kim says.

"Smashed to smithereens," Melanie adds.

"Speaking of cars," Kim says, "we're going to need your keys."

"We all have different bottoms," Robert says, ignoring Kim, "that's why we have to do whatever we can to—" Robert turns toward Kim. "What did you say?"

"Your keys. And your key card, too."

"Lindsay and I are talking," Robert says as he turns back to Melanie.

"Robert?" Kim asks.

"What?" Robert snaps.

"Fuck you."

As Robert turns toward Kim, Melanie grabs his arm and, with a deft twist, pins it behind his back.

"I don't know what you think you're playing at but—"

Robert's mouth hangs open, but no words come out as he struggles for air.

"What's wrong with him?" Melanie asks.

"I think he's having trouble breathing," Kim says as she withdraws the switchblade from Robert's ribcage. "A hole in the lungs will do that."

Robert keels over on the floor, gasping, bleeding, struggling to speak. Kim jumps off the futon. She picks up a submission stick leaning in the corner, telescopes it to its full length, and zaps Robert with a prolonged and powerful jolt. Melanie looks and then looks away. She takes a duffel bag and starts filling it with the packages of Bliss.

"What are you doing?" Kim asks as she retracts the wand and tucks it into her waistband.

"This comes with us," Melanie says.

"That's Bliss."

"You want to leave it behind so they can dose the next group that comes down the elevator?"

"I see your point, but…"

"Did you get the keys and the card?"

"Way ahead of you."

"Then grab his feet. He's coming with us."

Melanie hoists Robert by his armpits. Kim takes his feet but doesn't look happy about it. They carry the body that just a few moments ago was animated with desire. Now it's just a bloody bag of meat. They set it down again so Kim can swipe the door with the key card. When the light on the keypad turns green, Melanie pulls the door open and they carry him into the garage where a pair of corps stands, one on each side of the door, shooting the shit.

Melanie lets go of the body and Robert's head makes a sickening thud as it strikes the concrete. Kim kicks the corp closest to her in the knee, snapping ligaments. The corp screams as he goes down. Melanie aims a kick at her corp, but he blocks the blow, and shoves Melanie back into the door. While Kim uses the canvas strap of the duffel bag to choke out her corp, Melanie's meathead activates his submission stick.

"Lindsay!" Kim tosses the stick she'd used to zap Robert. Melanie plucks it out of the air and the weapon comes alive in her hands. She brandishes the stick at the corp and his eyes tell her this is a very bad idea. Melanie and the corp thrust and feint, but neither one of them wants to find out what happens when the electrified wands come into contact with each other.

Melanie swoops low but the corp is ready for it. She passes the stick from one hand to the other and hurls it at his head. The stick delivers a jolt that knocks the corp off his feet and when he hits the deck, he zaps himself again with his own stick, knocking him unconscious.

"You all right?" Melanie asks.

"Yeah. You?"

Melanie nods. A loud banging noise from inside Robert's office disrupts the silence.

"Shit," Kim says.

"Let's go," Melanie says.

Kim presses the key fob, flashing the headlights on a black pickup truck parked a few steps from the door to Robert's office. Melanie tosses the duffel in the back of the truck as Kim slides behind the wheel. Melanie climbs into the passenger seat. The clock on the dashtab reads 1:11, and she has no idea if it's day or night. Kim slams the truck into reverse.

"Where do you want to go today?" the computer asks.

Kim stomps on the gas as Melanie bubbles through the dashtab screen and shuts off the GPS. The truck bursts through the exit and into the LA night. The number of cars on the road astonishes Melanie. Who are these people? Where are they all going? For the millionth time it occurs to Melanie you're never really alone in LA. No matter where you're going or how the late the hour, there's always someone on the road alongside you, picking their nose, putting on makeup, grooving to some unheard music. She normally takes comfort in the anonymity. She couldn't live in a place where everyone was up in her business all the time, but just once she'd like to see the roads as empty as she feels inside.

Now that she's out of Evergreen, it dawns on her that she has no way of getting a hold of Trevor or Doyle. She knows Bill's number but doesn't have a tab. She can't go home and who knows where Abigail is. She feels like she should know what to do but doesn't have a clue.

"Hungry?" Kim asks.

"I could eat," Melanie lies.

"I'm starving."

Kim spots a taco shop just past the state casino and pulls into the drive-through. There's a line, but it moves quickly. They order a pair of California burritos and huge cups of agua fresca. Kim tears into her food like she hasn't eaten in days, which is probably the case. Melanie isn't hungry. Her mind keeps wandering to the Bliss in the back of the truck.

"You okay?" Kim asks as she polishes off her burrito.

"We need to find somewhere to crash."

"I know a place," Kim says. "My auntie has a spot in Koreatown."

Melanie nods. "There's something I need to tell you."

"You're in Make It Stop," Kim says.

"You knew?"

Kim shrugs. "Robert told me."

"Does anyone not know?" Melanie says, raising her voice because she can, because it feels good to lose a little bit of control.

Kim nods at the duffel bag in the bed of the truck. "You got plans for all that Bliss?"

"We should probably do something about that," Melanie admits.

"You think?"

"But I don't know how to get in touch with anyone."

"Don't you have a secret meeting place or something?" Kim wipes her mouth with a napkin and tosses it on the floor.

"Used to."

"And?"

"It got blown up."

The cab of the truck lights up with blue and red lights from a police cruiser that's pulled up behind them.

"Get out of the car with your hands up!" a voice calls out on the loud hailer.

"Quite the secret organization you've got," Kim says.

"Tell me about it."

BILL IS STAKED OUT AT Evergreen, drinking a cup of coffee and reading the paper, when a black pickup truck with the HNS logo on the door panel bounces out of the parking lot and goes screaming past him. Bill is inclined to ignore the truck, but then his dashtab squawks to life:

"Code Red. I repeat, Code Red. Lock down the facility."

Bill is monitoring the hospital's radio frequency, and puts two and two together.

It's Melanie. Has to be.

He tosses the paper into the passenger seat and stomps on the gas.

Bill catches up to the truck without much difficulty and gets close enough to make out her silhouette through the rear window, but he can't get a bead on where she's headed. The truck swerves into an all-night taco stand. Bill cruises past, circles around the block, and approaches from the opposite direction. Melanie and another woman he doesn't recognize sit inside the truck in the drive-thru line. He watches them get their food and prepares to follow, but they pull into the parking lot instead. It doesn't take a detective to figure out they're stopping to eat, but he keeps a close eye on them just to be sure. There's no point in ruining their meal, but all good things must come to an end.

After a few minutes, he pulls up behind the truck and flips the switch on the disco lights. Like a straight shot of dopamine.

Bill uses the mic to tell them to get out with their hands up, and they do. He opens the door and steps out of his vehicle, the mic cord stretched to the limit. "That's it nice and easy... Now turn around."

Melanie does as she's told. Bill flashes a smile.

"Miss me?" Bill asks.

"Can we lose the lights?" she asks.

Bill reaches into the sedan and shuts off the flashing lights. Melanie puts her hands down and so does Kim.

"How was rehab?" Bill asks.

"A real blast." Melanie opens the tailgate and pulls out the duffel bag. "I brought you a souvenir."

"For me?" Bill steps forward and unzips the duffel. There's enough Bliss in the bag to start an orgy at a mega church. He can sense Melanie's companion tense up and her hands are nowhere he can see them.

"Tell your friend to cool it," Bill says to Melanie without taking his eyes off the Bliss. It's the biggest score he's ever seen. Too bad he can't turn it in. He zips up the bag and turns to Melanie.

"You want to tell me about this?"

"INS is manufacturing Bliss and dosing patients jammed up in the system."

Bill lets this sink in. "They make this at Evergreen?"

Melanie shakes her head. "Colonial."

Bill whistles.

"That's where I'm going next," Melanie says.

"Where *we're* going," Melanie's friend adds.

Bill nods at the woman. "And this is?"

"A friend," says the friend.

Bill lets it slide. "What were you planning on doing with all this Bliss?" he asks.

"Giving it to you."

Good enough. Bill takes the duffel bag and throws it in the back seat of his sedan. He pauses at the driver's-side door.

"I'm glad you're safe."

"Sounds like you missed me," Melanie says.

"Sounds like it, doesn't it?"

Bill winks, gets in his car, and drives away. He scowls at the mirror, watching the taco shop get smaller and smaller. Sooner or later, he is going to have to tell Melanie the truth about him, before she finds out the hard way.

17

NEON HEARTS

KIM KNOCKS ON THE SECURITY door bathed in the glow of a pink neon sign. The light clicks off, Kim steps back, and the door slowly opens. A middle-aged woman with a commanding presence peers at Melanie with a kind smile.

"Jen," Kim says.

At the sound of Kim's voice, the woman's smile dissolves. She regards Kim with a look that tells Melanie this isn't the first time Kim's come here looking for help. "What do you want?"

"My friend's in trouble," Kim says, nodding at Melanie. "We need a place to rest. Just for a few hours, I promise."

"Your friend," Jen mutters as she pushes the gate open wider, but her smile reappears when she turns to Melanie. "Please, come in."

They enter a dimly lit lobby with music so delicate and low Melanie can barely hear it. The lobby is crammed with a counter, a small leatherette couch, and a water cooler. The three women fill up the tiny space.

"Who is she?" Melanie asks as Jen disappears down a hallway.

"My Aunt Jen."

"She seems nice."

Kim lays a death stare on her.

They follow Aunt Jen down a narrow, carpeted hallway even darker than the lobby with doors on both sides. Aunt Jen opens one of the doors and beckons them inside.

"Stay as long as you like," Aunt Jen says.

"Thank you so much."

"You're welcome, sweetheart."

Aunt Jen closes the door. The room is bathed in red light and furnished with a pair of massage tables. Melanie curls into a ball on one of the tables; Kim climbs onto the other.

"I'm sorry I dragged you into this mess," Melanie says.

"It's fine. You sure you're okay?"

"Yeah," Melanie says, too tired to sell the lie, but Kim isn't having it.

"Tell me."

"You know that first night in rehab?" Melanie says. "When it feels like the world has left you behind?"

Kim nods.

"It feels like that. It feels...like the end."

"Of Make It Stop?" Kim asks.

"Of everything."

"You're tired," Kim says. "You'll feel better after you get some rest."

"You're probably right." She's exhausted and isn't thinking clearly, but Melanie knows she'd feel better if she could get ahold of Trevor. Then it hits her. "Does your aunt have a tab?"

"I'm sure she does," Kim says.

There's a soft knock on the door and Aunt Jen enters with a tea tray.

"Something to help you sleep," she says.

Melanie and Kim each take a cup.

"Ask her," Kim says.

"Ask me what?" Aunt Jen says, suddenly suspicious.

"I'm sorry to bother you," Melanie begins, "but do you have a tab I could borrow?"

"Of course, sweetie. Let me get it for you."

Aunt Jen exits but returns almost immediately with an old boxy-looking tab and hands it to Melanie with great solemnity.

"Thank you," Melanie says.

"Drink your tea while it's hot." Aunt Jen side-eyes Kim as she leaves. "I'll need that back when you're finished."

"Of course," Melanie says. Now she really wants to know what Kim did to piss off her aunt, but that can wait. She starts bubbling through Aunt Jen's tab.

"What are you doing?" Kim asks.

"I think I found a way to get in touch with my people."

Kim walks over and looks over her shoulder. "TruLuv?"

"Long story," Melanie says. "What's this?"

Apparently, Melanie isn't the only one with a TruLuv account because when she calls up the site, images of Aunt Jen pop on the screen. She's all dolled up and every icon on her profile is bursting with notifications, an avalanche of hearts.

"Your aunt is a very popular lady."

"Gross." Kim climbs onto the other table and wraps herself in a sheet.

Melanie logs out of Aunt Jen's TruLuv account and into her own—well, Sonja's anyway—and quickly scans her messages. None of them are from Trevor, but a new message from the Truthbot catches her attention:

Sonja is lost and needs to be found.

—Truthbot

"You can say that again," Melanie says as she types out a message on her page for all to see:

Looking for tall, dark, and neurotic. I have something exciting to share with you.

If Trevor is still monitoring her account, he'll get the message—but is he? She knows very little about Trevor's life outside of MIS.

He likes writing code, hacking into hospitals, listening to the Dodgers, and is probably banging Viviana-fucking-Sanchez right now. It makes her sad that after carrying a torch for this boy for almost two years, he is mostly a mystery to her. She hadn't fallen for Trevor so much as the idea of Trevor—an idea, she now understands, that existed only in her head.

Melanie shuts off the tab and curls up on the table. She can feel the tears coming and she doesn't try to hold them in. Melanie cries as quietly as she can so she doesn't wake up Kim. She isn't someone who floats on top of her feelings. They inhabit her. Mad or sad. Drunk or sober. She's all in. That's the way it's going to be until she figures a way out of this mess.

TREVOR WAKES UP ON THE couch with a terrible feeling. There'd been no vision, no omen. No one had spoken to him in a dream, but he is filled with dread. He doesn't need a symbol or a sign to know what's it is because it's coming from him. He is both the signal and the source of this no-good feeling, which kicks off a round of bad person blues: I am shit, always have been shit, always will be shit. I make shitty decisions and do shitty things. I am shit to others and—

His tab is buzzing. That's what woke him. Not a dream. Not a premonition. There are only two people who have this number: Viviana and Doyle. Fifty-fifty.

If it's Viviana, he can still make everything right.

If it's Doyle...he doesn't want it to be Doyle.

He snatches the tab off the table. It's Doyle.

"Are you in a secure location?"

"Secure as any." Trevor's been camped out in Viviana's apartment. He's stuck around in the hope she'll return, but with each passing hour that hope feels more remote.

"That's not good enough," Doyle says.

"It's going to have to be."

Doyle sighs. "I'm only going to say this once, so listen up. I tried to cut a deal with Hansen. It didn't go well. Now HNS is on the warpath and none of us are safe."

Trevor stands and walks to the window. He peeks through the blinds, half-expecting to see Doyle down on the sidewalk. It's dark outside. A bus glides to a stop across the street and begins taking on passengers while cars flash by in the night. A man pushing a shopping cart down the sidewalk curses when the wheels of his cart catch the dead husk of a fallen palm frond.

"Is Viviana with you?" Doyle asks.

"No. She..." Trevor isn't sure what to say.

"She what?"

"I don't know where she is."

"Are you worried something has happened to her? Or is something else troubling you?"

"I don't know. She left..."

"If her heart is true," Doyle says, "you have nothing to worry about."

"Right." But is it? That's the question Trevor's been tormenting himself with. He's never felt this way before and it absolutely sucks.

"I'm going underground, and I suggest you do the same."

"Wait, what?"

"History will tell us if we were right or wrong, but at least we did our best."

Trevor can't believe what he's hearing. "You're quitting? What about Melanie?"

"She's on her own. We all are."

"After everything we've been through, that's it? Good luck and watch your ass?"

"You think this is easy for me?" Doyle asks.

"If your heart is true, you have nothing to worry about," Trevor says and ends the call.

Doyle has washed his hands of Make It Stop. He didn't call Trevor to warn him, but to say goodbye. Well, goodbye and good riddance. Doyle has disrupted his life for the last time.

That disruption is secondary to the upheaval Viviana has caused. Trevor knows what's in his own heart. But what's in Viviana's? He wants to believe—needs to believe—that he knows, but he doesn't.

VINYL SIGNS ADVERTISING SAME-DAY MOVE-IN specials plaster the stucco walls of Viviana's apartment building. It's the kind of place for people who crash-land in LA to chase their dreams, a place for people with no connections and fewer options, a place that will never give back your security deposit. Melanie knows these kinds of places well.

Melanie double-checks the address Trevor sent to her TruLuv account to make sure she's at the right place.

"This is it," Melanie says.

"What are we doing here?" Kim asks as she shuts off the engine.

"Well, Trevor, who I used to have a thing for, started shacking up with Viviana, who is a total hoe-bag, but now Viviana's MIA and he's up in her place freaking out."

"*Used* to have a thing?"

"Not a full-on thing," Melanie says, "but maybe a little bit, definitely, yeah."

"What about the dirty cop?" Kim asks.

"Bill? He's not dirty!" Melanie can't believe what she's hearing. Bill has been nothing but solid.

"What is he then? A good cop?" Kim sneers.

"I don't know," Melanie admits.

"You have a thing with him, too?"

Melanie shrugs. "Maybe?"

"How many people you got a thing for?"

"Right now," Melanie says with a wink, "just you."

Kim shakes her head. Before heading to the Valley, Melanie and Kim took turns taking showers in a tiny stall at the back of the massage parlor and ate their weight in scrambled eggs and sweet jasmine rice Kim's aunt had prepared in the kitchenette. After her shower, Melanie walked past an open room and saw Aunt Jen consoling Kim, who was quietly sobbing on her aunt's shoulder. Kim didn't see her, but Aunt Jen nodded and Melanie moved on. Kim's been quiet ever since.

They wait for someone to come out and slip through the entrance to the building, which is actually several buildings connected by stucco breezeways and high-traffic carpet. Dusty plants decorate the common areas. The drywall in the passageways is chipped and scuffed from careless movers banging into it with boxes, carts, and beat-up furniture. As they make their way up the stairs to the third floor, Melanie lays out the game plan.

"I'll keep Trevor engaged. You look around the apartment and see if anything seems strange."

"What's this Viviana like?" Kim asks. "Besides being a total hoe-bag…"

"Dangerous," Melanie says.

What does Melanie know about Viviana?

Not much. She's hot, fit, infuriatingly cheerful. She has a weakness for name-brand shoes, clothing, and makeup—things Melanie only cares about in the context of an assignment. Despite the fact that out of everyone at MIS Viviana was the only one who actually shopped at the Galleria, she is a damn good op.

As they approach Viviana's apartment, the door flies open. Trevor stands on the other side with a look of desperation that gives way to disappointment and then, finally, relief.

"You look terrible," Melanie says.

"Thanks."

Might as well get this over with, Melanie thinks. "I'm sorry I took your truck."

Trevor shrugs. "I'm just glad you're okay. Who's your friend?"

"New recruit."

"Make It Stop is over, Mel."

"Can we come in?"

Trevor steps aside and Melanie and Kim enter the apartment. He needs a shave and a shower, but he doesn't smell like he's been drinking, and she doesn't see any booze or drugs lying around. Trevor sprawls on the couch in front of an array of tabs connected to various devices. Aside from the hardware on the coffee table and the blanket on the sofa, the apartment is immaculate.

"What's this about Make It Stop being over?" Melanie folds her arms across her chest. Kim stands off to the side.

"I talked to Doyle a little while ago."

"And?"

"He tried to cut a deal with HNS."

"Um," Kim interrupts, "do you have any water?"

Trevor nods at the kitchen. Kim noiselessly goes through the cabinets looking for a glass while Trevor and Melanie continue their conversation.

"Where's Viviana?" Melanie asks.

"I don't know. She just…disappeared."

"Where did you see her last?"

"Here. Working out in the gym."

"And you think something happened to her?" Melanie asks.

"I don't know what to think."

Melanie takes a deep breath and lays it all on the line. "I think you need to consider the possibility Viviana isn't the person you think she is."

"What are you saying?" Trevor asks.

"Sometimes people leave."

"She wouldn't."

"People keep secrets."

"We had plans."

"Do you need me to spell it out for you? You told me Doyle thought we had a rat."

"The rat was Doyle!" Trevor shouts. "He was the one talking to Hansen!"

"Maybe he wasn't the only one."

"You think she was using me?"

"Since you put it that way—"

"I get it. You're jealous."

"Um, guys." Kim enters the living room from the hallway, holding a piece of molded plastic. "I found this in the bathroom."

It's a tester from a home pregnancy kit, and Melanie can see from where she's standing the result is positive.

"What?" Trevor asks, clearly baffled.

Melanie takes the tester from Kim and holds it up for Trevor. "You really don't know what this is?" Melanie is too exasperated for words.

"Your girlfriend is pregnant," Kim says.

Trevor doesn't take the news well. "I can't fucking believe this."

Why is it some men can't accept that the natural consequence of having sexual intercourse with a healthy, fertile female is the creation of a fetus? What makes that so hard to grasp? Hack into a corporation's private server? No problem. Coordinate a multi-agent mission? Can do. But the concepts of basic biology prove to be elusive for Trevor.

"Why me?" he whines, which Melanie cannot and will not tolerate.

Melanie breaks it down for him. "Listen, Trev. Chances are she doesn't want you to know so she went somewhere to take care of it."

"But—"

"No buts. This isn't about you."

That he understands but he doesn't like it. He gets up, retreats to Viviana's bedroom, and slams the door.

"You used to have a crush on this guy?" Kim says.

"Used to."

"If I were you, I'd stick with the dirty cop. That guy definitely likes you."

"He does, doesn't he?" Melanie says, just to hear herself say it, but Kim has given Melanie an idea.

BILL SITS IN THE FRONT seat of his sedan, staring straight ahead, asleep with his eyes open. It used to unnerve his buddies in his squad, but it comes in handy on a stakeout. Right now, he's dreaming about a sandwich his mother made for him when he was nine. At first, he thinks it's a tuna salad sandwich except they are out of tuna. He doesn't know how he knows this; he just does. She dices celery and onions but instead of tuna she chops up a thick slab of ham. This upsets Bill for reasons he can't explain when, thankfully, his tab buzzes. The sandwich dissolves. The detective awakes. Where is he? Who is he? He is receiving a call, a message from another world.

"Detective William Carlos Williams Redondo."

"Bill?" Melanie asks.

"Oh, hi, Melanie."

"Is that really your name?"

"Is that why you called? To ask me my name?"

"I need a favor," Melanie says. "I need you to find someone for me."

"You got a name? Date of birth?"

"Viviana Sanchez. I need to know if she's in the system."

Bill types the name into his dashtab, an elaborate setup that puts the rigs they install in LAPD cruisers to shame.

"Let's see…here you go…you're in luck. Looks like a Sanchez, Viviana, was detained yesterday."

"Where?" Melanie asks. She's trying to play it cool, but he can hear the excitement in her voice.

"Colonial General Hospital."

"Shit. Why there?"

"That's where they send all the Bliss cases. That's not official policy, just what I've heard."

"That doesn't sound like Viviana."

"Can't help you there."

"Thanks." Melanie ends the call. Bill stares off into the distance, wishing he'd asked Melanie if she intends to go to Colonial but already knowing the answer just the same. Bill starts the car and gets ready for the fireworks to start.

MELANIE IS GIVING KIM THE lowdown when Trevor emerges from the bedroom. He's shaved and showered and is wearing his favorite Exxon Dodgers T-shirt. He seems calmer now, more like his old self, but this isn't going to be easy.

"Any news?" he asks.

Melanie takes a deep breath. "I think we may have found Viviana."

"What does that mean?"

"HNS has her. She's at Colonial."

He goes back to the couch and sits, staring trancelike out the window. Several seconds pass before he's able to speak. "How?"

"I don't know," Melanie says. "You're just going to have to trust me."

"I have to get her out of there," he says, but he sounds eerily robotic, his mind a million miles away.

Melanie nods. "I'm going to help you."

"We're going to help you," Kim corrects her.

"I have an idea," Trevor says, and starts typing away on one of the tabs on the coffee table. "Display in holo mode," he says, and a three-dimensional hologram of the layout of Colonial General Hospital hovers in the middle of the room. The outlines of the hospital are in the same light blue that architects use in their plans.

"How did you do that?" Melanie asks.

"HNS scrubbed its servers of all information related to Colonial. But it's an old facility, built in 1965, and the architect is understandably proud of his achievement. I found the plans in an unsecured folder on the firm's database.

Melanie whistles.

"There's always a back door," Trevor says with a shrug. He's back to his coolly efficient self. There was a time when his frosty standoffishness drove Melanie crazy. Convinced it was a ruse, she'd tried to bully him into reciprocating her feelings. The intensity of her attraction was equivalent to his emotional unavailability. The harder he was to get, the more she wanted him. But it isn't a front. That's just how he is. Why has it taken her so long to understand that?

Kim enters from the kitchen with a pair of steaming mugs of tea. She hands one to Melanie and sits down on the floor. Melanie hadn't seen her get up nor heard her puttering in the kitchen. It's downright spooky how quiet she is.

"Thanks."

"No problem."

"Does any of this look familiar to you?" Trevor asks.

"Kinda," Melanie says, but the truth is it doesn't look familiar at all. She wasn't working for MIS when she went to Colonial, and this is the first time she's considered the layout. The hospital is one big tower with a central elevator and thirteen floors. The main entrance and lobby are easy to puzzle out. The next level up looks large enough to house the detention ward, which in her memories is massive. "I think this is the detention ward."

"Not anymore."

Both Melanie and Trevor turn to Kim. Trevor looks like he'd forgotten about her.

"You've been there?" he asks.

"More than once," Kim says with a touch of defiance.

"As a patient?"

"With Robert. Sometimes I went with him on his runs."

"Robert was working for HNS?"

Melanie nods.

"But not anymore?" Trevor asks.

She draws a line across her throat.

Trevor turns to Kim. "And you?"

"I was his favorite," Kim says, betraying no emotion what-soever. That was the hand she'd been dealt, and she played it. End of discussion.

Trevor fills the silence. "Do you remember the layout?"

Kim nods and moves closer to the holo to point out various features. She knows where everything is, from where they process the patients to where they make the drugs. She knows all the points of entry and is able to tell them where the security stations are located.

"That's a lot of corps," Melanie says.

"We're going to need more firepower," Trevor adds.

"What about Doyle?" Melanie asks.

"He's probably long gone," Trevor says without taking his eyes off the hologram.

"Is there a way to find out?"

"Sure, but I don't see the point." Trevor selects a tab from the pile in front of him and places a call but no one picks up. "He's not answering."

"So much for that," Melanie says.

"Hold on." Trevor hooks up the tab to a black box and flicks a switch. Crowd noise fills the apartment. People laughing, shouting, scraps of music. Trevor turns the volume down.

"What the hell?" Melanie asks.

"I put a tracker on Doyle's tab. That's how I knew about his meeting with Hansen."

"Aren't you sneaky," Melanie says.

Trevor bubbles through some screens on his laptab before pulling up a map and zooming in. "He's close."

Melanie looks over his shoulder to peer at the screen. They're closer than they've been in a week and they can both feel something, but whatever it is pushes them apart.

"What is it?" Melanie asks.

"He's at a place called Flanagan's. Looks like an Irish bar."

"Oh, my god," Melanie says. "Doyle went off the wagon."

18

FLANAGAN'S

MELANIE PULLS OPEN THE DOOR and steps into the gloom. She hears Doyle before she sees him sitting at the far end of the bar, laughing at the punch line of a joke—something about a man who goes to see a doctor about a penis growing out of his knee.

Melanie sits on the stool beside him, and Kim takes the seat next to her. Doyle quiets. An Irishman on a bender sidles up to Kim. He's dressed in work clothes and his shoes are speckled with concrete. He has the look of a man who's resolved to spend every last penny of his paycheck.

"Where ye from?" he asks Kim.

"Palo Alto."

"Paul O'Alto? I know him well." The man slaps the bar, laughing uproariously. "I've never shagged an Oriental. Is it true what they—"

In the blink of an eye, Kim has her knife out and pressed up against the Irishman's bloated neck. The woman is a magician with a blade. The man backs off and disappears into the murk. Melanie turns her attention to Doyle. His mood has gone from glib to glum, and he regards his empty tumbler with regret.

"What do you have to say for yourself?" Melanie asks.

"I fucked up."

"That's a start."

"More like an ending," Doyle says.

"It doesn't have to be."

Doyle turns and regards her with astonishment. "I'm not talking about my sobriety. Fuck my sobriety. I'm talking about Make It Stop."

"Is there something you need to tell me or are you just feeling sorry for yourself?"

"I'm only doing what's best," Doyle says.

"For you?"

"The organization."

"Yeah, well, great job."

"Right. Great job, me." Doyle raises the glass to his lips but it's empty.

Melanie swivels on the stool to give him her full attention. "What did you hope to accomplish by coming here?"

Doyle shrugs.

"We need you."

"It's over, Mel."

"They've got Viviana."

The news pains him and he closes his eyes for a moment. Melanie continues. "She's at Colonial and I think you know what that means."

"Fuck." If Doyle seemed broken before, he looks defeated now.

"We're going to get her out, but we can't do it without you."

"You don't need me."

"Yes, Doyle, we do. I need you."

Doyle shakes his head. Melanie stands.

"We're leaving. You can either come with us or keep this pity party going. What's it going to be?"

The bartender comes over and sets three shot glasses and a dusty bottle of Chadwick's on the bar. "Gent sent this over," he says as he pours out the shots. "Said to leave the bottle."

The three of them stare at the tableau before them. Doyle is the first to pick up a glass, then Kim, and finally Melanie.

"To Gary," Melanie says.

"To Robert," Kim adds.

"To Lindsay," Doyle says.

They clink their glasses together. Melanie catches a whiff of the whiskey. It smells like paint thinner mixed with diesel fuel. Doyle looks like he might gag. Kim is the only one who isn't affected.

"We don't have to do this," Melanie says.

"We can just leave these here," Doyle agrees.

"Spirits for the spirits," Kim says as she sets her drink on the bar.

"I'm sorry," Doyle says, as he takes notice of Kim for the first time. "Who are you?"

PART III
THE COLONY

18 HOURS AGO

19

PINK CLOUD

Viviana drives her white BMW 325 coupe down Moorpark Street in Sherman Oaks. She's wearing her favorite workout outfit and spent a fair amount of time putting her hair and makeup together before leaving her apartment for the last time. Although she'd made up her mind to go, there was a part of her that wanted Trevor to walk in and talk her out of it. She knows that would have only complicated things, but maybe she'd feel better about leaving if she'd told him to his face instead of sneaking away like this. Probably not, she reasons; it would have been awful. But could she feel any worse than she feels right now?

A black SUV overtakes her on the left and swerves in front of her. There's no time to lay on the horn because she has to grip the wheel and practically stand on the brakes to avoid rear-ending it. Two more SUVs swoop in from either side, boxing her in.

So, that's the score.

An HNS security officer in full riot gear pops out of the SUV directly in front of her and aims his assault rifle at the BMW. By the time he opens fire, Viviana is curled up in a ball on the floor of the passenger side of the coupe. As rounds riddle Viviana's windshield, she reaches into the glove compartment and detonates a smoke grenade. While the trigger-happy corp jams another clip into his rifle, pink smoke fills the BMW.

Time to make her move.

Viviana slips out of the car with a Glock in each hand. She emerges from the pink cloud and shoots the corp between the eyes. More goons pile out of the SUVS on either side of her. She pirouettes and squeezes off two more rounds, one from the weapon in her left hand, another from the weapon in her right. Both corps drop to the ground. The remaining corps open fire, but they aren't very well trained. As Viviana tumbles out of the way, the corps standing directly across from each other mow each other down.

"Cease fire!" shouts one of the corps.

Viviana takes him out.

"Get her!" yells the man in charge.

Another goner. This is almost too easy.

When she discovered she was pregnant, she wondered if she would be able to do this, but the fact of her pregnancy doesn't cross her mind at all. When she's finished, she isn't even winded and there are no more corps standing.

"Hello, luv."

Viviana turns and an Englishman in a blue suit bashes her in the face with the butt of an assault rifle. The last thing she sees before she goes under is the incandescent whiteness of his teeth.

20

FUCK-UPS ASSEMBLE

WHAT'S LEFT OF MIS MEETS in a nearly empty parking lot near LAX. The lot is lit but the marine layer is weirdly thick tonight, their vehicles little islands in the mist. Melanie doesn't like being out in the open like this. Feels weirdly vulnerable, though she supposes it would be worse if they were sitting in their cars. Being able to look everyone in the eye underscores the insanity of the endeavor. Four against HNS. What are they thinking?

"Let's get this started," Doyle says. His eyes are bloodshot, but he seems reasonably sober. Melanie hopes he's got some coffee in him. He nods at Trevor.

"Right," Trevor says, his voice catching. "We all enter the hospital at the same time. Doyle will engage the security at the main entrance and create a diversion. The bigger the better."

Doyle smiles crazily. Melanie can only imagine what he's got planned.

"You two," Trevor continues, turning to Melanie and Kim, "will go in the back way, infiltrate the detention level and extract Viviana."

Melanie nods.

"I'll enter the hospital the old-fashioned way—as a patient. Once inside the emergency room I'll find a way to access HNS's system and see what I can find. But remember, the key is to create as much chaos as possible."

"Easy peasy," Kim says.

No one laughs. Melanie loops her arm around Kim, shivering from the cold. It's always so much colder down here by the ocean at night. That's something else she's constantly forgetting about LA. What exactly has she learned during her time on the planet?

Not much, apparently.

"Any questions?" Trevor asks. He seems eager to get on with it.

"Where do we meet up afterward?" Melanie blurts since no one else has the guts to ask. Maybe they haven't thought it through. Maybe no one expects to make it out alive, but she doesn't want to die tonight.

Trevor hands everyone a burner tab. "Whoever gets out first can set up a meet, provided we aren't..."

"In jail," says Doyle, who seems more sober by the second.

"Or dead," Kim adds. She already has her game face on. She *always* has her game face on.

"Good luck," Trevor says.

Melanie feels ill at ease, as if something has come between her and the others. She doesn't know what it is exactly, but it prevents her from reaching out to Trevor and Doyle and telling them how much they mean to her. No one hugs or says goodbye. They all just drift to their vehicles.

"I'm driving," Kim says to Melanie.

"Sure," Melanie says, tossing her the keys.

"Melanie?" Trevor interrupts. "Can I talk to you for a sec?"

"I guess," Melanie says. She hopes Trevor will say something, anything, to dispel this pervasive feeling of doom but she isn't counting on it. There's a part of her that wonders if this feeling is a hangover from the Bliss Hansen injected into her. Kim said she'd have cravings, but what about withdrawals? Is that what this is? Or is it always going to be like this?

"There's something I need to tell you," Trevor says as they wander off into the fog, "and I need you to hear me out."

Melanie begins to protest, but Trevor cuts her off.

"It's about Bill."

"Not this shit again," Melanie says, suddenly angry.

"Your detective friend is not who you think he is," Trevor says.

"Trevor, I don't have time for your conspiracies."

"You talked to him earlier today, right? On one of my tabs at Viviana's apartment?"

"Yeah, so?"

"I traced the call and got his name—his real name—home address, everything."

"You can't do that, Trevor. He's a cop!"

"Not according to the LAPD. He doesn't show up anywhere in their system."

"You don't expect me to believe —"

"No, I don't, so I called him and confronted him about it."

"And?"

"Why don't you ask him yourself."

Trevor looks beyond Melanie and she turns to see a pair of headlights cutting through the fog. Bill's big brown sedan rolls across the parking lot and comes to a stop about fifteen feet away. The lights switch off and Bill steps out of the car.

"I'll let you two talk," Trevor says and walks away.

"So, it's true?" Melanie asks Bill to break the silence.

"I'm afraid so."

"What are you, one of those cop-loving creeps with a hard-on for handcuffs?" Melanie's pissed and doesn't see the point in trying to hide it.

"It's not like that."

"What's it like then?"

"My dad was a cop," Bill says with a shrug. "The shoe fit."

"But why?" Melanie is so tired of being lied to she almost regrets the question. It feels like the more she needs to know the truth the further away it gets.

"My sister," Bill says. "She was one of the first to OD on Bliss. I tried to get justice for her, do things the right way, but no one cared. She was just another dead junkie."

Melanie's head swims. "I'm sorry…but why me?"

"She was in Make It Stop."

Melanie gets it now. "Lindsay."

Bill nods.

Lindsay Moran, the poor girl she replaced on the ops team and whose identity she used for a cover story at Evergreen.

"I'm so sorry."

"Yeah, me too," Bill says.

Melanie wishes she had something to take the pain away, a bottle, a pill, a quick screw in the back of Bill's sedan. Is that the Bliss talking? A new idea worms its way into her brain.

"Were you really in the bomb squad or was that a lie, too?"

"That part was true. Why?"

"I want to introduce you to someone."

Melanie slips her arm in Bill's and walks him over to Doyle as he takes a furtive sip from a thermos.

"That better be coffee," Melanie snaps.

"Unfortunately."

"This is Bill. He was in the Army. He's going in with you."

"Now wait a minute…"

"He's good with explosives."

This gets Doyle's attention. "Oh, really? I've got a little something you might find very interesting…"

The two head off toward Doyle's car. Melanie can only shake her head. As she makes her way back to the HNS truck, Trevor drives by in the sprinter van, waving from the driver's seat as he heads out of the lot. Melanie climbs into the passenger seat of the HNS pickup.

"Can I ask you a question?" Kim asks.

"Sure," Melanie says.

"You trust these people?"

"Of course. Why do you ask?"

"Don't take this the wrong way, but after everything I've heard about Make It Stop, I was expecting something a little more... professional."

"Yeah, me too." Melanie says.

Kim cranks the engine, drops the shifter into drive, and burns rubber out of the parking lot.

21

COLONIAL GENERAL HOSPITAL

ONCE A RESPECTED MEDICAL FACILITY, Colonial General Hospital was on the brink of being shut down before it was sold to Health Net Secure, whose CEO, Derek Hansen, promised to restore the hospital to its former prominence as a first-rate caregiving institution.

That didn't happen. If anything, the quality of care worsened. It got so bad, Trevor recalls, ambulance drivers refused to take non-critical patients to Colonial. The ER was staffed by overworked residents and supervised by physicians no one else would hire. Hansen's first move was to make the drug and alcohol detoxification and rehabilitation center at Colonial a conditional release facility, and patients, who viewed the hospital as a kind of penal colony, referred to it as such. Then they started manufacturing Bliss at The Colony and everything got much, much worse.

Desperate souls still wander into its emergency room at night, and now Trevor will be next. Armed with a modified laptab and a straight razor, Trevor pulls into the guest parking lot outside the emergency room and kills the engine. He turns on the interior light, angles the rearview mirror away from him, and opens the razor. It had been his father's blade and it was extremely sharp. His father had kept a whetstone in the garage and would spend entire weekends sharpening the kitchen knives and gardening equipment while listening to the Dodgers on the radio. It was a skill he'd picked up from his own father, a handyman whose main line at the end of his life was knife sharpening. "The work is never dull," Trevor's grandfather was fond of saying.

Trevor smiles at the memory, holds the knife up to his neck, and nicks the tip of his earlobe. Blood pours down his neck. Taking care not to touch the wound with his hands, Trevor gets out of the sprinter van and crosses the parking lot to the emergency room. He goes through the sliding glass doors, passing a pair of EMTs, neither of whom give him a second look. He might as well be invisible, which is precisely what Trevor wants, what he's always wanted.

He proceeds directly to the admissions desk and addresses a bored-looking Filipina in hospital scrubs.

"I'm sorry to bother you," he says as his blood drips onto the counter, "but I seem to be in a bit of distress."

"IT LOOKS LIKE A LIGHTHOUSE," Melanie says as they approach the hospital. Colonial General Hospital rises out of the gloom like a tower of light. The first rehab center she went to down in San Diego was called The Lighthouse, which she thought was messed up. Sure, from land a lighthouse may *look* like a symbol of safety and refuge, but when you're bucketing about the storm-tossed seas of life it's the last thing you want to see on the horizon. A lighthouse means stay away. A lighthouse means crazy fucking danger. A lighthouse means change course or die. There's nothing subtle about a lighthouse.

No wonder Melanie only lasted a few days in that shithole.

"I always thought it looked like a jail," Kim says, taking the off-ramp. She whips the pickup onto a surface street, suspension rattling, and speeds past the hospital's entrance. She points the truck toward the back. It won't be long now. Melanie feels like she should say something like, "You ready to kick some ass?" but doesn't know how to pull that off without sounding corny. It sounds like something a dude would say, and a dumb dude at that.

"You ready to kick some ass?" Kim asks.

Melanie tries not to laugh, so it spurts out of her mouth like a cough, but a laugh is a laugh and it works its magic on her nerves.

"Problem?" Kim asks.

"Sorry," Melanie says.

Kim eases into an empty space next to the loading dock. She gets out of the car and Melanie follows. Kim moves with confidence and for that Melanie is grateful because the second Kim pulls open the loading dock door and steps inside, Melanie realizes she isn't ready for this.

They're in some kind of shipping and receiving area the size of a small warehouse with towers of boxes stacked along the walls that rise to the ceiling and more boxes piled haphazardly throughout the room. There's Bliss in these boxes. Melanie knows it like she knows her birthday. It's the smell that gets her. The aroma of the drug triggers something in her body that sends a message to her mind. *This is what you want. This is why you're here.* Sweet, seductive mindfuck.

"I-I can't do this," Melanie whispers.

"You got this." Kim says, latching on to Melanie's arm to prevent her from pulling away.

"The smell…"

"Put it out of your mind and breathe through your mouth."

"I can't," Melanie says, but Kim isn't having it.

"You're not listening," she insists, her eyes full of daggers. "Just. Breathe."

Melanie does what she's told and takes in a lungful of air. After three deep breaths, she feels a little bit better though better isn't the right word exactly because now what she feels is disgust instead of desire. Is she ever going to feel normal again or is feeling normal only something normal people feel?

"Can I help you?"

A tall, heavy-set man wearing a facemask, latex gloves, hard hat, and a safety vest towers over them. He holds a tab housed in an industrial strength case. He must be in charge here, a foreman or something.

"Where's Robert?" Kim asks.

The question doesn't make sense to Melanie. If Kim only ever came here with Robert, wouldn't this guy know that?

"Haven't seen him," the foreman says, his gaze traveling from Kim to Melanie and lingering there for what feels like a long time. It's hard to read his expression with the mask on.

"He said to meet him down here," Kim says.

"Pick up or drop off?"

"Pick up," Kim says. "You got something for me?"

The foreman takes his eyes off of Melanie long enough to consult his tab. "I don't have you on the list," he says.

"Robert probably forgot to call it in," Kim says. "I'll try the lab."

"You know where it is?" the man asks, his eyes back on Melanie.

"Of course," Kim snaps.

Melanie has to hand it to her: Kim doesn't suffer fools—even when she's full of shit.

Melanie sizes up the foreman. He's probably in his thirties but looks older. Behind him, more men package up boxes for delivery. They're all wearing paper masks.

"You got any more of these?" Melanie leans forward and taps the man's mask where his lips would be.

"Over there," the man says, nodding at the desk next to the time clock where the paper masks are stacked.

"Thanks." Melanie grabs a mask and slips it on. She hands one to Kim who does the same.

The foreman shakes his head as he walks away.

"Feel better?" Kim asks.

She doesn't, but it's easier to say yes.

VIVIANA COMES TO IN A darkened cell. She has no idea how she got here or how long she's been out. Her arms and legs are restrained, fastened to some kind of table, and it's too dark to tell if trying to tip it over will gain any kind of advantage or cause an immense amount of pain and hurt her baby. Once the panic subsides, the sadness sets in. Not for herself, or even her baby, which she hasn't reached a final decision about, but for Trevor, who will never know her true feelings for him. And how could he when she didn't know herself until this very moment?

She thought she could be strong, whatever that means, and do this herself, but those are just words, affirmations she'd told herself because she was scared out of her mind. Now she'd give anything to go back in time and be waiting in her apartment when Trevor walks through the door. She'd tell him everything and they'd figure out what to do. Together.

The door creaks open, letting in a shaft of light. The prick who'd knocked her out in the street enters the cell, but doesn't close the door behind him. Is he taking her somewhere?

He walks right up and looks her up and down. He doesn't seem drunk or high but...off. A little too happy to be here.

"Can I help you?" she asks.

"Oh, that's rich," the man says with a strong English accent. "Do you know who I am?"

"Should I?" Viviana asks. She honestly has no idea, but this man's identity is tied to his ego, and that's always a dangerous thing.

"Your colleagues at Make It Stop know who I am."

Viviana gets the sense he isn't bluffing, and with her cover blown neither should she. "I see."

"I'm afraid you don't, darling," the man says as he strokes her cheek, "but you will."

She doesn't know what this dude's trip is, but he's giving off a pervy vibe. If the bastard climbs on top of her, she's going to take her chances and tell him she's pregnant. It probably won't make a difference, but it's her best shot.

The man takes off his jacket and rolls up his sleeves but keeps his pants on. He opens a plastic case with care. This, Viviana realizes, is the object of his infatuation. It's written all over his face as he reaches into the case and removes a syringe.

Panic rips through her like an electric current as she realizes, too late, she would give up her life for this baby.

He probes her arm and when he finds the vein, he strokes it with tenderness. He swabs the spot with a cotton ball dipped in alcohol. She can hear the man's breathing as he primes the syringe. Viviana tenses, waiting for the needle to plunge inside her. She makes the mistake of looking up at the man, his eyes rolling back in ecstasy.

"Hansen?" a voice calls from the doorway.

Hansen stops. His expression goes cold. "What is it?"

A man so large he has to stoop to pass through the doorway enters the room. "MIS has breached the facility."

"How many?" Hansen asks.

"It's her," the man says.

"Fuck," Hansen whispers.

Melanie, Viviana thinks. Has to be. Only Melanie could make someone this angry.

Hansen takes a deep breath and returns the needle to the case. The two men exit the cell, but the door stays open and she can hear Hansen tell someone to take her to detention.

A pair of corps enter the room, decked out in riot gear. They disengage the gurney's wheel locks and push her out of the darkness.

"Come on, baby," one of them says, "let's go for a ride."

MELANIE FOLLOWS KIM DOWN A long, empty corridor with rows of lockers on the left, few of which seem to be in use.

"This feels familiar," Melanie says.

"Starting to come back to you?"

"I think so," Melanie says. They're on the detention level now.

"Here we go." Kim pushes through a heavy fire door at the end of the hall into a wide-open ward that Melanie recognizes immediately. It's been two years since she's been here, and although she's returned many times in her dreams, the reality is so much worse than her nightmares.

The ward is packed with people and nearly all of them are kannibals. She doesn't see any cots or makeshift camps like in Evergreen. Those who are able to stand huddle in circles, but most sit on the floor, propped up against each other or passed out where they lie. Whatever Melanie had prepared herself for, it wasn't this. This is awful. And then the smell hits her.

"Oh, fuck."

"Yeah," Kim says. "It's intense. You see your girl?"

Melanie doesn't answer. She doesn't know where to look. She keeps fixating on the piles of half-naked bodies. It's like the end of a zombie movie where the undead hordes are on the verge of taking over. If Viviana is here, she's in trouble.

"Hey!" Kim snaps.

"I'm looking!" The truth is Melanie is afraid of what she'll find. She never liked Viviana, but no one deserves this. No one.

Across the ward she spots a pair of corps in riot gear accompanying a trio of HNS workers covered in PPE. She watches a corp prod an unresponsive kannibal with a submission stick. When the body on the floor doesn't move, the workers drag it away. As the corps clear a path through the crowd, Melanie catches a glimpse of a woman sitting with her back against the wall, her hair hanging down in her face.

"There," Melanie says.

"Go," Kim says.

Melanie slowly crosses the ward, careful to avoid bumping into someone. She can feel Kim behind her and it's a good feeling. With Kim watching out for her, she feels strong enough for anything.

"Viviana," Melanie says, a notch above a whisper, but she doesn't respond. Melanie brushes the hair out of her face. *Please let it be Viviana*, and, *Please don't be a kannibal*, cycle through her thoughts.

It's her, but her eyelids are swollen and bruised, and her mouth is caked with blood.

"Viviana," Melanie says again, a little louder and a touch sharper.

"Oh!" Viviana jerks awake, startled and afraid.

"It's okay," Melanie says.

"Melanie? Is that you?"

"We're gonna get you out of here."

Tears stream out of the slits in Viviana's eyes. "Oh, Mel. I'm so sorry."

"It's fine," Melanie says, which is a stupid thing to say but how else is she supposed to answer? "Can you stand?"

Viviana nods and Melanie and Kim lift her to her feet.

"You must be Viviana," Kim says.

"Yeah," Viviana says, looking uncomfortable.

"Congratulations," Kim says.

Viviana doesn't understand. She looks from Kim to Melanie and sees the answer in their eyes.

"You know?"

Melanie nods. Viviana begins to tear up.

"We've got company," Kim says. Melanie turns and sees the pair of corps approaching, but now they're flanking Hansen and Applewhite, which she doesn't find nearly as upsetting as the sight of her cat sitting in the crook of Applewhite's arm. She loves that traitorous little bitch with her whole heart, but seeing Abigail here in this terrible place stupefies her with anger.

"Well, well, well," Hansen says, his teeth shining unnaturally, "just who we've been looking for."

THE FRONT OF COLONIAL GENERAL Hospital is made of tinted glass, so all Doyle sees as he approaches the building is his own ragged reflection. He's seen better days for sure, but how is he supposed to look? He flushed twenty-six years of sobriety down the drain. If Melanie hadn't shown up when she did, who knows where he'd be, or in what condition. He owes her this. He's alive. Who cares what he looks like?

The glass doors slide open with a hiss. Doyle shouts, "I need a wheelchair!"

The half-dozen or so people in the lobby look his way but no one moves except for a bored-looking corp sitting behind the welcome desk, and all he does is point to an alcove where four wheelchairs are nestled together like shopping carts. Doyle jerks one free and wheels it out the door and he doesn't stop until he reaches the trunk of Bill's sedan.

"Ready?" Doyle asks.

Bill lifts a CPR dummy out of the trunk and sets it in the wheelchair.

"Were you going to tell me why you have this in your car?"

Bill rips off a long piece of duct tape with his teeth. He seems confused by the question. "No."

Bill starts duct taping the dummy to the chair. Doyle goes to his car and removes a wad of Semtex from the trunk.

Bill stops what he's doing. "You had *that* in your vehicle?"

"Yep," Doyle says as he tapes the explosive to the dummy's midsection.

"But what if someone rear-ended you?"

Doyle shrugs. He'd prefer to focus on the detonator. Doyle hooks an eyebrow. "And?"

"It's your party," Bill says with a shrug.

"You're damn right it is."

Doyle pushes the wheelchair back to the hospital's front entrance, whistling Bartók. When he was in the Marines, he'd become intimate with the disposal of improvised explosive devices, which required he become an expert in how to make them. This one isn't large enough to do any significant structural damage to the building, but it will get plenty of attention. He pushes the chair across the parking lot and guides it up the handicap ramp because you can't be too careful.

"Fire in the hole!" he yells and gives the chair a hard shove into the lobby, cackling as he double times back to Bill's car.

AFTER BEING TOLD IT WOULD be hours before someone could give him a suture and he'd be better off going to an urgent care facility, Trevor thanks the redheaded nurse practitioner who'd slapped a bandage on his ear and told her he'd do just that; but instead of going home, he goes to the elevator and, using the key card he'd lifted while she took his blood pressure, rides it up to the third floor where the hospital's server room is located. He powers on his laptab and by the time the elevator reaches its destination, he's got the layout on his screen.

The office suite has seen better days. The high-traffic carpet gives way to dingy tile, bare fluorescent tubes burn with garish efficiency, and an unpleasant odor lingers in the air like a bad memory. Even though his eyes are glued to his screen, Trevor walks through the open office like he knows where he's going. The server room should be right over here, Trevor thinks, but something's wrong. The floor rises up underneath his feet as an explosion rips a hole in the ceiling and everything goes black.

"YOU GOT AWAY FROM ME once," Hansen sneers, "but it won't happen again."

The Englishman steps forward and the corps close in, submission sticks at the ready. Melanie refuses to be cowed by this cocky little man. It's Applewhite who has her worried. If he does anything to Abigail, she swears to God she'll...

"Bite me," Melanie growls.

"I'll do better than that," Hansen replies. "I'm going to give you another chartered trip to an island of bliss."

He produces a little plastic container the size of an eyeglass case and opens it, revealing a pair of disposable syringes that Melanie presumes are loaded with Bliss. Hansen takes one out and holds it up for her to see.

"You like? By the end of the week, there'll be thousands of these on the streets. It was my idea to package them in pairs so couples can trip the light fucktastic!"

"That's...insane," Melanie says.

"Isn't it?"

For a moment Melanie thinks Hansen's going to laugh, and then he does, a sharp barking sound.

"You are going to absolutely love this!" Hansen snaps the cap off the syringe and inspects its readiness.

Melanie feels her throat close and her mouth go dry. There is something terribly wrong with this man, she realizes. Something so irretrievably broken she almost feels sorry for him. How does someone slip so far down the ladder of humanity? She can think her thoughts but is powerless to put them into action. Whatever Bliss remains inside her system is enough to shut down all resistance.

"Are you ready for another taste?"

Melanie can't bring herself to refuse. The part of her brain that wants to be blissed out forever makes it impossible to form words.

"Melanie?" a concerned voice asks.

She's so focused on the syringe she doesn't know if it's Viviana or Kim who's calling out to her. She tries to answer but can only make what sounds like a low growl of base desire that rises in strength and intensity until she realizes this roar can't possibly be coming from her.

It's Doyle.

The fucker came through.

She pounces.

DOYLE DOESN'T HEAR THE EXPLOSION, but he sure as hell feels it. The blast flattens him to the asphalt, where he'd taken cover behind his car. The concussive force presses down on him like the hand of God. He's never felt anything like it and in its immediate aftermath—head numb, heart pounding, his body showered with glass—he experiences an epiphany: no drink could ever hope to compete with the mind-numbing, brain-stunning force of *that*.

The scene is eerily quiet. Doyle peeks his head over the trunk of the car. The entire front of the hospital is gone. The glass has simply disintegrated. Fires burn on several floors. The palm trees flanking the entrance blaze like tiki torches with flaming fronds dropping out of the sky like messengers of death. All of the cars and trucks in the parking lot have had their windows blown out, including his own. A single column of oily white smoke rises into the sky. Apparently, he's a bit out of practice in the improvised explosive department.

"Holy shit," he says but can't hear the words. He must have blown out his eardrums, too. He hopes the damage isn't permanent.

Doyle looks down and sees Bill lying on the asphalt, bleeding from a cut on his forehead. He tries to rouse him but gets no response.

He checks his vitals.

Nothing.

Shit, shit, shit.

Doyle opens the trunk, grabs his Mossberg tactical shotgun, and crosses the parking lot. He can feel the glass crunching underfoot but can't hear it, which is weird. As he approaches the wrecked lobby, he chambers a round. He keeps low to avoid the smoke. The spot where the wheelchair came to rest is just a black mark in the middle of the lobby. He doesn't see any casualties.

He doubts the elevators work and doesn't trust them to stay operational if they do. He heads for the stairwell marked with emergency signage directly across from the elevator. As he reaches for the door, the elevator slides open. It's filled with corps. Doyle lights them up, pumping round after round into the elevator car. Some return fire, the rounds pinging off the door behind him, but he keeps at it until all of the corps are down.

He puts his hand on the door to push it open, leaving a bloody handprint on the paint.

His blood. He doesn't make it very far and collapses on the stairs. He fumbles with his tab, types out a quick message, and hits send. What a terrible thing, he thinks as the device slips from his fingers, to never hear the round that has your name on it.

TREVOR LOOKS UP INTO THE night sky. It's cold and dark and the wind is blowing, and he can smell smoke. He's on his back surrounded by a halo of glass. Did he die?

An emergency light clicks on, solving the mystery of his existence. He's lying on the floor outside the server room at Colonial General Hospital, staring up into a hole in the ceiling that is not the sky but the floor above. About a dozen feet to his right, the floor drops off into nothingness. The glass wall is simply gone. From this spot on the floor, he can see the night sky and the beach cities south of the airport laid out before him like coins, orange and dull. It's like looking out of the mouth of a great snake.

Trevor's not alone. Lying next to him is an enormous man, bald and bleeding. Trevor has no idea who he is, and guesses he came through the hole in the ceiling. Sitting atop the bleeding man's chest is a black and white cat, licking at the blood dribbling down the man's neck. Trevor may be dazed, he may be confused, but he swears he recognizes the cat from his countless conversations with Melanie, her cat weaving in and out of the hologram.

"Abigail?"

The cat stops what it's doing and looks at Trevor. It's definitely her. What the hell is Melanie's cat doing here?

"Meow!" Abigail answers.

"Where did you come from?"

Trevor can make out the muffled sounds of gunshots. The ceiling creaks and sways like some massive erector set that could come toppling down at any second. In the distance, sirens wail. It's time to go.

He picks himself off the ground with a groan and tries to brush off the dust and broken glass, but there's so much of it he gives up. His head throbs—he's probably concussed—and his ear fucking hurts. He has no idea how long he's been out. Hopefully only a minute or two.

He locates his laptab. The screen glows and seems to work. He forces open the door to the server room and surveys the jumble. Everything's shifted around but the gear looks secure. He links his laptab to the server and starts bubbling through screens until he finds what he's looking for: a cache of files concerning the manufacture and distribution of Bliss. Materials shipped into the hospital, product pushed out. Everything.

"Meow."

"That's right, Abigail. We got 'em."

He scoops Abigail into his arms and waits for the files to download. Shouldn't take too long, but he feels a kind of unease that has nothing to do with his head injury. He turns and peers into the suite.

The big bald man is gone.

MELANIE PUSHES THE CORP OFF of her that she'd knocked out with his own submission stick. How strange the corps' gear doesn't protect them from their own weapons. She had the presence of mind to pull the unconscious corp on top of her when Doyle blew up the building. There's another one on the floor that she assumes Kim disposed of.

Light from an emergency sign cuts through the dust. Injured rehabees call out from underneath shifting mounds of debris. The able-bodied struggle to assist the wounded. The less fortunate cry out for help. One of the interior walls has partially collapsed and kannibals swarm out of the ward and into the hospital. Applewhite's nowhere to be seen, but Hansen darts through the doorway they used to reach the ward.

"There he is," Kim cries out.

There he goes, Melanie thinks, as Kim activates a submission stick.

Melanie turns to Viviana. "Can you walk?"

"Help your friend," Kim says. "I'll take care of Hansen."

"Wait!" Melanie calls out but it's too late, she's already another shadow slipping through the darkness.

"What's happening?" Viviana asks.

"We're leaving." Melanie pulls Viviana to her feet.

"Is…" Viviana hesitates but Melanie knows what she's thinking, what she's wanted to know all along, and she can't blame her one bit.

"Trevor's here. Doyle, too. Come on."

Viviana nods. She has trouble walking at first but quickly gets into a rhythm and they reach the exit in no time. By the time they get to the end of the hallway with the lockers, they're practically jogging. Halfway down the stairs, the sound of a gunshot from below echoes through the stairwell. Melanie stops and peers over the railing and sees two figures: one on the floor, the other kneeling. Kim and Hansen.

"Hey!" Melanie calls out and charges down the stairs. Hansen slips out the door, leaving Kim on the stairwell floor, clutching her knee.

"What did he do to you?!" Melanie asks, struggling to control her rage.

"What do you think he did? He shot me," Kim grimaces.

"Oh, my god," Viviana says as she catches up.

"Did he…" Melanie doesn't finish.

"No," Kim says. "He was about to stick me when you came along."

Melanie's not a doctor, but Kim's knee is a mess. Melanie rips off Viviana's shirt and uses it as a tourniquet.

"Kim knows her way out of here," Melanie says to Viviana, "and you're going to help her." She turns back to Kim. "Where's your tab?"

"In my bra," Kim says.

Melanie fishes it out. "See you outside."

She takes off before either one of them can talk her out of it.

THE WAREHOUSE LOOKS MORE OR less the same as when she left it: lights operational, structure intact, but several boxes have toppled from their stacks, their contents spread across the concrete floor. Melanie creeps through the mess, careful not to step on any of packages of Bliss. It would be so easy to pick one up and stash it for later.

Stop it.

She can't let her mind go there. She's got to keep it together and stay focused on Hansen. She can hear him shouting at her from across the warehouse, but as she crouches behind a stack, she accidentally kicks a roll of packing tape that goes rattling across the floor.

"There you are," Hansen calls out.

Melanie keeps moving. When Hansen comes to investigate, she needs to be somewhere else. She scuttles out of the way and takes cover behind another stack of boxes as Hansen heads toward the noise, stalking her.

"The first time we met," he says, taunting her, "I thought, *what's a nice girl like her doing in a terrible place like this?*"

He pounces on the spot where Melanie had been hiding, but she's moved on.

"One thing I've learned from people like you," Hansen says, "is you all think you're special. Your friend thought he was special—right up until the end. But I took care of that."

Melanie freezes. Is he saying what she thinks he's saying? He killed Gary?

Hansen slowly creeps her way. She can hear his voice getting louder. Melanie dials a number on her tab.

"But you know something?" he continues.

While she waits for the call to go through, she peers around the corner, and watches Hansen holster his weapon and take out the syringe.

"You're not nice, and you're not special."

Hansen makes his move but Melanie doesn't bother putting up a fight. Instead, she gives him the bird. Hansen slashes at her but his arm goes right through her because it's not Melanie he's attacking, but her hologram.

"What the…?"

Melanie races around he stack of boxes and rabbit punches Hansen in the kidneys. Hansen doubles over and she puts him in a chokehold, which enrages him. Hansen lashes out with the syringe, trying to stab her with the needle.

Melanie releases him and aims a well-timed kick at his head. Hansen tries to block the blow, which is smart, but he uses the hand holding the syringe, which isn't. It's a mistake Hansen instantly regrets as Melanie's foot drives his hand backward, plunging the needle into his eyeball, through the eye socket, and into his brain.

"That's for Gary," Melanie says.

Hansen drops to his knees. His hands fall away, the needle protruding from his eye.

Viviana and Kim finally show up.

"Ew," Viviana says when she sees Hansen.

"Gnarly," Kim adds.

"Oooooo," Hansen says as the drug takes hold.

Kannibals pour into the warehouse, drawn by the scent of the Bliss.

"We should go," Melanie says.

As the three ops slip out of the warehouse, Melanie looks back and sees the kannibals overwhelm Hansen, searching for the drug they can smell but can't do without. They tear at his clothes, his skin, the needle in his eye. It's a gruesome sight, ghastly and barbaric, but she needs to see it. For Lindsay and Morris and all the lives he ruined, but mostly for Gary. *Never let someone off the mat who's trying to put you in the ground.*

Melanie wonders if Hansen is in pain, if the shot of Bliss to the brain has put him in an opioid nirvana, a place where the pain of this world can no longer reach him.

Hansen screams.

So much for that.

TREVOR IS STILL IN THE server room, impatiently eyeing his laptab screen while he whispers under his breath. "Come on...come on..."

A message on the screen indicates the transfer of a file called KBLISS.DIST is at 99%. The second it reads "COMPLETE" Trevor stuffs the laptab in his jacket and scoops up Abigail. He warily makes his way through the ruined office. At the spot where he was knocked unconscious are two outlines in the carpet where he and his large companion had been resting. Had he crashed through the floor and landed on top of him? Is that what knocked him out?

Trevor continues on his way, but this time he takes the stairs. When he reaches the landing between the first floor and the bottom, he sees Doyle sprawled in a pool of blood.

Trevor calls out his name but he doesn't answer. Trevor sets Abigail down and checks Doyle's pulse. Nothing. His hand feels cool to the touch. Trevor picks up Doyle's bloodstained tab and reads the screen. He'd sent a message before he died. One word. MAYDAY.

Trevor checks his tab, but he doesn't have any messages. Who was he messaging and why?

"Meow," Abigail cries.

"I don't know either, girl."

"You might want to buckle up," Melanie says to her passengers as she stomps on the gas and goes tearing around the corner to the front of the hospital, which looks like a disaster zone. She can hear Kim grimacing beside her as she clutches her knee.

Melanie bears down on the hospital entrance where chaos reigns. Dozens of men and women wearing face masks and scrubs are at the scene, leading kannibals out of the hospital. Amid the confusion, she sees Trevor and Bill carrying Doyle.

"Is that Trevor?" Viviana asks.

Melanie doesn't answer because she sees what they don't: that motherfucker Applewhite staggering out of the hospital.

Well, she has something to say about that and goes careening toward the entrance. Trevor clocks the truck barreling down on him. Their eyes lock and she sees his fear turn to something else, a look so languid and purely Trevor that he owns it entirely. There's no name for this expression. It's just Trevor. What does he see in her eyes in that moment? Recklessness? Determination? Homicide?

Because she's not driving the truck anymore. She's aiming it at Applewhite.

Trevor and Bill skip out of the way. People in hospital scrubs scatter. Time grinds its gears as Melanie cycles through memories of those eternal nights in Evergreen, waiting for Applewhite to take her. But time slows for no one. Not Melanie and certainly not Applewhite—not this time—who doesn't see the truck until Melanie slams into him, sending the dumb brute pinballing into a concrete pillar that cracks his skull open. Melanie stands on the brakes to slow the vehicle before it too crashes into the pillar, crushing Applewhite's legs. He collapses on the hood of the truck and looks up at Melanie and finally sees who did this to him as his brains spill out of his cracked melon.

"Remember me?" Melanie asks.

Viviana and Kim spill out of the truck as the airbags go off. Melanie climbs on top of that big white balloon and rides it to the edge of the atmosphere.

22

INPATIENT

MELANIE WAKES IN A CLEAN, bright place, and for several moments her mind races about how wrong she'd been about the afterlife. If she'd known it was going to be just like rehab, she wouldn't have worried about it so much. But it's not just her thoughts buzzing around, she can fly, too, so off she goes never quite sure what's sky and what's cloud. Soaring softly and softly soaring and all of it so boring, boring, boring. She can hear the faint squeak of rubber-soled shoes on a freshly waxed floor, the smell of lemon-scented detergent and fresh gardenias. Melanie begins to suspect, and then to realize, this isn't a post-earth situation. She's in a hospital and the heavenly feeling comes not from finally being free of this disappointing body but from whatever drugs they've got flowing into her.

Then she remembers Kim and Viviana, who were in bad shape, and Hansen and Applewhite, whom she hopes are dead, thanks to her. That leaves Trevor and Bill and Doyle who are…she doesn't know.

She opens her eyes and sees Trevor standing over her with a bundle of flowers and a mournful expression that tells her everything she doesn't want to know.

"Doyle?"

"Didn't make it," Trevor says.

"How?"

"Corps got him, but not before he got a message out to some volunteers he'd recruited from other organizations."

"The people in the scrubs," Melanie says. "They were vigilantes?"

"Yeah, with their help we were able to get everyone out of The Colony."

"Did you know he was talking to them?" Melanie asks.

"No," Trevor says.

That was the old man's big secret. He wasn't collaborating with HNS, but enlisting the help of other outfits. Melanie can feel the tears spilling down her stupid face.

"What about Kim?"

"She's a fighter. She lost a lot of blood. If you hadn't gotten her out of there when you did, it would be a different story."

"Is she here?"

"She'll be by later."

"And Viviana?"

"Fine. Bill, too, incredibly. He's tougher than he looks."

Was that a crack? Melanie doesn't know and doesn't care, not when she doesn't know why she's in the hospital.

"What about me? Am I okay?"

Trevor laughs. "I wouldn't say *okay*, but yeah."

Melanie isn't sure how to say what needs to be said. She's just grateful he isn't handing her any of that bullshit about needing to rest and not getting too excited, all those annoying things people say to you in hospitals. If she wanted to pull the needle out of her arm (not that she would, it's all she has going for her) and leave the hospital bare-ass naked, Trevor would find a way to make it happen.

"Are you ready for some good news?"

"Please," Melanie says through a yawn.

She feels tired and fuzzy, like a caterpillar in a cocoon.

Trevor looks at her strangely. "Cocoon?"

"Oh, did I say that out loud?"

"You've been saying a lot of things," Trevor says.

"Just tell me something good," she said.

"I've got your cat."

"Abigail! You found her!"

"Something like that," Trevor smiles. He's so damn adorable when he smiles. Maybe being a dad will bring that out of him more. "There's more."

"Tell me," Melanie said.

"We were able to obtain all the evidence the Feds need to shut down HNS, hopefully for good. Hansen had a partner, the scientist who developed the drug, and apparently their partnership soured. He'd made a copy of all the data and was going to cut and run when we came along."

"And Hansen?" Melanie asks, just to be on the safe side.

"Dead."

"Applewhite, too?"

"Oh, yeah."

"Good." That's all that needs to be said about that.

"The DA has issued a warrant for Hansen's partner," Trevor continues, "but so far they haven't been able to locate him."

"He's flown the coop," Melanie says, which strikes her as funny even though it isn't.

"We have a lot of catching up to do," Trevor says, looking uncomfortable, "but I want to say thank you for getting Viviana out of there."

"I like her," Melanie says, "and she's smoking hot."

"I noticed," Trevor says.

"How long have I been out?" she asks, yawning again.

"Since last night."

"Where's my tab?" she tries to move her arms again but can't—not because she's tired and out of it but because she's shackled to the bed.

"What the—"

"You've been through a lot," Trevor says. "You need to get some rest."

Oh, *hell* no.

"Don't give me that," Melanie says, violently pulling on her restraints. "Get me some clothes and let's get out of here." Even as the words leave her lips, she knows neither of these things are going to happen. Trevor's face says it all. She's too tired, too spent. It takes just about everything she has not to cry.

"Listen, the data we discovered contained the chemical compound for Bliss as well as the breakdown for how it's made and what goes into it. The drug was designed to produce harmful side effects. In other words, they made it that way on purpose. The doctors here have been able to use the information to combat the effects of the drug. It's really very interesting. The synthetic opioid…"

"Trevor, am I in a detox ward?"

Trevor nods. "You're safe. This isn't a conditional release facility. We're not even in California. Doyle's distraction attracted a lot of attention."

"Where are we?"

"Arizona."

"Arizona!"

"We can leave as soon as the situation cools off and we get the drug out of your system."

"What are you trying to tell me?"

"You were exposed to Bliss."

"But I didn't—"

"It's mostly a precaution, the way the molecules…"

Melanie stops listening.

So, this is how it ends, she thinks. In like a hero, out like a junkie.

But how did it get into her system? She remembers the syringe sticking out of Hansen's eyeball. Did that really happen? She can see it plain as day, eating egg salad sandwiches with the crusts cut off with Hansen. But that's not right. Hansen is dead, like her mom. She's the one who made the sandwiches. There was a time when her lunches were the envy of her friends. Strange vegetables. Exotic fruits. Cheeses she still can't pronounce. Naturally, Melanie grew bored with them. Sometimes she wanted a bean and cheese burrito or a cup of ramen like everyone else. Then mom stopped making lunches. Sometimes Janet gave her money, but only sometimes.

Melanie hangs onto the memory of those lunches with her mother so they don't slip away, but thanks to the marvel of modern medicine the memory replays in her mind so vividly it might as well be happening now. She takes it all in, the ocean breeze, the crazy blanket with the zigzag pattern. They had separate thermoses, of course, with lemonade for Melanie and purple juice for her mother, which was obviously wine, but maybe not, let's keep this a happy memory and say it wasn't; and the light was beautiful and her mother so pretty with her sunglasses on so they could both forget about why she was wearing them; and the ants, of course there were ants, followed the zigzagging lines on the blanket like it was a maze that led to the promised land of the most fantastic sandwiches ever, the picnic blanket their little life raft in a sea of shadows. They say memories are stories the mind tells itself. She saw that in a video on her tab one night and the truth of it landed like a punch. But if she could hang onto this memory, and let the rest of them go, maybe, just maybe, she'll be okay.

23

AFTERCARE

Were all vigilante groups as dysfunctional as Make It Stop?

That's the question Melanie has been musing since she'd completed detox and started working full-time on her sobriety. After a little over two years of constant chaos with MIS, she's noticing how easy life can be without it.

For example, her morning ritual at the coffee shop is just that—a ritual with minor deviations. Sometimes there's a line; sometimes there isn't. Either way, she's out the door in five minutes or less with a hot cup of coffee. There's seldom any drama and these places are staffed with teenagers and college students. Even her recovery meetings run with clockwork efficiency, and they're led by volunteers who are junkies and drunks. So, what made Make It Stop such a clusterfuck?

She isn't sure she cares anymore. Her new life is so *easy* without MIS. As much as she misses Doyle and wishes Trevor the best in his new life with Viviana, she's embraced the boredom. Well, not boredom, but the day-to-day stuff normal people somehow find fulfilling. She's thrown herself into it and it's been fine. Almost fine, but she's learning to like it.

She's been teaching a yoga class twice a week and loves it. Being in her body and out of her head for ninety minutes twice a week has been pure bliss. Well, not bliss—she doesn't like that word anymore—but better than okay.

Three months have passed since they took down Health Net Secure. One month of inpatient rehab, another month of outpatient aftercare, and then a month on her own. She's seen Bill exactly once, when he came to visit her in Arizona. He likes her and she likes him, but she can't pursue him and her sobriety at the same time. That's the first rule of rehab: no new relationships, at least not right away. It's too easy to go off the rails when love and lust and sobriety get mixed together. And her experience with Bliss would only make things even more confusing. Was she feeling legit feelings for Bill or was it the drug? Maybe someday she'll know for sure, but not today and probably not tomorrow.

Her relationship with Trevor, on the other hand, is now squarely in the friend zone. She wouldn't sleep with Trevor in a million years, but she would die for him.

Like that wasn't totally morbid.

It's been one hundred days since she's had a drink, and she's come to the cantina where she'd had her first TruLuv date with Tosh, the guy whose phone she'd deep-sixed in the fountain, a memory that still makes her laugh. It was one of her ballsier stunts, not because there was any threat of retaliation but because she'd been sober. The scene that followed probably should have poisoned her memory of the place, but she really likes it here. There's something about sitting next to a gurgling fountain when the sun is bright and the weather cool with nothing better to do than sip a cup of tea that makes her feel like she's exactly where she needs to be.

"Is this seat taken?"

Melanie looks and sees Kim and Viviana standing behind her. She scrambles out of her chair and gives them both a big hug.

"What are you two doing here?" Melanie asks.

"We came to see you, actually," Viviana says

"There's something we want to talk to you about," Kim says.

"This sounds serious," Melanie says as she takes her seat. "I'm teaching a yoga class in an hour, so what's on your minds?"

"How is that working out for you?" Kim asks.

Melanie looks at the water splish-splashing in the fountain, coins gleaming from the bottom like submerged stars. This is the question she'd been avoiding, because once she asks it, she will have to live with the answer. It's human nature. Ask a rich man if he's rich enough and he'll spread out his arms and show you everything he has, but in the back of his mind the answer is always a resounding "no."

"Great," she says.

"We want to talk about Make It Stop," Viviana says.

"Make It Stop is over," Melanie says. "It died with Doyle. Plus, with Hansen gone, and HNS dismantled..."

"Hansen had a partner," Kim says.

"And he's looking for new opportunities," Viviana adds.

They both have their game faces on. For Kim, this is nothing new, but Melanie doesn't recall Viviana being so hard to read.

"And you're going to make sure it doesn't happen?" Melanie asks.

Viviana and Kim nod grimly.

"You can't be serious," Melanie says even though it's obvious they are.

"We can't quit now," Viviana says.

"You are serious—and pregnant!"

"We need to nip this in the bud," Kim says.

"You don't understand," Melanie says. "MIS was just some big, stupid dream in Doyle's head. It existed because he said it did. It wasn't real."

"No," Viviana says, "the best part of MIS is sitting at this table."

Melanie's scalp tingles and her heart begins to race, like she's on drugs only better. Because it's true, isn't it? Aside from Scary Gary, they were the best, and she suspects Kim would have given him a run for his money. Gary would have loved the challenge of trying to crack Kim's tough-as-nails exterior, and she would have loved to have seen it.

"I'll think about it," Melanie says.

"You'll do it," Kim says.

"Or else?" Melanie asks.

"We'll come to your yoga class," Viviana says.

"Every single one," Kim says.

"I'm a *great* yoga teacher," Melanie protests.

"Sure," Viviana says.

"What does that mean?" Melanie asks.

"We'll just wait and see," Kim says, laughing now.

Melanie gets up. "I'm going to use the restroom, and you're going to order something decadent, and when I get back, we'll talk about this some more."

Melanie crosses the patio and goes inside. She heads for the bathroom and nearly stumbles over the little table with the drawer stuffed with secret confessions. She'd forgotten all about it. She sits down at the table and closes her eyes. Perhaps there's a message inside the drawer that will inspire her, not a fortune like the kind they put in cookies, but something she needs to hear. She opens the drawer, takes out a note, and opens her eyes.

DON'T STOP

Melanie looks over her shoulder to make sure she isn't being watched, that this isn't some kind of setup, but no one is paying any attention to her and, besides, how could anyone know what's in her heart?

Scary Gary knew, but he's gone and isn't coming back. Kim knows. Viviana, too.

For today, that's more than enough.

She slips the note in her pocket and shuts the drawer.

ACKNOWLEDGMENTS

I SET OUT TO WRITE a dark story set in the near future, but I took so long that my imaginary future kept getting eclipsed by the actual future. Another problem with taking so long to write this book is that not all of the people who cheered me on along the way are here to see its completion. I've dedicated this book to two friends who are no long with us, people who fought the good fight until they couldn't fight it anymore. There are at least four others who inspired characters that have crossed over. Now they live on in your imaginations.

So many books and movies influenced *Make It Stop* it would take pages to list them all (including the one with the rule about not talking about it), but Sascha Pöhlmann's *Vote with a Bullet: Assassination in American Fiction* came into my life at the perfect moment.

I am indebted to early readers who helped me get the book into its present form: Sean Carswell, Dave Fromm, Hannah Gordon, Claire Harris, Siel Ju, John Leary, Joshua Mohr, Joseph O'Brien, Aaron Petrovich, Todd Taylor (*Razorcake* por vida!), and Sandra Younger. This book also benefitted from guidance from Amanda Johnston, Francesca Lia Block, and my agent, Peter McGuigan. I am also grateful to the team at Rare Bird Books, including

Hailie Johnson and Kellie Kreiss, but especially Tyson Cornell, who stood by the project during its long road to realization, and Guy Intoci, who helped me get it over the finish line.

I nearly abandoned this project several times and probably would have if the struggle at the heart of the book wasn't so similar to my own. I've never gone undercover or worked for an underground organization, but I wouldn't be alive today without the gift of sobriety. If you struggle with substance abuse and are thinking about quitting, believe me when I tell you it's not too late to make it stop.